KT-362-218

ADDICTED

AN OUTLAWS NOVEL

ELLE KENNEDY

piatkus

PIATKUS

First published in the US in 2016 by Signet Eclipse, an imprint of
New American Library, a division of Penguin Group (USA) LLC
First published in Great Britain in 2016 by Piatkus

1 3 5 7 9 10 8 6 4 2

A CIP catalogue record for this book
is available from the British Library.

ISBN 978-0-349-41194-1

Printed and bound in Great Britain by
Clays Ltd, St Ives plc

Papers used by Piatkus are from well-managed forests
and other responsible sources.

MIX
Paper from
responsible sources
FSC® C104740

Piatkus
An imprint of
Little, Brown Book Group
Carmelite House
50 Victoria Embankment
London EC4Y 0DZ

An Hachette UK Company
www.hachette.co.uk

www.piatkus.co.uk

1

"I miss our house." Sighing, Piper nestled her head against Lennox's shoulder and curled one arm around his chest. "Are you sure it's too dangerous to go back?"

She'd been asking that same question for weeks now. Lennox was getting tired of answering it, but of all the people he'd extended his protection to over the years, Piper was one of the few he had a soft spot for. She'd turned twenty a few months ago, and despite the hard life she'd lived, her youth and innocence had been preserved. Well, maybe not the innocence—even as she voiced the question, her hand was drifting seductively toward Lennox's waistband.

"It's too dangerous to go back," he confirmed. Then he chuckled and intercepted her hand before it could slide inside his pants. "And what you're doing is equally dangerous, love."

Her laughter warmed his ear. "Aw, come on, Lennox. How long are you going to hold out on me?"

Hmmm. Probably until he could look at her without seeing the bedraggled sixteen-year-old who'd shown up at his doorstep four years ago. He'd been twenty-three, and lusting over a teenager hadn't felt right. Sure, Piper had grown up since then, but it was still hard for him to reconcile the skinny kid he'd taken under his wing with the gorgeous woman she'd become.

Which was ironic, because he had no problems lusting over his best friend, and he'd known *her* since they were both in diapers.

As if on cue, a blond head across the room swiveled in his direction, and the object of his thoughts flashed him a mischievous wink. It was as if Jamie always knew when he was thinking about her, and he had the same sixth sense about her. Growing up together had created a bond between them. They knew each other inside and out.

Though in a moment, another man would hold claim to the *inside her* part.

He'd known it was bound to happen after he and Jamie moved to Connor Mackenzie's camp. In a world filled with danger and uncertainty, it was important to form alliances, and Connor was a valuable ally to have. Lennox was damn grateful for the man's assistance.

Connor's right-hand man, on the other hand . . . Lennox liked the guy, he really did, but Rylan's flirtation with Jamie was starting to wear on his nerves.

It was Rylan who was sprawled on his back right now, his chest bare as Jamie's fully clothed body straddled his on the frayed couch. He reached up to cup Jamie's breasts through her shirt, summoning a moan from her rosebud lips. Even though her blue eyes went hazy with pleasure, they stayed locked with Lennox's.

If any other woman were looking at him like that, all heavy-lidded and visibly turned on, Lennox would have sprinted over there and joined the party. But he knew Jamie wasn't sending an invitation. She simply got off on being watched.

Watching was all he was capable of doing anyway. Jamie had been his best friend for more than twenty years. She was the only person in this fucked-up world who he trusted implicitly, who he could confide in and count on. After everything they'd been through, their friendship was rooted in feelings. Respect, admiration, affection . . . all those pesky emotions were too dangerous to bring into a sexual relationship. Sex was fun, but it was complicated as hell when feelings were involved.

And these days, life was already complicated enough.

For twenty-seven years, Lennox had lived and struggled in the free land, labeled an outlaw by the Global Council that ruled the Colonies with an iron fist. In order to prevent another war and ensure that the remaining natural resources weren't squandered, the council was all about population control and enforcing rigid restrictions on its citizens. If you didn't live in one of the four council-run cities and follow their rules, then you were considered a threat.

Lennox had never been too good at following rules. Except one: keeping his hands off his best friend. He'd already suffered too much loss. His parents, his friends, and now, thanks to an ambush by the Enforcers, his house. Jamie was important to him—he'd be damned if he lost her too.

He shifted his gaze from Jamie and Rylan, focusing instead on the back corner of the barn, which was stacked to the rafters with furniture and other random junk. The rest of the room had been cleared out and cleaned, the large space empty save for a couple of couches and an assortment of ratty old armchairs.

It was a far cry from the setup at the old place. Lennox didn't want to depress Piper by admitting it, but he missed their house too. It was hard to consider any place "home" in the free land, but that cozy split-level had come damn close. He and Jamie had stumbled upon it after Enforcers ran them out of their camp on the coast. They'd fixed it up, scrubbed it down, and turned it into a place where other outlaws could come and bask in the little freedom they had left. Booze, sex, conversation. Simple joys, really, but thanks to the war that had devastated the globe forty years before, joy was hard to come by these days.

"I'm serious," Piper insisted, and then her lips brushed the side of his neck. "The sexual tension is killing me."

Lennox chuckled again. "Xander and Kade are in the lodge," he told her. "I'm sure they'd be happy to help you relieve some tension."

She sighed again, her fingers absently tracing the raven tattoo on his forearm. "You're no fun, Lennox. You never want to entertain me."

He reached out and tweaked a strand of her brown hair. "I'm not here to entertain you, love. I'm here to take care of you."

"Yeah, I guess that's true." Her voice softened. "And

you've taken really good care of me, Len. I can never repay you for everything you've done."

"Seeing you happy and safe is the only repayment I've ever wanted," he said gruffly.

That got him another kiss—a loud smack on his cheek. "Ha, you're such a softie. I don't know why you bother acting like a badass all the time. Everyone can see right through you."

He could have corrected her, pointed out that he didn't *act* like a badass—he *was* a badass. He'd killed. He'd stolen. He'd betrayed people he'd cared about. Because that was what it meant to be an outlaw—you did everything in your power to survive.

Piper had never seen that side of him, the one that valued self-preservation above all else. He'd done his best to shield her from it, leaving her at home when he went out on supply runs, sending her away when he needed to put a bullet in someone's head. He hoped to keep shielding her, but like with everything else in this world, he knew that was probably hoping for too much.

"Anyway, since you insist on being mean to me, I'm going to track down Kade," she added, hopping off the couch. "Night, Lennox."

"Night, love."

As she headed for the door, he fought the urge to go with her, reminding himself that she would be fine trekking through the camp in the dark. She was armed, and Connor and his men had secured the hell out of the wilderness resort. The huge property was hidden in the mountains, rigged with motion sensors and explosives, and monitored by security cameras, which trumped all other luxuries. If the generator was low on fuel, Connor ordered everything else to be powered down—lights, heat, anything would be sacrificed to keep the security system operational.

Even so, it was hard for Lennox to accept that this place was truly safe. The Enforcers who policed the cities and searched the Colonies for outlaws were an ever-present threat, and one he never underestimated. Even when he was balls deep in a beautiful woman, he was still painfully aware that an Enforcer bullet could strike the back of his head at any moment. He just hoped those bastards had the decency to let him climax before they pulled the trigger.

"Rylan," Connor called from the door. A second later, the camp leader strode into the barn with a scowl on his face.

Without missing a beat, Rylan untangled himself from Jamie, his scuffed boots hitting the barn floor as he rose to his full height.

Lennox was impressed by the way Connor's men obeyed him on instinct. The man was a natural-born leader and protector, even if he was a prickly asshole a lot of the time. Lennox knew that if anything ever happened to him, Con would protect Jamie and the girls, no questions asked.

As Jamie's companion abandoned her for his leader, Lennox saw a slight pout form on Jamie's lips, but she didn't voice a complaint. Con and his woman had been away from camp since dawn, and everyone had been on edge awaiting their return. The two of them had gone to see Reese, the leader of a small town several hours east, with whom both Connor and Lennox had a reluctant alliance.

Reese was unpredictable on good days and down-right vindictive on bad ones, so Lennox never knew what to expect when he paid a visit to her self-pro-claimed kingdom.

"I need you," Connor barked at Rylan. Then he glanced Lennox's way. "You too, if you've got the time."

Lennox rolled his eyes. "What else do I have going on?" He'd been bored to tears since he and the women joined up with Connor's group.

Before, they'd been surrounded by people. Nomads who stayed at the house for a while before traveling on, strangers who needed a bed for the night, friends from other outlaw communities in West Colony.

Here, Connor discouraged visitors. He wasn't keen on letting anyone *leave* the camp either, unless it was for a meeting with one of their allies, or a supply run. But they'd stocked up on enough shit to last them through the winter, so as far as Connor was concerned, there was no reason to step foot outside camp.

Lennox, on the other hand, was itching for action. And sex. Christ, he needed a good lay. With Piper and Jamie off-limits, Layla was the only available woman at the camp, and though he'd screwed around with her several times already, he enjoyed a little variety in his life. He'd been tempted to finagle his way into Connor and Hudson's bed, but the couple didn't seem inclined to include anyone but Rylan in their bedroom activities.

Fuckin' Rylan. The man got to screw the delecta-ble Hudson *and* the woman Lennox had fantasized about for years. Some guys were just born lucky.

As he stood up, Jamie marched in his direction. Her pale blond hair fell over one shoulder, hovering right above her cleavage. She had fantastic tits—which she never failed to remind him of, probably because he'd spent a good portion of their adolescence ragging her about her flat chest. She'd had the last laugh, of course, transforming from a scrawny girl to a curvy, sexy-as-sin woman right before his eyes.

Truthfully he would've screwed her back then, flat chest and all. Jamie had been his first crush. He sure as hell hadn't been hers, though. She'd had all the boys in their camp panting over her, and she'd known just how to keep them wrapped around her little finger.

"I want to come to this meeting," she announced.

Lennox smirked. "You weren't invited."

"Screw that. We're a team. I go where you go."

"Things are different now, love. You and I don't run things anymore. Connor does."

Her blue eyes flashed. "Screw that," she repeated.

"You're just pissed because you didn't get to sit on Rylan's dick." He chuckled.

That got him a hard slap on the arm. "I don't care about Rylan's dick right now. I just don't want to be kept out of the decision-making process. Blind obedience isn't my thing, Len."

She was right—she'd always had a mind of her own, and that was one of Lennox's favorite things about her. The woman was outspoken, smart, and stubborn as fuck.

"It's not mine either," he admitted. "But we're playing by a new set of rules. Connor took us in, and now we've gotta do what he says." He tipped his head. "Unless you want to take off on our own? Because I'll do it, if that's what you think we should do."

She went quiet for a beat. He could see her shrewd

brain working. Then she raked one delicate hand through her hair and sighed. "Not this close to winter. If we want to find a new place, we're better off waiting till spring."

He nodded. "Agreed. But that means we defer to Con until then. Ergo, you need to go to your cabin while I find out what he has to say."

"I hate it when you *ergo* me."

A grin sprang to his lips. "Bullshit. You love everything about me."

She responded with a grudging smile of her own. "Yeah. I do." Then she reached around him and smacked him on the ass. "You better hustle, babe. Don't want to keep our mighty leader waiting."

Lennox was still grinning to himself as he left the barn. Darkness instantly enveloped him, the smell of pine and earth filling his nostrils. The camp was too damn rustic for his liking, but hey, at least the cabins were clean and cozy, the security was top-notch . . . and Jamie was here.

She was really the only thing that mattered, if he was being honest. He could be living in a volcano, inhaling ash and bathing in hot lava, and he'd be perfectly content with it as long as Jamie was by his side.

2

Lennox tracked down Connor and Rylan to the front porch of Connor's cabin, which was situated less than a hundred yards from the main lodge of the abandoned resort. One lit candle sat on the ledge of the porch, casting the occasional flicker of light over the shadowy backdrop of the mountains beyond the trees. Lennox had never liked the mountains. He preferred the coast, the salty scent of the ocean and the warm sand beneath his toes, but his days of living near the shore were long gone.

The earthquakes that ravaged the globe after the war had left most of the coastal cities underwater. The ones still standing were in shambles and inhospitable, though according to Connor's woman, the Global Council was apparently in the process of forming a new colony on the west coast.

Speaking of Con's woman, Hudson was perched on the edge of Connor's chair, her long blond hair falling over one slender shoulder.

Shit. Jamie wasn't going to be pleased when she heard that Hudson was allowed at the meeting while she'd been excluded, but Lennox wasn't surprised to see Hudson there. Connor didn't let her out of his sight if he could help it.

Hudson surprised him by hopping to her feet once Lennox reached the steps. "I'll leave you boys to it." She planted a kiss on Connor's lips before straightening up. "I'm going to see what Jamie is up to."

As she sauntered off, Lennox couldn't help checking out her tight ass, which earned him a low growl from Connor.

He turned back, blinking innocently. "Your woman's hot, Mackenzie. Men are gonna look."

Rylan grinned. "And some men are gonna touch." He jerked a proud thumb at his own chest, triggering a snort from Connor.

"Keep bragging and your touching days will be over."

Rylan mimicked Lennox. "Your woman's hot, brother. Men are gonna brag."

Connor rolled his eyes before turning his attention to the figures that came up beside Lennox.

"Hey," Xander greeted the group. He clapped Lennox on the arm, then climbed the steps and hopped onto the railing. Lennox had known the bearded outlaw for years, long before Connor and his boys had moved to the area, and it still surprised him to see Xander among the group. He had no idea how Con had managed to convince the nomad to settle in one place.

Kade walked up next, nodding at Lennox as he leaned against the railing next to Xander.

Pike was last, propping his hip against the door, his surly gaze focused on Connor. "What does she want?"

As usual, Pike got right to the point. The man never minced words.

Connor ran a hand over the dark stubble lining his jaw. "You."

In a rare occurrence, Pike reacted like a normal person instead of the emotionless robot Lennox had grown accustomed to. The man's eyebrows shot up, his mouth twisting in a frown. "Me?"

"And him."

Connor nodded toward Rylan, who reacted like the sex-crazed fucker he was.

"Hell yeah. She wants us to service her? Sign me up." Playful blue eyes shifted to Pike. "I don't mind sharing, but if you want to sit this one out, I won't cry myself to sleep about it."

Lennox snickered. It was no secret that Rylan had been trying to get into Reese's pants for a while now, but the woman was a total ballbuster and wanted nothing to do with the blond outlaw. Lennox wasn't sure why, considering that Reese had no problem fucking everyone else, himself included.

"She doesn't want your dicks." Connor looked unusually cheerful as he shot down Rylan's hopes. "She wants your fists."

Pike's frown deepened.

"Foxworth's having some trouble protecting itself," Connor explained. "Two ambushes in the last three months."

"Enforcers?" Xander said sharply.

Connor nodded. "One run-in with an Enforcer unit, and then a bandit attack not long after."

All the men sneered. Bandits were the lowest form of life in the Colonies. They were men without morals.

They roamed the free land, robbing, raping, and generally posing a nuisance to the outlaws who were trying to make a life for themselves in this shitty world.

Lennox hesitated for a beat before speaking up. He still wasn't sure how much to confide in the group— all the secrets he knew would take years to divulge— but now that he was living at their camp, he didn't feel right withholding certain pieces of information.

"Reese has deals in place with the Enforcers, Con. She bribes them and they stay away. Why would they attack her town all of a sudden?"

Connor didn't look surprised by the intel. "I guess those alliances are on shaky ground. Shit's changed since Commander Ferris took over the unit."

"What does she need us to do?" Gone was the mischievous look in Rylan's blue eyes. He was all business now, hard and menacing.

"Train her people. Only a handful of them know how to fight. Most can't even shoot a weapon." Connor leaned back in his chair, looking unhappy. "She wants you and Pike to spend a few weeks in Foxworth and work with her people, show them everything you taught all those recruits back when you two were still part of the army group."

Pike didn't look thrilled by the idea. "Can we say no?"

Connor's voice roughened. "She lent us her chopper so we could rescue Hudson from the Enforcer compound last month. We owe her."

"Then give her something else," Pike grumbled. "I've got better ways to spend my time than to teach a bunch of clumsy hacks how to shoot a gun."

"This is what she wants. It's *all* she wants. Trust me, I tried to negotiate, but she wasn't having it."

Rylan interjected. "Hey, it's not the worst favor she could've asked for." He turned to Pike with a careless grin. "A few weeks at Foxworth, sparring during the day and screwing at night? Not a terrible gig."

Pike still looked unconvinced.

"What's the real deal here?" As always, Connor seemed to read his man's mind. His sharp gaze fixed on Pike, who responded with a stiff shrug. But Connor was like a dog with a bone. "You don't want to go. Why?"

Lennox watched in fascination as the most tight-lipped bastard he'd ever met caved under Connor's shrewd hazel gaze.

"Don't want to leave Hope," Pike muttered.

There was a beat of silence. Then a loud snort from Xander, who'd just lit a cigarette from his perch on the railing.

Connor was equally dumbfounded. "Are you kidding me? You want us to face Reese's wrath just so you can stick around here and hang out with your fucking *pet*?"

Lennox swallowed his laughter. The pet in question had caught him by surprise when he first showed up at the camp. Apparently Hudson and Pike had found themselves a wolf pup, who they were now raising and teaching to do their bidding. To Lennox's amazement, Pike was scarily gentle with the furry beast, and it was rare to see the man around camp without Hope scampering at his scuffed boots.

"She's in training," Pike said tightly. "If I leave, it'll screw up the routine we have going."

"Hudson knows the routine—she's been doing it with you," Connor pointed out. When Pike shrugged again, the leader cursed. "Is this seriously going to be an issue?"

After a beat, Pike swore under his breath. "Fine. I'll go."

"Damn right you will." Connor shifted his exasperated gaze to the railing. "You too, Kade."

The dark-haired man looked startled. "Why me?"

"Because you fight like shit," Connor said bluntly. "Wouldn't hurt to brush up on your hand-to-hand combat skills."

Kade nodded in resignation. He was only twenty-four and looked it, with his lean frame and boyish features. The guy had been living in West City up until he escaped a little over a year ago, and he'd yet to develop the hard edge that the other men possessed. That every outlaw possessed.

In all honesty, Lennox wasn't sure what Kade really offered to the group. Xander had vouched for him, though. And the first time Xan brought Kade to Lennox's house, Lennox had watched the city boy tag-team a curvy blonde with Xan as if he'd been in the free land for years.

"I'm going too, then," Xander said immediately.

"No." Connor's tone invited no argument. "I need you here."

Xander's features tightened.

Lennox didn't claim to be a mind reader like Connor, but he was perceptive enough to figure out the reason for Xander's unhappiness. Kade was still green, and Xander had taken the guy under his wing. Someone would need to look out for Kade at

Foxworth, but neither Rylan nor Pike was up for the job. The former would be too busy chasing pussy, while the latter would no doubt find a shadowy place to hole up in and avoid any social contact.

Connor yet again proved to be the leader Lennox always knew he was by saying, "Lennox will go and keep Kade company."

Lennox raised an eyebrow. He wasn't used to other people making decisions for him, but he decided not to argue. He *could* use the change of scenery. Besides, the way Xander's shoulders relaxed told him the man would appreciate it if he went along.

"No problem," he said easily.

Connor looked pleased. "Good, then we're all on board." He rose from his chair and addressed the group. "You leave tomorrow night."

3

"Seriously. What's the deal with you and Lennox? You're really not sleeping together?"

Jamie wiggled out of her jeans and turned to grin at Hudson, who was sitting cross-legged on the twin bed in Jamie's cabin. No matter how many times she insisted that she and Lennox were simply friends, Hudson still raised the subject every time the two women were alone together.

"Nope, not sleeping together." Jamie folded her jeans and carefully placed them in the top drawer of the weathered dresser.

Lennox always teased her about her need to maintain tidiness and order, but it wasn't a compulsion or anything. So many things in this world were out of her control, but this was one thing she *could* control. Putting away her clothes, eliminating clutter.

Stupid as it might be, Jamie equated living out of a backpack with admitting defeat—it was like saying it was inevitable that they'd be forced to run again.

Fuck, she was tired of running. Her entire childhood had been one frantic getaway after the next, a constant cycle of packing up and moving somewhere new. Sometimes, if the Enforcers were breathing down their necks, packing wasn't even an option.

There had been times when Jamie was tempted to beg her parents to surrender to the council and move to the city. Because really, the people in West City lived a good life for the most part. Everyone was assigned a job suited to his or her skills. They were given clean, spacious accommodations. They ate well-rounded meals in the dining halls and had lots of free time to socialize and roam the city.

For the majority of citizens, all those perks were appealing enough to allow them to overlook the truth—that they were living in an oppressive environment, wrapped up in a pretty package under the guise of freedom.

Jamie's parents had reminded her of that each time she cried about abandoning camp, and it was a reminder she clung to whenever life got too hard. The citizens *weren't* free. How could they consider themselves free when they were unable to leave the city gates without written permission and an Enforcer escort? When marriages needed to be approved by the council, or outright arranged if a citizen remained unmarried by the age of thirty-five? When girls were sterilized when they reached childbearing age, except for those chosen to breed?

Thinking about the breeding laws always resulted in sending a chill up Jamie's spine. She couldn't stomach the notion of being sterilized against her will. Having the right to bear a child stolen away from her . . . that alone was enough to make her want to burn West City to the ground.

"But . . . why not?"

Jamie snapped out of her thoughts. "Why not what?"

"Why aren't you sleeping together?" Hudson repeated.

"Because we're friends."

"So? Rylan is my friend, and I sleep with *him*."

The remark wasn't meant to be hurtful, but Jamie couldn't fight the pang of resentment it evoked. It was no secret that Connor and Hudson fooled around with Rylan sometimes. And although Jamie knew it shouldn't make her jealous, it did, damn it.

From the moment she'd met the sexy blond outlaw, she'd come to think of him as *hers*. Which probably wasn't fair to Rylan or the women he slept with, but Jamie's heart was as stubborn as the rest of her.

It also didn't help that Hudson was drop-dead gorgeous *and* had landed one of the sexiest men in the colony. Jamie couldn't deny she'd fantasized a time or two about Connor's intense eyes and rock-hard body, but at the same time, she couldn't bring herself to hate Hudson. The woman was fun to be around, and she'd been nothing but kind to Jamie since they'd met.

Still, sometimes Jamie wanted to shake her by the shoulders and say *share the wealth, girl*.

"Lennox and I aren't like that," she said absently. "We never have been."

"Never?" Hudson looked doubtful. "Haven't you known each other for years?"

"Since we were kids. Our parents were friends, and Len and I grew up together in an army camp."

"Wait—was the People's Army still around at that point?"

"No, it was officially disbanded five years after the war. But unofficially it was around for years after that. Even now there are groups who still keep trying to drum up support for a new People's Army."

"I hope they get it."

Jamie couldn't hide her surprise. "You realize that could mean another revolution against the council? Which means your brother might get caught in the cross fire."

"Not if he leaves the city first." Determination lit Hudson's gray eyes. "I'm working on making that happen."

This time, Jamie made an effort to mask her reaction. She wasn't entirely comfortable with the fact that Hudson's twin brother, Dominik, was the head Enforcer of West Colony. Dominik and his men had been feared and vilified by outlaws for as long as Jamie could remember. They were known to be ruthless sons of bitches, and they'd only gotten worse over the past couple of years.

According to Jamie's parents, when the Enforcer unit had been formed after the war, the initial goals had been to protect the citizens, police the Colonies, and round up outlaws. The Surrender Law had been put into effect, which meant that outlaws were offered the choice to reintegrate into society or else face execution.

But with a new commander leading the military now, things had changed. The Surrender Law had been abandoned. Now outlaws were killed on sight.

Hudson claimed that the rising violence among the Enforcers was due to a drug cocktail the commander was giving the men, but Jamie was skeptical. Those assholes had always been violent, and she had trouble sympathizing with Hudson whenever the woman spoke about Dominik. If it were up to Jamie, he and his men would all be wiped off the face of this razed, blackened earth.

"I know you don't like hearing about him." Hudson shifted awkwardly, proving to be more perceptive than Jamie had given her credit for. "But he's my brother. I still love him."

"I know."

"He's trying to make things right."

Jamie didn't answer, but her thoughts on the matter hung between them like a cloud of radiation. *I'll believe it when I see it.*

Hudson sighed. "Okay, enough about Dom and more about Lennox." She flashed a smile, but it looked forced. "So you've known him forever and you never got together. Which raises the question . . . *why*? You do realize he's insanely attractive, right?"

"I hadn't noticed." She rolled her eyes. "Of course I know he's attractive, you idiot."

The tension dissolved as Hudson burst out laughing. "Good, because I would've been concerned if you didn't. That man is fucking gorgeous."

No argument there. Lennox was one of the sexiest men she'd ever met. That messy dark hair, chiseled features, magnetic silver eyes . . . Shit, and his body? It had been designed for pure *sin*. Jamie would have to be blind not to notice how attractive her best friend was.

If she was being honest, there was a period of time when she'd noticed far, far too often.

"Uh-oh, you're blushing." Hudson pounced instantly. "Ha! You two *did* hook up!"

"We didn't." She shrugged. "But I wanted to at one time."

"I knew it!" Hudson leaned back on her elbows, wearing an expression of sheer delight. "When was that?"

"When I was sixteen, I think. So Lennox would have been eighteen. We were living on the coast at that point, and one night—it was late, way past midnight— I caught Lennox sneaking away from camp. I was curious, so I followed him down to the beach." Jamie wiggled her eyebrows. "And then I hid behind a tree and watched him jerk off."

Hudson hooted. "Oh gosh, really? Did he know you were there?"

"I don't think so. I mean, he didn't give any indication that he knew. But holy shit, it was the hottest thing I'd ever seen," she admitted.

Even now, years after the fact, she could easily conjure up the memory of Lennox on that beach. His long body stretched out on the sand as he propped himself up on one elbow. His pants undone. The pleasure stretching his features taut as his strong hand worked his cock in slow, almost seductive strokes.

Jamie ignored the shiver of heat that shimmied up her spine. "After that, I lusted hard for him. I started flirting with him more, trying to catch his interest." She gave another shrug. "But he continued to treat me like a sister, so yeah, it was pretty clear he wasn't interested. Then I fell in love with this other boy at camp and forgot all about Lennox."

"Well, that's no fun." Hudson's disappointment was unmistakable.

"It was better that way. Lennox never stuck with one girl for very long. He just fucked her and then moved on to the next one. Trust me, he would've broken my heart. At least this way I still had him in my life."

"I guess."

Jamie grinned as another memory surfaced. "He was such an ass sometimes, though. He might not have wanted to screw me, but he was crazy protective and liked to make my life difficult. That boy I was into? Lennox beat the shit out of him after he found us making out in the woods. Then I fell for this other guy who treated me terribly, and Lennox pounded on him too. Oh, and I was in love with this older guy for a while—poor thing used to crap his pants when Lennox was around, which was hilarious because this guy was five years older. But Lennox had a reputation by then for watching out for me."

Hudson snickered. "It sounds like you've been in love a lot."

She considered it. "I guess I have. I tend to fall hard for people. And super fast."

"I'd never been in love before Connor," Hudson confessed. "But I fell fast for him too."

"Of course you did. That man is smoking hot." Jamie pulled her shirt over her head, then unclasped her bra as she searched for something to sleep in.

It wasn't until she glimpsed the slight flush on the other woman's cheeks that Jamie realized her nudity was the source of Hudson's discomfort. She always forgot that Hudson still wasn't used to the lack of modesty in the free land. But Jamie had stopped being modest a long time ago. Growing up in a camp full of people and having to share quarters more often than not had pretty much erased any shyness or self-consciousness she might've felt. "Oops, sorry. I keep forgetting you're from the city."

"Oh, it's all right. I don't know why it still surprises me." Hudson's cheeks turned redder. "By the way, that visit to Foxworth? I have never seen so many naked bodies in one room before."

Jamie laughed. "Reese hosted a party for you, huh?"

"Yep. We didn't stay long, though. Connor wanted—" She stopped abruptly, then grinned. "Well, you know what he wanted."

"I can imagine." And *only* imagine, because although Connor had been a frequent visitor to the whorehouse, Jamie had never had the pleasure of sleeping with him.

Sparing the other woman from seeing her bare tits, Jamie turned away and slipped an oversize T-shirt over her head. It was one of Lennox's, with a huge hole on the sleeve, but it was soft and worn and her favorite shirt to sleep in.

"What'd you think of Reese?" Jamie asked. She knew that most women found the reigning queen of Foxworth incredibly intimidating.

Hudson surprised her by saying, "I liked her. She's smart. Calculating. Looks like she knows how to get shit done. Well, I guess she must, since they've been living in that town for years and the Enforcers have left them alone." She paused. "Until recently, anyway."

Jamie's spine stiffened. "Is that what Reese said? Enforcers have been sniffing around and causing trouble?"

The blonde nodded. "I'm sure Lennox is going to tell you all about it after he's done with Con, but I might as well fill you in now. Reese wants Rylan and Pike to go to Foxworth for a while to train her people how to fight. There were some attacks on Foxworth, and now everyone is on guard."

Rylan was leaving?

It annoyed Jamie that her first thought was about Rylan leaving, and not concern for the people of Foxworth. "When are they going?"

"Soon, I imagine. I'm sure Connor and the others are figuring out the details now."

But clearly they'd already finished, because a sharp knock sounded on the door, followed by Lennox's deep voice. "Jamie. Need to talk to you."

Hudson slid off the bed as the door swung open. She greeted Lennox with a smile, then squeezed Jamie's arm and flitted out the door.

The moment they were alone, Jamie narrowed her eyes at Lennox. His serious expression told her everything she needed to know. "You're going with them."

He nodded.

She nodded back. "All right. When do we leave?"

A pained look crossed his features. "You're not coming with us."

"Are we really starting up this bullshit again?" She flopped down on the edge of the bed and crossed her arms. "I deferred to you about the meeting, but you're not going to win this one. I go where you go."

It was the pact they'd made when they were kids, and each of them had spoken those words time and again over the years.

"We'll be gone for weeks, love. And Foxworth is apparently taking some heat from Enforcers. I'd rather you stayed here where it's safe."

She lifted her chin in defiance. "No."

"Jamie—"

"*No*," she repeated. "I'm coming with you."

"What about Piper and Layla?" he countered. "You're perfectly okay leaving them alone?"

"Connor and Hudson will be here to watch over them. I told you, Len—you can't win." She shrugged. "Besides, this training thing could be useful for me. It's been a while since I got in any target practice."

Lennox snorted. "You can shoot better than anyone I know, Pike and Rylan included."

He had her there. The adults at the camp they'd grown up in had made sure every single child knew how to shoot a weapon. Jamie and Lennox used to take their rifles into the woods and set up targets, and by the time she was seven years old, she could blow a glass bottle right out of the sky while both she and the target were in motion.

"Fine, then I'll work on honing my combat skills." She refused to back down. "Either way, I'm going with you."

A crease of unhappiness dug into his proud forehead, but Jamie knew he was close to capitulating. Lennox didn't like letting her out of his sight and they both knew it. And that was fine by her. His overprotective bullshit annoyed her sometimes, but when it came down to it, she and Lennox were a team and always had been.

"Fine," he grumbled. "You can come."

She snickered. "You say that as if you're giving me permission. But sure, you can keep thinking you're in charge if it makes you feel better."

His lips quirked in an exasperated smile. Then he walked over to the bed and captured her chin with one big hand before dipping his head to kiss her cheek. "Night, love. We'll talk more tomorrow."

The soft brush of his warm lips on her skin made her smile. Lennox was always so tender with her, which was ironic, considering that it was no secret that he liked rough sex. Jamie had seen him pound into women with fervor, use his lips and hands and teeth to let out his sexual aggression.

She was one of the rare people who got to experience the gentle Lennox. The sweet Lennox. She would've missed out on that if the two of them had gotten sexually involved, because going to bed with Lennox would've come with a choice: sex or friendship.

Times like these, when he ran a tender hand over her cheek and gazed at her as though she meant the world to him, she was glad she'd never been forced to make that choice.

Rylan could tell that Connor had more to say. While the other men headed off in different directions, he remained on the porch, studying his best friend's serious eyes.

Usually Con was a lot harder to read, but tonight he

was conveying his unease as clearly as the neon lights that had once lit up city billboards. Rylan remembered being shown a picture of a place called Vegas when he was a kid, and how his eyes had grown larger than saucers when he saw all those lights, shining bright even at night.

Nowadays, nights were shrouded in darkness unless you were lucky enough to find a place with a generator or access to the power grid. Or if you lived in the city, where modern conveniences were given freely to the citizens who toed the line.

"What's on your mind?" he asked the camp leader.

Connor rose from his chair and joined Rylan at the railing. He stared into the dark forest for a moment, opened his mouth, then closed it when soft footsteps sounded from the path on their right.

They both turned to find Hudson approaching the cabin. "I'm exhausted," she announced as she climbed the steps. "You coming to bed?"

Connor gave a brisk nod. "Give me a second, sweetheart. I need to talk to Ry."

"Don't take too long." She glanced at Rylan. "You've got five minutes and then I'm dragging him inside. He's exhausted too, but he'll never admit it."

"Of course not. We're men, baby. We can never admit to having anything less than go-all-night stamina." Rylan waggled his eyebrows at her.

Laughing, she stepped closer and threw her arms around him in a tight hug. "Night, Ry."

Rylan squeezed her back, planting a kiss on the top of her head. The other man watched the exchange without a hint of jealousy in his eyes. He turned into a possessive asshole whenever anyone showed interest in Hudson, but never around Rylan. Maybe Connor was confident that Rylan would never try to steal his woman. Or maybe Con just suspected what Rylan had never voiced out loud—that he had no interest in settling down. Ever.

Either way, it didn't matter why his friend trusted him. He enjoyed his visits to their bed, and as long as Con was willing to share Hudson, Rylan was happy to accommodate them.

The moment Hudson was inside the cabin, Connor finally voiced his thoughts. "Reese is lying to me."

"Huh. Okay." Rylan's gaze sharpened. "You think there weren't any attacks on Foxworth?"

"No, the attacks were real. I spoke to her people. They confirmed it."

"They could have been lying too. You know everyone there follows Reese's lead." Which never failed to get him hard, seeing the power Reese wielded over her people.

Something about that woman turned Rylan on something fierce. He found it insanely bothersome that she didn't return the interest. He could rock the woman's world, if she'd just let him.

Connor was shaking his head. "I know when I'm being lied to. Her people were telling the truth. She wasn't." His hands curled over the wooden ledge, frustration etched into his features. "Her request for training . . . something about it sounded off."

"What do you think she's up to?"

"No clue, but there's definitely something brewing in Foxworth." Con shrugged. "I need you to find out what it is."

Rylan offered a rueful grin. "If you need to me to

set up some kind of honey pot operation—or would it be honey dick?—then you might be shit out of luck. My natural charisma doesn't work on that woman."

The other man chuckled. "Guess you'll have to dip into your other bag of tricks, then. I don't care how you get the intel, just get it done. I'm not happy about sending people to Foxworth when I know Reese is cooking something up."

"I'll do what I can," he promised.

"Good, now I should probably get inside before Hudson comes out and—"

A loud crash sounded from the vicinity of the trees. In a heartbeat, both men had their guns out of their waistbands and aimed at the dark forest. Since the entire camp was rigged with trip wires, Rylan tensed, expecting an explosion to light up the sky at any moment, but the night went silent again.

Frowning, Connor slid the radio out of his belt. "Xan, you at the lodge?"

A static-ridden response came back. "Yeah."

"Check the cameras in the east woods. We heard a crash."

There was a long beat of silence, then, "Think it was a branch. A few of those dead trees we need to cut down took a beating during the thunderstorm the other night. I'm seeing lots of branches on the ground."

Connor relaxed. "Gotcha. Thanks."

They kept their weapons trained for several more seconds before lowering them. It probably *had* been a fallen branch, Rylan decided. The chances of anyone sneaking into the camp without setting off one of the motion sensors or explosives were pretty damn slim.

Tucking his gun away, Connor headed for the cabin

door, then halted when he realized Rylan was still at the railing. He slanted his head and said, "You coming in or what?"

Rylan barked out a laugh. "Your woman's tired."

A wicked gleam entered Connor's eyes. "Yeah, but nothing puts her to bed faster than a screaming orgasm. Been a while since we gave her one."

Rylan's dick was hard in a nanosecond. Yeah, it'd been a couple of weeks since he and Connor tormented Hudson's sweet, delectable body.

Jamie had already gone to bed, so it probably wouldn't be gentlemanly if he woke her up to finish what they'd started in the barn. But damn, he could use a good lay right now. Orgasms were one of the few rewards in this dangerous, fucked-up world. Made living in it a bit more tolerable.

With a grin, he gave Connor a slap on the shoulder. "Lead the way, brother."

4

The group gathered in the courtyard the next evening after the sun had set. While the men loaded gear into the Jeep, Jamie hugged Layla and Piper good-bye before pulling Hudson aside.

She checked that the other women were out of earshot, then said, "Take care of them for me."

"I will," Hudson promised.

"And keep an extra eye on Piper. Girl's as stubborn as a mule, and she doesn't always follow orders."

The blonde grinned. "Don't worry. I'm used to dealing with stubborn asses." She cocked a head toward Connor, who was issuing some last-minute orders to Pike.

Jamie snickered, and the sharp sound startled the one-month-old wolf pup at Hudson's feet. "Aw, wolfie, don't be scared." She knelt down and patted Hope's soft head. When a pair of eerie blue eyes peered up at her, a shiver ran up Jamie's spine. "Jesus, her eyes freak me out."

Hudson scooped up the wolf and nuzzled her dark fur. "Don't say that. You'll give her a complex."

That triggered another snicker. "Don't take this the wrong way, but . . . you and Pike are fucking insane. You realize she's a wolf and not a person, right?"

"Agree to disagree."

Hudson stuck out her tongue, then ambled off toward Connor and Pike. The latter plucked the furry bundle from Hudson's arms and whispered something in Hope's tiny ear. Which only made Jamie gape, because, really? The man barely said a word to the human beings around him, but he was whispering sweet nothings to a *wolf*?

An engine roared to life behind her. She spun around to find Lennox straddling his Harley. "You riding with me or in the Jeep?"

Jamie hesitated. Pike was now straddling his own bike, which left Rylan alone at the Jeep, tossing gear inside. She glanced back to Lennox, who seemed to already know the answer.

"Gotcha," he said dryly.

For some stupid reason, she found herself on the defensive. "It's a long drive. Figured I'd ride in comfort so I don't show up to Foxworth with a sore ass."

Lennox smirked. "You and Ry alone in a car for five hours? Bet you'll still be showing up at Foxworth with a sore ass, love."

She gave him the finger, but he just laughed and started the engine. A moment later the powerful machine disappeared down the path.

Lennox had been mocking her about her crush on Rylan for more than a year, though she supposed she deserved it. She was twenty-five years old, too damn old for girlish crushes, but . . . damn it, Rylan was sexy as hell, not to mention the most likable man she'd ever met.

She headed for the Jeep and threw her duffel bag in the back. When Kade came up beside her, she battled a spark of disappointment. She thought he'd be on one of the motorcycles.

Just when she'd resigned herself to riding alone in the backseat, the dark-haired man beat her to the door. "Mind if I sit back here? Xan and I were fixing the barn roof all day and I want to stretch out and sleep."

"It's all yours." She gestured to the torn seat.

Kade climbed into it, then rested his head on one of their bags and closed his eyes.

She and Kade were around the same age, but she didn't know him well. He'd been part of Connor's group for a year or so, but there was something seriously haunted about his dark eyes, as if he hadn't quite left the city behind him.

"Ready?" Rylan's deep voice sounded from behind her.

She walked up to the passenger's side. "Yep." She was more than ready, actually. Sitting up front with Rylan for the five-hour drive? Hell yeah.

He grinned as he slid behind the wheel. "You're the sexiest copilot I've ever had," he drawled.

The compliment brought an uncharacteristic flush to her cheeks. Damn it. She was so gone for this man.

Pike signaled something to Rylan before speeding off on his Ducati, and the Jeep quickly followed suit. Rylan kept the headlights off as he steered down the long path winding along the mountain.

Jamie wholly approved of the location of their camp. The entrance to the main road was overgrown with foliage, and Connor and his men had removed any road signs that had once directed visitors to the resort. The place was completely hidden from view, high enough on the mountain and shielded by forest so that nobody on the road could see the lights in the cabin and main lodge.

But while the isolation boded well for safety, it got to a person after a while. She was looking forward to being at Foxworth and interacting with people again. It was rare for large groups of outlaws to congregate in one place, but Reese's town had a population of nearly eighty, at last count.

As they followed the motorcycles down the dark, quiet road, she and Rylan chatted for a bit, then settled into silence as he loaded a CD, which was another rarity. Jamie hardly ever got a chance to listen to music, but the Jeep had an older-model CD player that miraculously still worked, and she leaned back in her seat as music floated out of the speakers. They were three songs into the album when she realized how depressing the music was, chock-full of twangy guitar and lyrics about heartbreak and misery.

"Are you trying to depress me?" she teased.

He chuckled. "Pike and I stole this Jeep when we were making our way out of the south. Damn thing only had three CDs in the glove box. This one is the most uplifting, believe it or not."

"Does this music have a name?" she asked curiously.

"Country." He shrugged. "It's not terrible, but I've

listened to this shit so many times it's a miracle my ears haven't exploded."

They went quiet again as the singer crooned about his lady and a trailer and a field of buckwheat. After thirty minutes, the album ended and Jamie swiftly intercepted Rylan's hand before he could load the next one.

"Oh my God. No more!" she begged. "I'm ready to hang myself here."

"Fine, then as my copilot, you need to entertain me in other ways so I don't pass out like this asshole back there—" He jerked a thumb at Kade, who was out like a light. "Know any games?"

"I know all kinds of games." She winked at him.

Rylan's blue eyes instantly smoldered. His tongue came out to moisten his bottom lip, and it was so sexy it sent a bolt of heat right to her core.

"Yeah?" he prompted, those eyes continuing to gleam.

"Oh yeah."

She slid closer and rested her hand on his groin, shivering when she felt him hardening beneath her palm. She gave a slight stroke, and his hands tightened around the steering wheel. Another teasing stroke, and a groan escaped his lips.

Rylan rocked his hips and thrust into her hand. "Fuck, baby, you're killing me. Undo my pants."

Feminine power. It was a heady thing.

Jamie had been fourteen when she realized how much power a woman truly possessed. The men at her camp, her father included, were the toughest, baddest dudes she'd ever known. They hunted to feed the group, fought off bandits and Enforcers, did everything they could to keep everyone safe. The women had been equally tough, but with young children in the camp, the role of caretaker naturally fell to the females.

To Jamie it had always seemed that the men commanded more power—until the day she'd kissed a boy for the first time and watched him turn into a puddle of mush at her feet. In that moment, the toughest boy she'd ever met would have done anything for her. Ripped the shirt off his back to keep her warm, walked on hot coals to keep her safe, stepped in front of a bullet to keep her alive.

In a world where you had to utilize every skill in your repertoire, the realization that sex and seduction could be used as a tool had been a goddamn eye-opener.

But she didn't have an agenda at the moment. She didn't want to use Rylan or persuade him into doing something for her. She just wanted him. Period.

Smiling, she slowly dragged his zipper down and slid her hand inside his pants. He jerked when she curled her fingers around his heavy shaft, then moaned when she dipped her head and brought her tongue out for a taste.

Keeping one hand on the wheel, Rylan threaded the other one through her hair and choked out, "I like this game."

It was midnight when they finally neared their destination. About a mile out of Foxworth, Lennox slowed the bike and conducted his usual sweep of the area. He'd been there numerous times and had never encountered any trouble before, but he'd be a fool to take the seemingly secure surroundings at face value. The West City Enforcers were well trained—they knew how to remain invisible, and they excelled at biding their time until the opportunity for an ambush presented itself.

But there was no trouble to be had tonight. A sharp whistle from Pike confirmed that the area was clear, and Lennox sped up toward the huge steel gates surrounding the little town. On the east end of the main gate was a raised landing to accommodate an armed guard, who monitored all arrivals. Another guard manned the back gate, while several others patrolled the perimeter. It was a twenty-four-hour security detail, and every guard reported directly to Reese.

Lennox stopped in front of the gate, which was over ten feet high. Reese's group had laid claim to Foxworth about four years ago; it had taken nearly half that time to erect the gates, which had involved hauling in sheets of metal from nearby factories and shipyards in order to complete the project. He wholly approved of their efforts. As much as he'd loved his old house, he'd never felt entirely safe there. At Foxworth, he always felt safe, which was all sorts of fucked-up, because he knew damn well that safety was nothing but an illusion.

The dark-clad figure standing above the entrance trained his rifle at the approaching motorcycles. Rylan waved from the front seat of the Jeep. With the vehicle's top down, the guard had a clear view of him.

A second later, a metallic grinding filled the night

air as the gate slid open and two of Reese's people waved the convoy in.

Lennox drove into a gravel-lined courtyard littered with dozens of other vehicles. He killed the engine and glanced around, noting that not much had changed since his last visit.

Foxworth was nothing more than one street with a town square and park in its center, and one- to three-story shops lining both sides of the wide lane. The gates had been built to enclose just the main stretch; there were several very nice properties in the surrounding area, but Reese wanted everybody close by, so storefronts and boutiques had been converted into living quarters. The town's rec center served as a gathering place, and there was even one restaurant that was completely operational.

Foxworth was downright paradise compared to some of the other communities Lennox had visited.

He removed his helmet and slid off the bike, turning toward the Jeep as Jamie popped out of the passenger's seat. She was surprisingly light on her feet. Then again, she'd just spent hours in a car with the object of her affection.

Annoyance clamped around Lennox's windpipe. He tried to force it away, but the vise only squeezed tighter when Rylan stepped out. His jeans were unzipped.

So that was why Jamie was so chipper. She'd blown Rylan on the ride over.

Lennox met Rylan's eyes and nodded at the man's crotch. With a wink, Rylan zipped up and wandered toward Kade to help him unload the Jeep.

Knowing Jamie's mouth had been on Rylan brought

simultaneous jolts of heat and resentment. Jamie knew her way around a man's cock, so damned if the thought of her sucking someone off didn't turn him on.

Sadly, Lennox would never be lucky enough to experience that magic mouth on *his* dick. He'd gone to great lengths to preserve their friendship by solidly keeping sex out of the equation.

"I was hoping you'd be here." A throaty voice sounded from his left, and then Reese appeared and tugged him toward her for a hug.

She looked as gorgeous as ever. Her hair, the color of burnished copper, streamed over one shoulder in long waves. Black pants and a tight black tee hugged her endless supply of curves, showing off a pair of spectacular tits and an ass he'd dug his fingers into on more than one occasion.

Lennox kissed her cheek, then pulled back and examined her. Her brown eyes, usually shrewd and alert, were lined with exhaustion.

"You look tired," he said frankly.

Reese sighed. "I am tired. Sloan and I butchered a cow today. Took hours."

Sloan was Reese's number two. The burly, bearded man served as her shadow, which was why Lennox wasn't surprised to find him lurking a few feet away, his watchful gaze fixed on his queen.

"I'm glad you're here." A slow smile curved Reese's full red lips. "I was starting to get bored."

He grinned. "What, the forty-odd dicks in this place aren't enough to satisfy you?"

"Not like yours." She swept her gaze over his arms, chest, and groin, then licked her lips. "Fuck, I'm *really* glad you're here."

"What about me?" came Rylan's careless voice. "Happy to see me?"

In the blink of an eye, Reese's demeanor went from seductive to displeased. "Rylan," she said coolly.

"Reese." The blond man bent his tall frame to kiss her cheek, and though she let him, she didn't seem to enjoy it. "You look beautiful as always, my queen." He gave an exaggerated bow that made Reese roll her eyes.

"Thanks."

One syllable was all she spared before dismissing Rylan from her gaze. Shifting around, she leaned up on her tiptoes to press her mouth to Lennox's.

The kiss was brief but molten hot. Reese's tongue curled around his in a teasing stroke before she nibbled on his bottom lip and murmured, "Come find me later, honey. We've got lots of catching up to do."

As she drifted off to greet Pike, Rylan let out a heavy sigh. "Tell me your secret, brother. How do you get her to stick her tongue down your throat like that?"

He snickered. "Easy. I don't annoy her."

"I don't do it on purpose," Rylan protested.

Lennox couldn't disagree. Rylan was the least annoying person he'd ever met, yet Reese was constantly swatting him away like a bothersome fly buzzing around her head. Lennox couldn't even begin to figure out why that was. Reese was a strange creature, happily welcoming some men into her bed, while being incredibly selective about others.

Jamie joined them, carting her duffel bag in one hand. "Where are we sleeping?" she asked Lennox. "The usual place?"

He nodded in response. Whenever they came to

Foxworth, the two of them usually crashed in adjoining rooms that had once made up the office and waiting area of a law firm.

"I'll drop our bags off." He relieved her of the duffel, cursing when he felt its heft. "What the hell did you pack in here, love? Bricks?"

"We're here for a month," she said defensively. "I brought a little bit of everything."

Lennox smothered a sigh. Traveling with Jamie could be a pain in the ass sometimes.

She glanced at Rylan. "You guys aren't starting the training stuff tonight, are you?"

"Hell no. We can start tomorrow." Rylan's blue eyes danced impishly. "Tonight we party."

5

"You asked him to come, sweetheart." Sloan voiced the gruff words after Reese had directed yet another dark glare in Rylan's direction.

She gritted her teeth at the unwelcome reminder. Yes, she'd requested Rylan's presence. Yes, she'd all but threatened to cut off Connor's balls if he didn't send Rylan and Pike her way. But that didn't mean she had to *like* it.

"Because I need him," she muttered in response. "He and Pike understand combat—they'll be able to teach our people everything they need to know."

"Your people," Sloan corrected.

She smiled wryly. "I might give the orders, but they all know I don't make a single decision without your input."

They reached the front stoop of the two-story building Reese called home. Sloan stopped by the rail and fixed those serious hazel eyes on her.

His steady gaze unnerved her, as it always did when she found herself the focus of it. Only two people had the ability to read her, to dive into her mind and know exactly what she was thinking. One of them was dead. The other was very much alive, and far too willing to use that skill to his advantage.

"Remind me again why we don't like him," he said.

The mocking note in his tone grated on her nerves. "Because he's a wild card. And we don't like wild cards."

Sloan nodded.

She knew what he really wanted to say. That Rylan's total recklessness and unpredictable nature reminded her too much of Jake. Which was the truth—the similarities between the two men were damn near eerie. They even shared a physical resemblance with their fair hair and blue eyes. Jake had been smaller, though, only a few inches taller than Reese, and lanky in contrast to Rylan's broad, muscular frame.

If she was basing her opinion on looks alone, she would've fucked Rylan's brains out a year ago. Didn't matter that he reminded her of her dead lover, because her dead lover had been one of the sexiest, most magnetic men she'd ever met. Jake might have turned into a tyrant by the time he died, but her attraction to him had remained stronger than ever despite that.

No, it was Rylan's complete lack of self-preservation that concerned her. His inability to walk the path of least resistance. The way he dove headfirst into danger without a single thought to his own well-being or that of others. She suspected he fed off the thrill, the adrenaline high, and maybe that worked well for him, but it wasn't the way Reese operated.

"We need to be smart about how we handle this," she told Sloan. "Keep an eye on him while he's here."

"You think Connor was suspicious?"

"I know Connor was suspicious." She cursed under her breath. Connor was a major thorn in her side sometimes. The man was too perceptive for his own good, not to mention a ruthless motherfucker. If he caught so much as a whiff that she might be placing his men in danger, he wouldn't hesitate to slit her throat.

Her gaze drifted toward the small building that housed the recreation center. Rylan and Pike were already headed in that direction. From the carefree spring to Rylan's long stride, she knew exactly what he'd be doing when he got there. Dropping his pants and sticking his dick in the first available pussy.

And that was just fine by Reese. Let him screw to his heart's content. Rylan's sex drive bordered on addiction, and she was happy to provide him with all the sexual distractions at her disposal. Her girls enjoyed his company. They'd keep him busy enough that he wouldn't think too hard about everything else going on around him.

"What do you need me to do?" Sloan said in a low voice.

The question didn't surprise her. She and Sloan had been through hell and back together—the man did whatever she asked. There was no line he wouldn't cross for her.

"Do what you do best," she answered, arching a playful eyebrow. "Pay attention and keep your mouth shut."

He flashed a rare grin. "Just the way I like it."

* * *

The rec hall was bustling with activity when Lennox arrived after stashing his and Jamie's bags. A few dozen people filled up the space, holding various containers of alcohol and in various states of undress. Pulsing bass music blasted through the room. It shook the walls and the linoleum floor beneath Lennox's heavy boots as he made his way through the crowd.

Several women wandered over to greet him, and he smacked kisses on their cheeks before continuing toward a group of familiar faces.

Beckett broke out in a wide grin at the sight of him. "Len! My man! You made it." The tattooed mechanic slapped Lennox's arm in greeting before yanking him in for a hug.

Lennox grinned at his old friend. "You know I don't pass up any opportunity to come here. Hey, Trav."

Travis stepped forward to bump his fist against Lennox's. "Good to see you, man."

He shook hands with a few of the other guys, who he was friendly with but not close to—Nash, Davis, and Rick.

"Heard your place got ambushed by Enforcers," Nash said sympathetically. "Fuckin' blows, man."

"Yeah, wasn't too happy about that," he admitted.

"So you and your girls are living with Connor now?" Davis looked intrigued.

Lennox nodded, accepting the whiskey bottle Beckett passed his way. He took a deep swig and welcomed the burn that hit his stomach. Reese had the best booze, high-grade stuff she smuggled in from the city. It was potent shit.

"How's that working out for you?" Davis pressed when he didn't elaborate. "Connor's woman there too?"

"Where else would she be?"

"Hot as hell, that one," Rick drawled. "Con wouldn't let anyone touch her when she was here."

Lennox thought about Hudson's tight body and flowing golden hair, and could understand exactly why Connor would want to lock that shit up. "Do you blame him?" His attention was diverted when loud laughter echoed from the vicinity of the pool table. "Well, fuck me. When did you get the table refelted?"

Last time he'd visited, the green felt was in tatters after decades of use. Sinking a ball in any of the pockets had been like navigating a damn minefield.

"Last week," Beckett revealed. "Sloan and Trav were out on a supply run and came across an abandoned pub about a hundred miles south."

Travis rolled his dark eyes. "Sloan wouldn't leave until we'd stripped every billiards table in the place. You should've seen how carefully he was slicing off the felt. Like he'd rather cut off his own finger than bring Reese an inferior product."

Lennox had to laugh. It was no secret that Sloan would walk through fire for Reese, but the man's unwavering loyalty was intense sometimes.

"Beck!"

The men turned as Jamie flew up to the group. Blue eyes shining happily, she threw her arms around Beckett, who lifted her off her feet and hugged her tight.

Seeing Jamie look so happy flooded Lennox's chest with warmth. Maybe it was a good thing he'd allowed her to come along. They'd been through too much shit lately—losing their home, losing their close friend Nell . . . Fuck, now his chest was aching, because he was suddenly hit with the memory of Jamie sitting on the floor, tears streaming down her cheeks as she held Nell's lifeless body in her arms.

The ambush on their house had been an unwelcome reminder of how fleeting life in the free land could be. People died. They always fucking died. But even knowing that, Lennox felt wrecked every time he was forced to grieve for someone he'd cared about.

Tonight wasn't about grieving, though. It was about seeing old friends and having fun. Enjoying a rare respite from the bullshit beyond Foxworth's gates.

"I missed you," Jamie told Beckett before planting her lips square on his mouth.

Beckett slipped her some tongue, then lowered her down and slung an arm around her shoulder. "Missed you too, babe." His hand nonchalantly eased lower to cup her left breast over her tight black tank.

In retaliation, she reached out and squeezed one of Beckett's sculpted pecs, hard enough to make him wince.

"No fair," the dark-haired man griped. "My tits aren't as big as yours. It hurts when you do that."

"Oh, you poor man. We should find out if there're still doctors around who perform boob jobs. Did you know people actually used to do that? I think they were called plastic surgeons or something."

Lennox watched the exchange with amusement. He and Jamie had known Beckett for years, long before the man had settled down in Foxworth. He'd been a nomad when they first met, fixing up old cars he found on the road, roaming the colony alone, and interspersing the months of solitude with visits to Lennox's for some booze and female companionship.

Beck and Jamie had fooled around more times than Lennox could count, but it had never bothered him. Maybe it was because he knew she didn't have feelings for Beck. Or any of the other men she'd been with, for that matter. They were just a lay to her, a good time.

Her infatuation with Rylan was another story. Jamie looked at him the way she'd looked at all her boyfriends growing up: as if they'd hung the god-damn moon.

Lennox didn't like that. He knew Jamie better than she knew herself. She loved to be in love, but more than that, she *wanted* to be in love. She wanted the same thing her parents had—a partnership, someone to build a life with.

It was more than evident to Lennox that Rylan wasn't interested in finding a woman to settle down with. He just wanted to fuck around, but Jamie was oblivious of that harsh truth. Sooner or later she'd try pushing Rylan into something serious, and the man would bail and leave her with a broken heart. Lennox could see that disaster coming from miles away, but he'd yet to find a way to broach the subject without pissing Jamie off.

"Come dance with me," she urged Beckett.

He waggled his eyebrows. "Only if it's naked dancing."

She offered a compromise. "How about we start with the dancing and work our way up to the naked part?"

"Deal." Beckett lifted her into his arms and carted

her toward the center of the room while Jamie laughed in delight and locked her hands around his neck.

Lennox watched as the other man set Jamie on her feet and shoved one hard thigh between her legs. A second later, they were tangled up together, bodies moving seductively to the music.

He shifted his gaze in time to see Reese arrive. Sloan was at her heels, but remained standing near the door as Reese settled on an empty couch in the far corner of the room. She cocked her head at Lennox, who quickly excused himself and wandered over to join her.

The moment he was beside her, Reese curled her legs under her and rested her head on his shoulder. "So, how is it living under Connor's thumb?" she asked dryly.

"Pretty good, actually. They have a solid setup, fully stocked for winter. It's a good place to regroup while we decide whether we're taking off on our own again."

She peered up with a frown. "Don't do that. Seriously, Len. Stay there, or come live here with us. It's not safe anywhere else."

"It never was."

Her tone was grim. "It's even worse now."

Lennox searched her face. "Enforcers giving you trouble?"

Reese hesitated, as if she didn't know how much to share. Then she nodded. "Yeah, a bit. Sloan nearly killed the last rep who came by."

"Shit. That's no good." He knew Reese had a shit ton of alliances in place with certain higher-ranked Enforcers. Lennox was privy to way more information than he'd told Connor, but he planned on filling his new leader in eventually.

The Enforcers used Foxworth as a campsite of sorts during their colony sweeps. It wasn't an arrangement Lennox or any of the others were comfortable with, but it was the price to pay for the Enforcers' silence. Reese gave the assholes beds, booze, and broads, and in return, Foxworth was immune. The outlaws living there weren't rounded up or reported to the council, and Foxworth was allowed to continue to thrive.

"What'd the bastard do to piss off Sloan?" Lennox asked curiously.

"He tried changing the terms of our deal." Her jaw was tighter than he'd ever seen it. "The piece of shit wanted to 'borrow' one of my girls so they'd have a fuck toy during their colony sweep."

Lennox frowned. "You're kidding me."

"No joke. I told him there was no way in hell he was taking anyone out of Foxworth. He got pissy, aggressive. Started throwing his weight around, but Sloan shut it down."

"How?"

She snorted. "Knocked the bastard out cold. It was a total shit storm when he came to. He wanted to execute Sloan on the spot, but I threatened to go to his commander and tell Ferris all about our little deal."

Which would be like signing his death warrant. Commander Ferris strictly forbade any contact between his soldiers and the outlaws. Lennox had never met the man, but he'd heard Ferris was ruthless as hell and known to execute his own men if they disobeyed orders.

"The asshole and his troop took off, but I didn't like

the way we left things," Reese admitted. "Another rep came by a few weeks later, apologized for his man and said the deal stands, but there was tension there. I didn't like that either."

He didn't blame her. Antagonizing the Enforcers would only lead to a war. Reese had a good thing going with them right now, so it was best if she found a way to preserve the alliance.

"Anyway, enough business," she said flippantly. Her hand found its way into his lap at the same time she pressed her lips to the side of his throat. "I have a surprise for you."

"Oh, really?"

She nibbled on his neck, and a hot shiver of anticipation raced up his spine. It'd been far too long since he slept with a woman as passionate as Reese.

"Surprise," a throaty voice said.

Fuck. Make that *two* passionate women.

Lennox twisted his head as a stunning brunette with catlike eyes approached the couch. Decked out in a black corset and a teeny scrap of fabric that constituted a skirt, the woman lowered herself onto Lennox's lap and brushed a seductive kiss on his lips.

"Tam," he groaned into her mouth. "Didn't know you were here."

"Well, now you do." Dark eyes gleamed impishly at him. "I'm heading out tomorrow morning, but you know I can't leave the colony without seeing my favorite badass."

He was flattered. Tamara ate men for dinner and spat them right out, so the fact that she had a soft spot for him was, frankly, a relief. The woman was a legend in the free land. A smuggler, she was an out-law's go-to for anything his heart desired, but the prices she charged for her services were damn steep. She also wouldn't hesitate to shoot someone down if they betrayed her. Hell, she was capable of doing it just because they'd annoyed her or caught her on a bad day.

Luckily Lennox didn't annoy her often. Didn't annoy anyone, for that matter. He wasn't being naive when he said he didn't have any enemies among his fellow outlaws. He was well liked by everyone, and he used that to his advantage.

"Where you off to?" he asked as she ran one hand down the center of his chest.

"South Colony. I need a vacation."

He snickered. Only Tamara could get away with saying shit like that. She had the means to do it too. With her connections, she could sunbathe nude on any beach on the globe, in full view of the Enforcers.

"I wish I could go with you," Reese grumbled.

Tamara grinned at the other woman. "You should. Ditch this shit hole and travel the Colonies with me. Think of all the trouble we could get into."

"Plenty of trouble to be had here." Reese brought her hand to Lennox's belt and slowly undid the buckle.

A second later, she had his zipper down and was holding his jeans open for Tamara, who wasted no time sliding *her* hand inside them.

Lennox groaned as warm fingers encircled his rapidly hardening cock. Tamara pumped him slowly. Reese leaned in to suck on his neck.

Every man in the room was staring enviously in their direction. Including Rylan, who caught Lennox's eye and tipped his head in an unspoken question.

"Rylan wants in," Lennox murmured.

Reese stiffened, lifting her head to frown at him. "No fucking way."

He tried another angle. "I hear he's good with his tongue . . ."

"Oh, he is," Tamara confirmed.

"I don't care how good he is," was Reese's muttered response. "This is a private party. He's not invited."

Lennox shot a rueful look at Rylan, giving a slight shake of his head. The blond man rolled his eyes before turning to say something to Pike.

Ah well. He'd tried. Rylan was on his own tonight. And Lennox, well, he was suddenly being tugged to his feet by the two women, Tamara's hand still buried inside his jeans.

"We want you to ourselves tonight." Reese brought her mouth to his ear, flicking her tongue over the lobe. "And you better not be tired from that long drive, because we expect you to last all goddamn night."

A wicked grin lifted his lips. That sounded fucking phenomenal.

Or rather, it sounded like phenomenal fucking.

"I'll see what I can do."

6

When Jamie approached the huge lot behind the town square the next morning, she knew without a shred of doubt that she was going to enjoy every single second of the Foxworth combat training.

Rylan, in all his masculine glory, was stripped down to a pair of jeans and scuffed black boots, his bare chest and golden hair gleaming in the sunshine.

She suddenly wished she'd fooled around with Beckett last night instead of spending the time catching up and shooting pool with him. If she'd gone to bed well fucked, then maybe her body wouldn't be pulsing like an electric current right now, aching for action.

Speaking of well fucked . . . Lennox looked more relaxed than ever as he strode up to her. He'd disappeared with Reese and Tamara yesterday, and Jamie didn't need to guess what the trio had been up to all night. The answer was right there in Lennox's heavy-lidded gray eyes.

"Had fun last night, did ya?" she teased.

"Reese and I had a lot of catching up to do," Lennox said with a wink.

Three stone walls no more than four feet high enclosed the north side of the town square, and Lennox hopped up on the wide ledge of the back wall. His body was angled so that he was facing the parking lot rather than the bronzed statue in the square behind them. The statue was a man on a horse, but the engraved letters on the plaque at the base had been scratched off. Jamie figured the guy was probably a war hero. Maybe from one of the battles that had been fought long before the final war that had led to the formation of the Global Council.

"I'm sure." She climbed up beside him, unable to keep the amusement out of her voice. "And Tamara? Catching up with her too?"

He shrugged. "She left for South Colony this morning. Someone needed to send her off with a bang."

Jamie snickered.

Their attention turned to the lot, which today was serving as an impromptu gun range. Rylan and Pike had already set up targets in various sections of the lot. Now the two men stood near a large wooden crate, checking the arsenal of handguns and rifles stashed there. Jamie wasn't sure how Reese had accumulated so many weapons, but there was no point in asking the woman. Reese never divulged her secrets if she could help it.

The first group of trainees trickled in. According to Beckett, of the eighty people living in Foxworth, only about twenty of them knew how to shoot a gun. The other sixty were clueless, and Rylan and

Pike were splitting them up into groups of fifteen for the training sessions.

Jamie raised an eyebrow at the amount of young faces she was seeing. Normally she only spent time with Beck, Travis, and a few other close friends, so she hadn't realized there were so many kids in town. Half of the first group was made up of teenagers.

Two skinny boys who couldn't have been older than fourteen were laughing to each other as they walked up. One jabbed the other in the ribs, which led to a lighthearted shoving match that had them cackling.

"Were we ever that young?" she asked Lennox.

He teasingly pinched her arm. "Yep."

"Are you sure? Because I feel so old now. Actually, I felt ancient even when I was their age." She nodded toward the exuberant boys.

"You're twenty-five, love." Lennox grinned. "Hardly what anyone would consider ancient."

Rylan's easygoing drawl drifted over from the target range. "Everyone grab a gun," he was telling the new arrivals. "Hold it. Get used to the weight of it in your hands. Then we'll show you how to load the magazines."

Jamie chuckled as every boy eagerly reached for a handgun. The girls seemed more reluctant, except for one dark-haired teenager who snatched up a slate-gray Glock as if it were a rare piece of chocolate.

"We should have brought Piper," Jamie mused. "She could have benefited from these lessons."

"Rylan can teach her when we get back," Lennox answered in a firm tone. "I don't like her being out in the colony."

"Uh-huh, sure. More like you don't want her witnessing all the debauchery here in Foxworth."

It didn't surprise her when Lennox didn't offer a denial. He couldn't, because he was as protective of Piper as he was of Jamie.

"What, you think Piper's innocent eyes can't handle the sight of you screwing Tamara from behind while she's going down on Reese?"

"That's not what happened last night."

"No?"

He broke out in a wolfish grin. "If you must know, Tamara was riding my face while Reese rode my cock."

The crude confession sent a jolt of lust straight to her pussy. She had no doubt that Lennox had made Reese and Tamara very happy last night. She'd seen him in action before, and damn, her best friend had no problems in the sex department.

"Braggart," Jamie accused.

"Right, like you weren't doing the same thing with Beckett and Travis." Lennox paused, donning a faraway look for a moment. Then he let out a rough curse.

"What's wrong?"

"Nothing." His voice sounded pained. "I was just remembering the last time Beck and Trav were over at the old house."

She remembered it too. Vividly. The two men had driven her wild that night. Beck pounding her pussy while Trav pounded her ass . . . A shiver ran through her as the delicious memories rose to the surface.

Beside her, Lennox shifted as if in discomfort. "How many times did you come that night?"

"God, I can't even remember. Three? Four?"

He grunted out a noise.

Jamie turned toward him, armed with a grin, but the smile died on her lips when she saw his eyes. They were molten, gleaming with raw heat that caught her off guard. It was a look she'd seen often, and one he wore well. A look that dampened the panties of any woman lucky enough to be the focus of that deep, intense stare.

But Jamie wasn't usually on the receiving end of it. Her nipples puckered into tight buds as the heat on Lennox's face singed right through her shirt. Sizzled right to her core. A strange current crackled in the air between them as their eyes locked.

"Len?" she said uncertainly.

His tongue came out to brush his upper lip. Jesus. Either she was completely misreading the situation, or Lennox was actually—

"*Never* point your weapon at someone!" Pike's sharp voice snapped in their direction. "Treat every gun like it's loaded, even if you're sure it isn't."

"Seriously, don't fuck around with these things." Rylan spoke up in agreement, but his voice was far gentler than Pike's. "You wouldn't believe how many innocent suckers have had their brains blown out by 'unloaded' weapons." He air-quoted that, then stepped up to one of the boys and nudged the kid's gun barrel in a safe direction with no human targets in sight.

Jamie liked the easy way Rylan interacted with the teenagers. Pike was too harsh, but that was to be expected, seeing as the man was a coldhearted robot. Rylan was the more personable, down-to-earth of the two, and the kids in the group seemed to respond to that.

"Shouldn't you be over there?"

Lennox's voice had her glancing back at him. It was clear that whatever moment they'd just shared had passed—his usual lazy expression was affixed firmly on his face. No trace of heat whatsoever.

But she knew she hadn't imagined his arousal before. It had been there, clear as the cloudless blue sky above them. Was it her, though? Had *she* been the one to stir his libido, or had he simply gotten off on the idea of Beck and Travis tag-teaming someone? Maybe he'd swapped her face for another woman's as he'd pictured her sandwiched between two men.

That seemed likelier the more she thought about it. She hadn't lied to Hudson when she confessed that Lennox had never shown even a hint of sexual interest in her. So it was hard to imagine that *now*, after twenty-odd years of knowing each other, he'd suddenly decided he wanted her.

It was probably better if he didn't. She'd put her attraction to Lennox to bed a long time ago. She was focusing on other men these days.

"That's one of the reasons you wanted to come here, right?" Lennox added, an edge in his voice. "To brush up on your own training?"

She flushed at the reminder of the lie she'd told him. It had been an excuse for her to spend time with Rylan, and they both knew it.

"I'm more interested in the hand-to-hand stuff," she said, shrugging. "Maybe the knife training too. I already know my way around a gun."

Lennox didn't answer. Tension stretched between them, so thick she could slice it with the knife hooked to her belt, but she didn't know how to make it better.

For the next hour, they watched the training in complete silence, and it wasn't long before Jamie found herself yawning. Rylan and Pike were busy teaching the group how to hold the weapons in a simple two-handed grip, how to provide leverage against the recoil, the proper stance to use when aiming at a stationary target. Nobody had even fired a gun yet.

By the time the trainees were allowed to discharge their weapons, Jamie had reached her boredom breaking point.

"Want to grab something to eat?" she suggested.

With a curt nod, Lennox slid off the ledge and held out his hand to her.

She took it, curling her fingers around his as he helped her to the ground. The tension was still there. She got the feeling he was mad at her, which only triggered a burst of irritation, because she hadn't done a damn thing to deserve his anger.

"Everything okay?" she asked tightly.

His head jerked in another nod. "All good, love."

Bullshit. But she wasn't in the mood to argue or pry. Lennox was like Rylan in many ways—easygoing to the max and oozing sexuality—but he also had his Pike moments of broody intensity. She'd learned never to push him when that moody cloud entered his eyes.

They headed down the cracked cobblestone sidewalk toward the large corner restaurant at the far edge of Main Street. The bright red sign had once read MERYL'S FAMILY RESTAURANT, but someone had crossed out the MERYL's and spray-painted GRAHAM's on top of it. Seeing it always made Jamie chuckle.

"Graham better be cooking up some burgers," she said as Lennox opened the door for her. "Beck said Reese and Sloan were butchering at the farm the other day."

The wind chimes hanging on the doorframe tinkled to signal their entrance. Sure enough, the delicious aroma of beef and deep-fried goodness filled Jamie's nostrils.

Foxworth had an operational farm beyond the town gates, which was run by an older couple who preferred farming and solitude to the constant activity in town. Reese assigned people to work shifts at the farm, but Jamie had never visited the place. It would've made her feel too guilty to look at all those sweet cows knowing she was going to eat one. Apparently the farm had started out with fifteen cows when Reese's group settled in the area, but last time Jamie was in Foxworth, Reese admitted they were down to three.

"What are they going to do when the beef runs out?" she murmured to Lennox, who was guiding her to the long counter across the room.

He shrugged. "Hunt more, I guess. There's lots of game out in these woods."

They slid onto a pair of tattered vinyl stools and greeted the outlaw woman behind the counter.

"Holy shit," Jamie exclaimed, gaping at the pretty brunette. "You absolutely weren't this big when I saw you a month ago, Bethany. You look like you're going to pop any second!"

Bethany rubbed a rueful hand over the enormous

bulge of her stomach. "I know, right? Feels like I'm way too big to only be six months along, but I don't have anyone else to compare it to, so maybe it's normal?"

Jamie didn't have a source of comparison either. There hadn't been a single pregnant woman in her camp growing up, and she and Lennox had never run into one during their travels. Bethany was the first and only woman she knew who was brave enough to get pregnant in the free land, and Bethany's decision brought a tug of envy to Jamie's heart.

She wanted children too.

She really, really did.

The one time she'd confessed it to Lennox, he'd laughed gently and told her she was crazy for wanting to get knocked up. Not only was the free land fraught with danger and hardship, but the Global Council strictly prohibited procreation. Only the hand-picked breeders and studs in the cities were allowed to increase the population, and every pregnancy was carefully monitored.

Outlaw procreation was even more of a concern to the council. The Enforcers rounded up the pregnant women they found, and if they discovered any children in the free land, the parents were killed and the child was whisked away to the city.

So yes, it was a dangerous desire to harbor. Jamie was well aware of that. But the longing was there. The need to put down roots and bring new life to the world was embedded deep inside her, and seeing Bethany's rounded belly and rosy glow only intensified the urge.

"Maybe it's twins," Lennox suggested, waggling his eyebrows.

Bethany paled. "Oh hell, don't say that, Len. I don't think I could handle it. And Arch would faint on the spot."

"He'd lose his shit," Lennox agreed with a laugh, before going serious. "Your man taking good care of you, love? Do I need to have a chat with him?"

Bethany rolled her eyes. "Arch and I are doing just fine. We're both excited for this baby, both pulling our weight."

"Good." Lennox nodded briskly.

Jamie hid a smile. She knew Lennox would've kicked Arch's ass if it turned out he wasn't supporting Bethany. Lennox was everybody's champion, but that was one of the things Jamie loved most about him. He'd lay down his life for the people he cared about. Hell, he'd lay down his life for strangers, depending on the circumstances.

"What can I get you guys?" Bethany asked. "Burgers and fries or beef stew. Take your pick."

"Burgers and fries," they said in unison.

The brunette grinned. "Coming right up." She disappeared into the back to place their order with Graham, the grumpy, bushy-haired cook who had the tendency to call Jamie "little one" even though he couldn't have been a year or two older than her.

The wind chimes over the door gave another melodic ring as Beckett and Travis strode inside. Jamie waved at them, then hopped off the stool to join the two men in a red vinyl booth by the window. Lennox slid in beside her, stretching one arm along the back of the booth, his fingertips lightly grazing her shoulder.

"Hey, Bethy! Burgers!" Beckett held up two fingers toward the counter, gesturing from him to Travis.

"Ever heard of the word *please*?" was Bethany's dry retort.

"Only in bed," he called back. "It's always *please, Beck, fuck me harder. Please, Beck, gimme your cock.*" He feigned a confused look. "Why? Does it have meaning in another context?"

Bethany grinned at him. "I'm spitting in your food, sweetie. Just keep that in mind when you're eating, 'kay?"

Beckett turned back to the group. "She won't spit in my food. She loves me too much."

Jamie laughed, but made a mental note not to take a bite out of anything on Beckett's plate. The man might have women panting over him, but Bethany wasn't someone you should ever underestimate.

Muffled gunfire sounded from the town square, causing Travis's green eyes to shift toward the large front window. "You guys catch any of the target practice?" he asked.

Lennox nodded. "The kids are eager to learn."

"They don't see a lot of excitement here," Travis admitted. "Reese doesn't let them go on supply runs. At least not yet."

"I don't blame her. It's dangerous outside these gates." Lennox absently ran his hand over Jamie's shoulder as he spoke, sending a peculiar shiver along her flesh.

She snuck a peek at his fingers. Long and callused, masculine but graceful. Her gaze slid to his wrist and forearm, resting on the swirls of ink tattooed on his golden skin. The black, red, and orangey designs extended all the way up to his solid biceps. Random pieces he'd accumulated over the years, when they'd been lucky enough to find a tattoo artist during their travels.

His other arm was also inked, but not a full sleeve. Just intricate lines and curves on his forearm, with streams of text hidden within the design. Jamie focused on one line in particular, the unmistakable capital letter inked in gorgeous calligraphy.

J.

He had her initial tattooed on his body. And she had his: an L on her right calf, surrounded by tiny flowers and twisty vines.

Nobody had ever picked up on that. Not Piper or Layla. Not Nell, the good friend they'd lost during the attack on their house. But Jamie had never thought anything romantic of the gestures. She and Lennox were best friends. There was nothing wrong with marking that friendship on their skin.

Right now, however, he didn't feel like a friend. He felt like a brooding, sexed-up man who'd essentially ravaged her with his eyes earlier.

She had no idea how to respond to that.

". . . drinking restrictions too," Beckett was saying.

Her head snapped up. "Wait—repeat that? Are you seriously saying Reese limits how much those teenagers are allowed to drink?"

"Yep." He grinned. "She's a cruel mistress, our Reese. But hell, I can't argue with that. Alcohol and teenagers don't mix well."

"Drunk kids do stupid things," Travis agreed.

Jamie poked Lennox in the side and said, "Drunk adults do stupid things too."

"Bullshit," he retorted. "I can handle my alcohol."

"Uh-huh. Sure." She glanced at the two men across from them. "Ten."

Beckett's lips twitched. "Ten what?"

"That's how many shots Len can handle before he turns into a slurring, bumbling mess."

That got her another protest from Lennox. "Bull-shit!"

Travis looked intrigued. "And how'd you come to this conclusion, sweetheart?"

"Years and years of research," Jamie answered. "First time I noticed it, we were—what, sixteen, Len?"

He grumbled.

"Mr. Cocky over here challenged me to a drinking contest one night, so we stole a bottle of rum from his dad's tent." Jamie stopped, laughing. "Scratch that—*I* stole a bottle of rum from his dad's tent, because Len was too much of a pussy to do it—"

"We flipped a coin," he cut in, his eyes dark with irritation.

She ignored him. "So we took the bottle and snuck down to the beach. We were living on the coast at that time."

"She matched me shot for shot," Lennox admitted, albeit grudgingly.

"And when we got to ten shots, Dumb-ass over here tried to fight a tree."

Beckett and Travis howled with laughter.

Lennox pinched her shoulder, then gave it a little

smack. "There was a goddamn animal in that tree. I told you, I *saw* it."

"Oh, sweetie," was all Jamie said. Then she rolled her eyes and addressed the other men. "After that, I kept count whenever he drank, and it was the same every time—ten drinks and Len does something crazy."

Beckett's demeanor sobered as he looked from her to Lennox. "Must be nice."

She wrinkled her brow. "What's nice?"

"Having history with someone." There was a profoundly sad chord in his tone. "My folks died when I was eight. I was alone in the colony after that."

Jamie hadn't known, and her heart squeezed at the pain she saw in Beckett's eyes. "I'm sorry, babe."

"It's all good. I survived." He shrugged.

"Our parents died too," Lennox said gruffly, his silvery gaze finding Jamie's.

"How?" Beckett asked.

She swallowed as the memories surfaced. "Both our moms died of pneumonia. Lennox's dad too. It wiped out most of our camp, actually. Started off as a cold, eventually turned into chest infections, then pneumonia. We had no meds, no antibiotics, and no way of getting our hands on them. All the Enforcer storage stations in the area had been looted clean."

Lennox's warm hand squeezed her shoulder. "Jamie's dad survived. So did a few others, but about a year after that, we were ambushed by bandits."

"They shot my father," she said flatly.

A pall fell over the booth, and not even the arrival of their lunch could ease the tightness in Jamie's chest.

She missed her parents. She knew Lennox missed his too.

God, why was this world so fucked up?

She felt Lennox soften beside her. Then he brushed a reassuring kiss on her cheek, and with that one moment of tender contact, the tension that had plagued them before faded away like a wisp of smoke. They were good again. She still wasn't sure why they'd ever been *bad*, but she wasn't about to question the abrupt shift. She just leaned in closer and borrowed strength from the strongest man she'd ever known.

The first day of training wrapped up at sundown. Might be too soon to tell, but Rylan had noted some real progress among the trainees, especially the teenagers. They'd been eager to learn and, oddly enough, treated their weapons with far more respect than many of the older folks.

The kids handled the guns with a level of seriousness that Rylan appreciated, as if they had true awareness for the power they held in their hands and the gravity of that responsibility.

The adults had taken that responsibility for granted, wasting ammunition even when it was clear they weren't prepared to hit the target.

Rylan found the discrepancy between the age groups pretty fucking interesting.

"You got this?" he asked Pike, who was in the process of closing up the gun crate.

Pike nodded in response.

"Thanks, brother. See you in the morning."

He left Pike in the dark lot and headed for the sidewalk. Large stone planters lined the cobblestones, and while they might have been overflowing with flowers at one point in time, the planters now served as cisterns to collect rainwater. Rylan paused in front of one and dipped his hands in the cool water.

He splashed his face, then brought his cupped hands to his bare chest and let the water pour over his sweaty flesh. It had been a long day. His ears were still ringing from the continuous bursts of gunfire, and calluses had formed on his fingers from holding a gun for so long.

"Well?"

He turned at the sound of Reese's voice. She approached him in lazy strides, but that laziness was belied by the sharp gleam in her brown eyes.

"Well what?" he asked easily.

"Think any of my people have potential?"

"Everyone has potential when it comes to guns." He rolled his eyes. "It's not too difficult to master the concept of point and shoot."

His mocking tone made her shoulders go rigid. Her *bare* shoulders, because she was wearing a tiny half top that revealed a helluva lot of cleavage and her flat midriff. Tight, dark blue jeans rode low on her hips, and Rylan fought the urge to slide a hand under her waistband and cup her pussy. Stroke it. Then tug the jeans right off, sink to his knees, and shove his tongue inside her.

It took some effort to will away an erection. Reese would probably cut his balls off if she knew where his thoughts had drifted. So would Sloan, who was lurking ten feet away and watching them with a frown.

Rylan had promised Connor he'd work his magic

on Reese, but if he was being honest, he had no fucking idea how to do it. The woman went out of her way to avoid him, and when they *did* interact, her bodyguard was always around.

"I need you to take this seriously," Reese said coldly. "My people have to learn how to defend themselves."

"Don't worry. They'll learn. But if you want me to speculate about their potential, then it's the hand-to-hand combat that'll be the true test."

She nodded.

Keeping his eyes on her, he grabbed the discarded T-shirt he'd tucked into his waistband and used it to mop up his wet chest. Reese's gaze followed the movement of his hand, resting on his pecs before raking over his abs. Her expression lacked the normal flash of lust that most women conveyed when his bare chest was on display.

This woman was so goddamn infuriating. Rylan had wanted her from day one, but all he'd ever gotten from her was dismissal. Disgust. Scorn.

And yet he continued to offer himself up to her like some kind of sexual sacrifice. Continued to face the brunt of her sharp tongue and cold rejections. Maybe it was the challenge of wanting someone he couldn't have. Craving someone who was so damn untouchable turned him into a determined motherfucker.

"You nailing him?"

When she frowned, Rylan cocked his head toward the ever-silent Sloan.

Reese smirked. "Maybe. Maybe not."

"You were with Lennox last night."

The smirk widened. "Was I?"

"You were." He slipped the shirt over his head, smoothing the fabric down his chest. "I bet he fucked you and Tam good."

Reese looked intrigued as he took a step toward her. "Where are you going with this, honey?"

"Just wondering when it'll be my turn." He took another step. She was a tall woman, but tiny compared to him. He always forgot how much shorter she was until he was standing this close to her. Looming over her.

She didn't seem fazed by the disparity in their sizes. She simply tilted her head to meet his eyes and pressed one hand to the center of his chest. "You want a turn, huh?"

The heat of her palm seared through his shirt and sped up his heartbeat. "You know I do, gorgeous."

Her lips curved ever so slightly. "And then what?"

Rylan blinked.

"What happens afterward?" she prompted, her delicate fingers stroking a slow circle around his left pec. "Let's play this out. We get naked. You shove that big cock of yours inside me."

Her fingertips brushed his nipple. When she pressed down hard, a jolt of lust shot through him.

"You fuck me as hard as I know you can. We come." Her fingers traveled to his other pec, rubbing his other nipple, which hardened beneath her touch. "Maybe we fuck again." She pinched the tight bud, and a groan left his lips. "We come again. And then what?"

It was damn near impossible to concentrate when

she was toying with his chest, when her warm fingers were sliding up to his neck to stroke the taut tendons there.

"Then what?" she repeated sharply.

He snapped out of his lust-drenched stupor. "I . . . don't know."

Reese offered a knowing smile. "Yes, you do. Or rather, you know what you're hoping for. That after I open my legs to you, I'll open my mouth. I'll tell you all my secrets, and then you can go running back to Connor so he can say 'good job' and pat you on the back."

Rylan's jaw tensed.

Her laughter just pissed him off further. "We both know that's your agenda."

"I've had the same agenda since the moment I met you." He smirked. "Me, you, naked."

"Yes, but this time your end goal is more than just a couple of orgasms." She dropped her hand to her side and stepped back. "And for the sake of argument—even if you weren't acting as Con's spy? I still wouldn't spread my legs for you. You're trouble, Rylan."

He regained his composure, flashing a wicked smile. "Trouble's fun."

"Trouble gets you killed."

Before he could blink, her hand snapped out and covered his groin.

"When I'm around, honey? This stays in your pants. I don't want it." She gave him a teasing squeeze and he almost came in her hand. "I don't need it."

"Reese—"

"Keep me updated on my people's progress," she

cut in, her voice a cheerful chirp. "I expect daily reports, *gorgeous*."

She squeezed his cock hard enough to make him moan, then released him so abruptly that his dick wept from the loss.

With a soft laugh, she sauntered off in Sloan's direction, leaving Rylan cursing after her in frustration.

7

"Don't block with your dominant hand. You want to be ready with that right cross even as you're deflecting my attack," Lennox explained to the teenage boy he was sparring with.

After four days of training, Rylan and Pike had decided to split the morning crowd into two groups: one was honing target shooting skills with Rylan, the other learning basic fighting moves under Pike's tutelage. Lennox had been recruited to help out. He'd been paired with Randy, a sixteen-year-old who hadn't known not to tuck his thumb into his fist until Lennox showed him the harmful error of his ways.

"But you came at me from the right," Randy protested. "My first instinct is to use my right hand to block."

"Then you need to develop some new instincts." Lennox grinned and came at him with his fist again.

This time Randy used his left forearm to block, but he wasn't fast enough. Lennox's fist connected with the kid's solar plexus, sending him sprawling ass-first on the pavement.

"Can't we do this on the grass?" Randy complained. He rubbed his ass as he awkwardly rose to his feet. "The field behind the high school would give me a nice, soft place to land every time you lay me down."

Lennox snickered. "Helpful tip: If you find yourself surrounded by bandits or Enforcers, chances are, it won't be in a fluffy meadow. It'll be on a supply run or on the road. So get used to cracking your head against the pavement, kid."

Grunts, heavy breathing, and the sounds of fists slamming into flesh echoed all around them. Pike and Beckett were working with their own teenage novices; the others had been paired off to practice the blocking techniques Pike and Lennox had demonstrated at the start of the lesson. Jamie had joined the fold too, sparring with Kade about fifty yards away. She was laughing her sexy ass off as she managed to sweep Kade's legs out from under him for the tenth time in a row.

Connor was right—Kade definitely needed work if a tiny thing like Jamie could get the best of him.

Randy followed Lennox's gaze, then snorted. "I guess I don't feel so bad anymore," the teenager remarked. "That guy can't block for shit either."

"Kade's a city boy. Still has a lot to learn."

"What'd he do in the city?"

"I'm not sure. Never asked him, if I'm being honest. But I assume he was assigned a job like all the other citizens." Though Lennox wasn't sure what kind of job Kade would've been suited for. The guy didn't have Xander's technological prowess, so the tech sector was out. Didn't seem to have any farming or trade skills, so that was out too. A teacher, maybe? Something in administration?

"He's lucky Connor Mackenzie took him in. Citizens are weak. They can't survive out here on their own."

The observation summoned a wry smile. Spoken by a kid who didn't know the difference between an uppercut and a jab.

"Come on, let's take a water break," Lennox suggested.

They grabbed two water bottles from the large cooler near the curb. One of Lennox's favorite things about Foxworth? Ice-cold water. Along with protection and immunity, Reese's hush-hush deals with West City's officials also involved unrestricted electricity from the city's power grid. The Enforcers who visited Foxworth required certain comforts, after all, which meant the food and water in town was refrigerated.

As Lennox welcomed the icy stream that slid down his throat, Randy spoke up again. "Hey, I've always wondered—why does Connor go by his full name? Whenever someone talks about him, they say Connor Mackenzie."

"Not so much anymore, actually. But there used to be another Connor in the area, so the last name made it easier to figure out which Connor you were referring to." Lennox remembered the other Connor being a scary mountain man, but the guy had left the area a couple of years ago.

"I don't know my last name," Randy admitted.

"Not everyone does." Lennox only knew his because his parents were born before the war, during a time when surnames still mattered.

Anyone born postwar didn't have much use for surnames. And while the citizens of West City were given ID badges, most outlaws didn't have proper identification. Some possessed birth records, but those were usually just papers handwritten by their parents, listing the child's name and date of birth.

"Do you know yours?" Randy asked curiously.

Lennox nodded. "Murphy. My dad said it's an Irish name."

The kid donned a blank look. "Irish?"

"Yeah. Meaning it originated in Ireland."

The explanation didn't bring comprehension. Randy simply looked more confused, causing Lennox to narrow his eyes. "You don't know geography? How the world used to be before the Colonies were formed?"

Randy shook his head.

"You serious? Reese doesn't teach you guys that shit?" It surprised him, especially since there was a still-standing library about three miles from Foxworth, full of prewar texts that the younger residents could benefit from.

"Reese says the past doesn't matter," Randy explained. "The other adults think so too. They always tell us they're preparing us for the future."

Lennox supposed he understood that. Truthfully there wasn't much to be gained from dwelling on the past. Knowledge, yes, but history and geography didn't exactly aid in one's survival. His and Jamie's parents had thought it was important, though. At their old camp, all the kids had attended daily classes, where they learned not just the skills that were advantageous to outlaw life, but topics that helped them understand the world that existed before them.

"Hit me like you mean it, baby . . ."

Lennox turned his head toward Jamie's mocking voice. He stifled a laugh when he glimpsed Kade's frazzled expression. The former city boy wound his arm back and lunged for Jamie, but she was too spry for him. She feigned left, then jabbed her elbow in the center of his throat before dancing away.

"I fucking hate you," Kade grumbled.

"No, you don't. You love me. Everyone does." Raising her hands in surrender, she marched up to him and planted a kiss on his cheek. "All right, I'm taking a break now. It's been a pleasure kicking your ass."

She sauntered off, leaving a gale of melodic laughter in her wake.

Randy's eyes glazed over as he unabashedly ogled Jamie's tight ass, which swayed seductively beneath her black leggings. "Think she'd be into me?" the kid asked.

Lennox could barely contain his laughter. "How old are you again?"

"Sixteen."

"Yeah . . . that might be too young for Jamie's blood. She likes men with a little more experience in the saddle."

Randy hesitated. "Is she your woman? The two of you showed up here together last time too."

"More like a sister," he said vaguely. "We've known each other forever."

"But you've, uh, had sex, right?"

"Nope." Though God knew he'd had sex with her in his mind a thousand times already.

But that needed to end, damn it. His dirty imagination had gotten him in trouble the other day, when he forcibly had to stop himself from mauling her in the town square. The memory of Jamie's naked body sandwiched between Beckett and Travis had triggered a bout of lust he hadn't been able to control. Jamie had seen it, and it had scared her. Even worse, it had put a strain on their friendship, making shit awkward between them.

He hadn't liked that. At all.

Kade drifted over, mopping his sweaty face with the bottom of his shirt. He must have heard the tail end of their conversation, because he grumbled, "Your *sister* just gave me a beat-down. Who taught her to fight like that?"

"You're looking at him."

"Yeah?" Kade's head tipped to the side. "Then chug the rest of your water and teach me some shit, because there's no way I'm letting that teeny blond demon win another fight."

Randy started to laugh, but the sound died midchortle, replaced by a choked noise.

Lennox followed the teenager's gaze to see what had clammed him up. A petite girl with a long brown ponytail stood next to Pike, listening attentively to whatever instruction he was giving her. It was the same girl who'd been dominating the target practice, Lennox realized.

"She's cute." He offered a pointed look. "And age-appropriate."

Randy's cheeks took on a reddish hue. "Uh, yeah . . . she's all right."

Lennox and Kade exchanged amused glances.

"What's her name?" Kade asked.

"Sara." The flush deepened. "She and her dad moved here a few months ago. Sloan ran into them on the road and brought them back." Randy awkwardly tilted his head to the left. "That's her dad over there."

Shit. Sara's father was one big motherfucker. At least six-five, with a shaved head and hawklike brown eyes that monitored his daughter's every movement.

"He's kinda overprotective of her," Randy mumbled.

Kinda seemed like a grave understatement. But at least it made sense now why Randy was ready to shit his pants every time he looked at Sara.

Lennox sighed. "You want to spend time with her, huh? But you're afraid of her father."

"Wouldn't *you* be? He's a giant. And he never lets her out of his sight."

Lennox thought it over. "You want my advice? Forget him."

The kid gaped at him. "Um . . . yeah, right."

"I'm serious. If you want to get to know her, get to know her. Scary Dad over there ain't gonna kill you just for talking to her."

"He might."

"Nah." Kade grinned and backed up Lennox. "Just make sure to keep your pants zipped around her, and you'll be fine."

Lennox shrugged. "Besides, if he does kick your

ass, who cares? Bruises fade. Broken bones heal. Life's too short, kid. If you really like this chick, then you've gotta make a move. You might never get the opportunity again."

Randy went quiet, mulling over the advice. Then he set his jaw in determination and raised his hand in the air. "Nice hit, Sara!" he called out.

She whirled around, her ponytail a brown blur. The girl she'd just knocked on her ass was clambering to her feet, but Sara's surprised gaze was focused on Randy. "Oh. Um. Thanks," she called back.

Lennox pressed his lips together to smother his amusement. Kade seemed to be doing the same. Sara's dad, on the other hand, didn't look at all pleased by the exchange. The man glowered at Randy, who simply waved politely.

"You've got balls, kid," Kade murmured.

"Big brass balls," Lennox agreed. He smacked Randy on the shoulder, unable to fight the pride in his chest. "Okay, time to get back to work. You can cheer me on while I kick Kade's ass."

As they walked back to the fighting area, Kade's low, knowing voice met Lennox's ears. "You should take your own advice."

Randy kept walking, but Lennox stopped, warily turning toward the other man. "What the hell does that mean?"

"It means I'm not as oblivious as everyone thinks." Kade offered a wry smile. "You want her, Len."

He decided to play dumb. "Who?"

"You know who." Kade went quiet for a beat. "I'm not sure what's holding you back, but whatever it is, I doubt it's as bad as you think, man. Life's too short, remember?"

Lennox gritted his teeth as the other man threw his own words back at him, but for the first time in his life, he didn't have a sarcastic retort or a careless remark to toss back.

"A bunch of pussies, that's what they are," Rylan announced, his irritated voice echoing in the cavernous loft that Beckett and Travis shared.

Lennox had to grin at the disgust twisting the other man's handsome features. It was rare to see Rylan drop his careless facade, but clearly the day's training had gotten to him. Lennox didn't blame him—there *had* been a shit ton of complaints floating through Foxworth these past four days.

Rylan turned the bone-handle knife in his hand a few times as he studied the wooden beam ten feet away. "One kid said he had a sore *finger* from pulling the trigger so many times. Can you fucking believe that?"

With a look of sheer disbelief, he gripped the handle so his thumb was pressed to its side, pulled his arm back, and lunged forward to hurl the knife.

The blade hit the beam with a *ping* but didn't connect with the wood, instead clattering to the weathered hardwood floor.

"Miss!" Beckett crowed. "You're up, Len."

Lennox studied his target, a wooden post that extended from floor to ceiling and was about a foot wide. The loft had an open-concept setup, with brick walls, exposed beams, and rusted piping. Beck and

Travis's sleeping quarters were on one side of the room, while the other end featured couches, a bar area, and plenty of space for the night's activity— knife throwing.

It was a small crowd tonight, not a party by any means, unless you counted the private party currently happening on a nearby couch. The two half-naked women tangled together there were drawing more than a few lustful glances from the knife-wielding men.

Lennox took a step back. Then another, this one at a forty-five-degree angle to his right. A second later, he wound his arm back and released the blade of the hunting knife when it was vertical to his target. The blade sliced into the wood as if the post were made of soft butter.

"Hit!" Beck exclaimed. He passed over the whiskey bottle so Lennox could take a swig.

Shit, he really wished he wasn't so good at this game. The rules were rather ridiculous—instead of taking a shot each time he missed, the thrower drank when he hit his mark. Lennox wasn't sure who came up with that, but it definitely wasn't to his advantage. He was very, very good with a knife. Which meant he was going to get very, very drunk tonight.

Behind him, Rylan was still griping about the gripers. "And that guy that helps Graham in the kitchen? He said he's sitting out tomorrow because squinting at the targets hurts his *eyes*. What the hell is wrong with these people? I've never met a more pathetic, sheltered crowd."

Pike took his turn, then tipped the bottle to his

lips after his knife hit its mark. "There are some pretty decent fighters in the afternoon group," he relented. "That chick Sam got me under her today."

Rylan hooted. "Bullshit. You *let* her do that because you wanted her under you. You're gonna be balls deep in that one tonight, brother."

Pike didn't deny it.

"Sam's a wildcat in bed," Beckett revealed with a grin. "She'll scratch and claw the hell outta you."

Pike looked intrigued, and Lennox tried not to roll his eyes. The bastard got off on sex with a side of violence. Shocker.

"Seriously, though," Rylan said, his face growing strained again. "What do we do about these fuckers? I don't think I can deal with another three weeks of this bullshit complaining. You'd think we're doing them a disservice or something." Sarcasm dripped from his tone. "Gee, assholes, *so* sorry we're teaching you how to defend yourselves. Ungrateful pricks."

Lennox snickered. It was his turn to throw again. He let the knife fly, then watched as it pinged off the post and bounced on the floor. Thank fuck. He'd hit his last seven targets, and his head was starting to feel foggy from the subsequent whiskey shots. But not foggy enough to stop an idea from forming.

"This is what you should do," he told Rylan, then nodded toward Beckett, who was flipping his knife in his left hand.

Rylan snorted. "What, throw knives at their heads and scare them into submission?"

"Make it fun. Turn it into a game." Lennox paused as he worked over the details. "No, a competition.

Split them up into teams and have them go up against each other. You can award points or some shit. Give 'em prizes."

"That's not a bad idea," Rylan said slowly.

"Could work," Pike grunted. "Might shut them up."

Rylan taunted his friend. "Thought their bitching didn't bother you . . ."

"No, it's fucking annoying, bro. I just don't see the point in bitching about the bitching."

Lennox laughed.

"Up again, Len," Beckett said.

Crap. He was getting too drunk for this. Might need to bow out of the game soon, unless he wanted to explain to Reese why he'd accidentally flung a knife at one of her people's throats.

Judging the distance to the post was getting difficult, thanks to his alcohol-hazed vision. Even as he took his shot, he had no idea if he'd moved far enough back for the knife to make a complete rotation, but to his dismay, the blade slammed into the post. Dead center.

Beckett grinned at him. "Drink."

Eight shots in less than an hour. Jesus. He needed to slow down.

Ten drinks and Len does something crazy . . .

Jamie's teasing comment from the other day buzzed in his mind, summoning a strangled laugh. She was right—excessive drinking screwed with his head. Damn woman knew him too damn well.

The men went another round, which, unfortunately, led to Lennox slugging back his ninth shot of whiskey.

When it was Rylan's turn, the man grumbled, "I

am not as drunk as I need to be. Swear to God, I'm taking a drink even if I miss this—"

No sooner had the words left his mouth than a knife whizzed through the air from behind him. The blade nearly clipped Rylan's ear off before connecting with the beam he'd been aiming for. The steel vibrated wildly as it lodged itself into the wood.

Everyone turned to see who had launched the blade, and Lennox snickered when he spotted Reese and Jamie. The women were standing by the door thirty feet away. Reese was clearly the perpetrator, because she gave Rylan a dainty little wave, which only made Lennox laugh harder.

"I see you haven't won her over yet," he said.

Rylan just grinned. "The night's still young."

Across the room, Reese arched one eyebrow. "Pike, Rylan," she called out. "I need to talk to you."

The two men wasted no time walking over to her. A moment later, the trio left the loft while Jamie wandered over to the group. She stopped to kiss both Lennox and Beckett on the cheek, then headed for the tall table that served as a makeshift bar counter. Lennox watched as she poured herself a drink and stood close to Travis, who wrapped one muscular arm around her shoulders and whispered something in her ear.

"Game over?" Beckett asked him.

"Fuck yes." Shit, was he slurring? "I haven't been this wasted in ages."

So wasted, in fact, that he stumbled over to the nearest couch and dropped his ass onto it. Chuckling, Beckett sat next to him, the whiskey bottle still firmly in hand.

Someone put on some music. Lennox wasn't sure

who, but he welcomed the sultry drum and bass beat that suddenly echoed through the room. A few other people drifted into the loft. Nash, with a pretty blonde by his side. Davis and Rick, who grabbed drinks and then stood to the side, chatting among themselves. Travis and Jamie were dancing now, their hands lazily roaming each other's clothed bodies as Travis thrust one thigh between Jamie's legs and ground against her.

Lennox's dick stirred at the sight. He hadn't gotten laid since that first night with Reese and Tamara, and the booze was making him horny.

Beside him, Beckett didn't miss the enormous bulge straining beneath Lennox's zipper. He laughed, then offered a mischievous smile. "Need a hand?"

As the alcohol pounded through his blood, Lennox leaned back with a smirk. "Do your worst."

"My best, you mean." Still grinning, Beckett slid closer and undid Lennox's pants.

He released a husky groan the moment his rock-hard cock met the other man's waiting hand. Beckett gave a slow pump. Lennox's eyes rolled to the top of his head.

Fuck. That felt good.

His dick agreed, pulsing incessantly in Beckett's hand. Lennox wasn't into screwing men, but a hand on his cock was a hand on his cock.

And damn, that hand knew exactly what it was doing.

Beckett stroked the sensitive underside of Lennox's dick, then twisted his fist around the head and slid it down to the base in a sharp stroke.

"Jesus," Lennox choked out.

Beckett chuckled.

Pleasure zipped down Lennox's spine and grabbed hold of his balls when he caught Jamie watching them. Even with her body wrapped around Travis's, all her attention was focused on the two men on the couch. Fascination danced in her blue eyes as they followed the fast motion of Beckett's hand.

Lennox winked at her, then closed his eyes, losing himself in the arousal overtaking his body. When a warm, wet mouth closed around him, he jerked, slitting his eyes open to find Beckett kneeling over him. The colorful tattoos covering both of Beck's arms rippled as his sculpted muscles flexed, as he braced one hand on the couch and wrapped the other around Lennox's shaft.

Lennox dragged his palm over the man's buzzed hair. "Fuck yeah. Suck me."

Another groan slipped out when Beckett tightened the suction and engulfed his entire length with one deep swallow. His eyes fluttered shut again. Beck's stubble abraded his thigh as the man's mouth sucked him hard and deep.

Blow jobs from men were a more savage affair, Lennox had found. Faster, rougher, involving cunning confidence that he appreciated. Beck didn't tease. He wasn't gentle. He just went to town on Lennox's cock until his balls drew up so tight they damn near disappeared.

He was too drunk to delay his release. He wanted to come. Now. He dug his fingers into the scratchy sofa cushion and thrust his cock deeper into Beckett's mouth. His hips snapped up as he fucked the man's face, feeling the orgasm rise to the surface and—

His eyes flew open at Jamie's approach. He'd sensed her presence, and the release that had been seconds from spilling over froze in his body like a bullet stopping in midair.

Jamie's blue eyes blazed with undisguised interest as she asked, "Is this a private party or can anyone join in?"

8

Walk away. Every rational part of Lennox's brain screamed for him to do that. No, to come in Beckett's warm mouth, *then* walk away.

But his split second of hesitation cost him.

The other man released him and lifted his head, licking his wet, swollen lips before greeting Jamie with a wicked smile. "I think the party just started, baby."

In the blink of an eye, Beckett sat up and tugged Jamie onto his lap. Her short filmy skirt rode up, revealing firm, pale thighs that made Lennox's heart beat a little faster. He'd seen her naked before. Hundreds of times. He'd seen her crying out with pleasure and trembling in orgasm. But it had always been from afar, and never with his cock hanging out, hard enough to cut stone.

"Don't stop on my account," she drawled. "Look at that big dick, Beck. It's dying for your mouth again."

Her eyes rested on Lennox's jutting erection, which grew impossibly harder. Shit, her appreciative gaze was a goddamn ego boost. He knew he was well endowed, but this was the first time his best friend had ever acknowledged that.

With a chuckle, Beckett slipped his hand under her skirt. "Dicks are fun and all, but this is where it's at, baby." His hand moved beneath the silky fabric, and Jamie's answering moan almost caused Lennox to blow his load.

Screw it. He was already in this deep. His cock was on display for Jamie's gaze to devour, balls aching so badly he was in genuine pain. Kade's advice to take what he wanted buzzed in his mind. He couldn't do it, though. At least not in the way his body demanded him to.

But . . .

"Lift up her skirt," he said roughly.

Jamie's eyes widened. He understood her surprise. Although he'd watched her with other men before, this was the first time he'd spoken during one of those encounters. The first time he'd interfered.

He wasn't opening that door. He *wasn't*. But damn it, the opportunity was there. The door wasn't open, but it was ajar. Only a small crack, and God help him, but he was powerless to resist from stepping through it.

Beckett's dark eyes gleamed. He bunched Jamie's hem between his fingers and slowly dragged it upward.

With every inch of smooth skin exposed to his gaze, Lennox's mouth went drier and drier. But his cock was leaking. He rubbed the pad of his thumb over the precome pooling at his tip and used it to slick his throbbing shaft. Jamie's eyes remained glued to his groin.

Sensing that Lennox was in charge, Beckett went still. He'd pushed Jamie's skirt all the way up to her waist, revealing her skimpy black panties, but now he waited for further instruction.

"Cup her pussy," Lennox ordered in a low voice. "I want to know how wet her panties are."

The other man obeyed, then released a groan. "Soaked."

Lennox watched as Beck stroked his palm between Jamie's thighs. When he lifted his gaze to her face, he saw that her cheeks were flushed with arousal. But her eyes . . . they flickered with confusion.

"What's the matter, love? You don't like what he's doing to you?"

The taunt had the desired effect. She parted her thighs even wider and narrowed her eyes at him. "I'd like it better if he was fucking me with his fingers. And if you put your hand on your cock while he did it."

Lennox smiled. "Beckett?"

"Hmmm?"

"Take her panties off."

The other man smacked Jamie's bottom. "Lift up, baby. Let's get these off."

Jamie rose from his lap, still watching Lennox even as Beckett tugged at the scrap of underwear. The silky fabric was dragged down her legs, then flicked away. Beckett brought her back into his lap. One arm came around her waist, long fingers splaying across her flat belly.

"Part those pretty pussy lips with your fingers, Beck. Spread her open so I can see."

Beckett's palm moved lower, skimming the top

of Jamie's mound. Two fingers slid up and down her slit before he did what Lennox asked. He parted her folds, then dipped the tip of one finger inside her.

"So fucking wet," Beck informed Lennox.

Yeah, he could see that. Her pussy was glistening. It was so damn beautiful. Pale pink and delicate, with a tiny little clit that Beckett was now rubbing with his index finger.

Lennox grabbed hold of his stiff shaft. When he gave it a lazy stroke, Jamie's eyes darkened from light blue to smoky cobalt. There was something oddly familiar about what was going down, and it took him a moment to pinpoint it.

They'd been here before, he and Jamie.

Years ago, she'd worn that same expression of primal lust as she watched him stroke his own dick. She thought she was being sneaky. Creeping after him in the middle of the night, hiding behind a tree while he jerked off. But Lennox had known she was there—and he'd taken full advantage of that knowledge. Instead of a quick jack-off session on the beach, he'd dragged it out, turned it into a performance Jamie wouldn't soon forget.

He'd been eighteen then, and already painfully aware that Jamie was the most important person in his life. If he didn't keep her at a distance, he risked losing her. That night he'd allowed himself to be a little risky. He'd known that letting her watch was as close as they'd ever come to actually screwing, and so he hadn't let on that he knew she was there. He'd let her watch every dirty second.

"You want me to make her come?"

Beckett's voice drew him back to the present. To

yet another illicit encounter with Jamie that Lennox suspected would end the same damn way—with him coming hard enough to forget his own name.

"Not yet." His voice sounded hoarse, gravelly. He cleared his throat. Gave his dick another stroke. "Play with her clit. Tease her."

Beckett smiled wickedly.

Fuck. This was such a bad idea. Alcohol really did make Lennox do some seriously stupid things sometimes. But he was helpless to stop it.

He kept his gaze on Jamie's face. He memorized every last detail, gauged her responses to learn what got her off. When Beck used a featherlight touch on her clit, he was rewarded with breathy noises. When Beck rubbed harder, she gasped. When he slowed down again, she moaned.

Lennox squeezed the head of his cock, trying to prolong his release. Now that Jamie was here, he didn't want to shoot off too early. He wanted to savor every goddamn second.

His gaze lowered to the blunt male fingertips rubbing circles around Jamie's swollen flesh. "Look at that hot little clit," Lennox murmured. "You want his tongue on it, love? You want him to suck on it?"

Her breasts rose beneath her tank top as she took an unsteady breath. Lennox wished he'd ordered Beck to strip her completely, but there was something seriously naughty about the fact that her shirt and skirt were still on. It drew all his focus to her pussy, and he hissed when he noticed the wetness coating her inner thighs.

"He's not going to lick you." Lennox gave his cock another tug as he vocalized the decision.

"Why not?" A husky, desperate whisper.

"Because then I'd lose my view." He moistened his lips. His hand continued to work his shaft. Fast enough to make her eyes glaze over.

"I think she wants your cock," Beckett murmured. "You gonna fuck her or what, Len?"

"No." He laughed when both Jamie and Beckett groaned in disappointment. "*You* are. Two fingers, Beck. More if she can take it."

Jamie visibly shivered as Beckett's rough hands pushed her thighs farther apart, a move that provided Lennox with an even hotter view. Christ, her pussy was drenched. He had to fight not to lean in and shove his face between her legs. He wanted to taste her. He wanted to lash his tongue on her clit while he finger-fucked her. He wanted to hear her scream his name.

Not gonna happen, bro.

Nope. He supposed he had to take what he could get.

"Beckett," he warned when the other man took too long to obey.

Beck moved his lips to Jamie's neck, chuckling softly. "Len is getting impatient," he teased. "Should we give him what he wants or piss him off even more?"

Jamie looked mighty interested in the latter. Winking at Lennox, she twisted her face toward Beckett and the two of them exchanged a long, passionate kiss.

Lennox groaned in frustration. He saw a flash of tongue. The noticeable clenching of Jamie's thighs as Beckett captured her lower lip with his teeth and bit gently. The man's hand was fisted in Jamie's pale hair, angling her head to drive the kiss deeper.

Their mouths devoured each other for what felt like hours, until Lennox growled impatiently. "Cock teases," he bit out.

They turned to grin at him, Jamie's pouty lips glistening from Beckett's kisses.

Christ. How messed up was it that in all the years he'd known her, he'd never kissed this woman? A peck on the lips, sure. Lots of cheek action. The occasional forehead kiss.

But a real, soul-melting kiss with greedy tongues and racing hearts? Lennox wasn't fortunate enough to know what that felt like. He could imagine it pretty well, though. And . . . fuck, just the thought of Jamie sucking on his tongue the way she'd sucked on Beckett's was enough to speed up his pulse.

"Shove your fingers inside her, goddamn it." The command was ripped from his throat as he jacked himself with renewed vigor.

Beckett finally did what he was told, pushing two long fingers into Jamie's wet heat. Deep enough to make her cry out.

"Holy fuck," she croaked, even as her lower body arched to accept the intimate intrusion.

Beck's body was moving too, jean-clad thighs rocking beneath Jamie as the man ground his dick against her ass.

Lennox was more interested in Jamie. The fire in her eyes as Beckett increased the tempo, his fingers thrusting over and over again while his thumb tended to her clit.

"Ride his hand," Lennox commanded. "I want you to come all over his fingers."

"What about you?"

Her voice was so soft he could barely hear her. "What's that, love?"

"Where are you going to come?" Jamie's expression grew tortured. She squirmed in pleasure as Beckett's fingers filled her in deep, hard strokes.

"Where do you want me to?" He hadn't meant it as a taunt, but somehow it sounded that way.

Jamie's lips parted to release a strangled moan. "Inside me."

His entire body froze. His heart stopped beating.

The ache in his balls was downright painful, and his hand was trembling wildly around his shaft. Sweet fucking God. He wanted that more than he wanted his next meal, his next breath. Just to plunge inside her and screw that tight pussy until he came inside her. Until he filled her up with his seed and then watched it drip down her thighs, marking her from the inside out.

"No." He spoke so sharply even he had to wince. Softening his tone, he rasped, "I think I'll let Beck finish what he started."

Lennox rose from the couch, surprisingly steady on his feet. His jeans were still on but unzipped, his dick out and at face-level with Beckett, who groaned when Lennox guided it toward him.

"Let's see how well he multitasks," Lennox murmured to Jamie. He peered down at Beckett with mocking eyes. "Think you can make both of us come at the same time, man?"

Beck growled and reached for Lennox's cock

with his free hand. "You better fucking believe it." His other hand remained firmly lodged between Jamie's legs. Two fingers, thrusting hard enough to make her bounce in his lap.

A warm mouth took Lennox in deep, summoning a low groan. He was vaguely aware of the attention they were attracting. Travis and Nash leaning against one of the exposed beams, their hot gazes fixed on the trio. The two girls who'd been going at it before had stopped what they were doing, also watching in fascination.

Beckett's tongue glided along Lennox's shaft to get it slick, but there was no need. He was oozing precome, so close to bursting his vision had gone misty. But not misty enough that he didn't see Jamie. She was *all* he saw.

Her big blue eyes. Her lush mouth. Her graceful neck arching as she breathlessly rode Beckett's hand.

The dark male head bobbing up and down Lennox's cock captured Jamie's attention. Moan after moan escaped her lips. Then she started to beg. "Suck him all the way down, Beck. Get him close."

Jesus Christ. Beckett was now deep-throating him. Stars flashed in front of Lennox's eyes, and his hips pistoned as he drilled Beckett's hot mouth.

"Goddamn it, love," he hissed at Jamie. "I don't come until you do. Let me see it."

Her gaze burned into him, thick with desire. She reached down and rubbed her clit, delicately at first, then faster, rubbing in tight circles as she sank down onto Beckett's fingers.

"Len . . ." His name slipped out on a shaky breath. "I'm almost there."

He cupped the back of Beckett's head, stilling the man's greedy pulls on his dick. The base of his spine was tingling. He was seconds away from losing control.

"Give her another finger," Lennox ordered.

The answering male moan vibrated in Lennox's cock, nearly sending him over the edge. He clenched his ass cheeks to stop the release, focusing instead on the hand between Jamie's thighs. Beck's fingers, three of them now. Slick from Jamie's juices as they stretched her open and fucked her to an orgasm that made her shudder.

Her moan of abandon triggered Lennox's release. He spilled into Beckett's mouth in long, pulsing jets, while his gaze stayed locked with Jamie's. While his heart pounded and his mind imploded, the pleasure so intense he could barely stay on his feet.

Jamie's breathing was as shallow as his as she shook uncontrollably on Beckett's lap. The other man groaned loudly and Lennox's dick slid out of his mouth. "Coming," Beckett choked out.

Lennox barely registered the man's climax. With his own orgasm fading away, the realization of what he'd done crashed into him like a lead weight. He hastily tucked himself in his pants and zipped up, focusing his gaze anywhere but on Jamie. He sensed her watching him, though. Felt her confusion and uneasiness hanging in the air. Heard her unspoken questions.

But he had no answers for her. Just his own personal dose of agitation, and the awful suspicion that he'd screwed everything up.

* * *

Reese stopped in the middle of the sidewalk outside Beckett's loft. "Got lots of complaints today," she said with a frown. "My people say you're riding them too hard."

Neither Rylan nor Pike looked at all repentant, not that she'd expected them to be. Connor and his men were cold, ruthless pricks. Pike, in particular, but the description also extended to Rylan. The man used his killer grin and disarming southern drawl to fool everyone he met into believing he was harmless.

"Your people are weak." Pike was curt and to the point.

"And all they do is whine," Rylan added in annoyance. "You'd think they've never been knocked around before."

"They haven't," she retorted. "They're kids who've had their parents protecting them all their lives."

"Lucky them."

Rylan's bitterness caught her off guard, because it was rare to see him lose the Mr. Charming act. It suddenly occurred to her that she didn't know anything about his background except that he'd once trained army recruits. Connor wasn't one to volunteer many details about his men.

"What about the older ones?" Pike mocked. "What's their excuse? We had four no-shows today, and about twenty assholes crying about their sore muscles."

She stifled a groan, but it was hard to suppress the wave of self-reproach that crested inside her. She'd been too easy on some of the newer arrivals and she knew it. When Jake was in charge, he'd been a total hard-ass, damn near tyrannical when it came to the outlaws he took under his protection. He'd trained them, pushed them, made sure they could wipe their own asses without requiring assistance.

Reese's approach had been similar, at least at the beginning of her reign. Lately she'd been trying to ease up on her people. After a while it got tiresome knowing that everyone thought she was a raging bitch.

But damn it, she'd allowed them to get too soft.

Rylan narrowed his eyes when he noticed her expression, and she cursed her face for revealing her worries. His voice lost its edge as he said, "Don't worry, gorgeous. We have an idea about how to make this less of a chore for them."

"How?" she asked suspiciously.

"We're thinking of turning it into a competition. Breaking them up into teams and having them go up against each other." He shrugged. "We can come up with different events for them to compete in. Short- and long-range targets, moving targets, sparring, knife skills, that sort of shit. They can rack up points and we'll declare a winning team at the end."

She had to relent. "That's not a bad idea."

"It'd be better if there was a prize at the end, something they're all fighting toward. Any ideas?"

Reese thought it over for a moment. "Beef," she decided.

Rylan's mouth quirked up. "I'm trying to figure out if that's a euphemism or not."

She rolled her eyes. "Literal beef. We're not butchering again until the end of winter, so we're rationing all the meat we have. We can give the winning team steaks. You know, some choice cuts of meat."

Pike nodded. "Good plan."

She couldn't figure out if he was being sarcastic—it was impossible to judge the man's tone. But she decided to treat it as a sincere comment. "Fine. Go ahead with the plan, then."

"We done here?" he said curtly.

"Yes."

Pike left without a word, stalking down the darkened street until he disappeared from view. He usually stayed in one of the town houses on the outskirts of the town, where he kept to himself. That was how he operated—took care of business and then got the hell out. She'd always appreciated that about him.

Rylan, of course, lingered. "So we're in agreement about this competition thing?"

"I just said so, didn't I?" she said irritably.

His blue eyes gleamed. "Seal it with a blow job?"

"Good night, Rylan."

She spun on her heel and went to join Sloan, who'd been standing by one of the broken streetlamps watching the exchange. Without a backward glance, the two of them headed to her brick building and climbed the narrow staircase to the second floor.

Rather than turn on the lights, Reese lit a couple of candles and collapsed wearily on the huge futon in the center of the room.

Sloan leaned against the wall. The damn man never sat. Sometimes she wondered if he even slept. He had a bed in the next room, but fuck if she'd ever seen the sheets messed up.

"Teresa."

The name, uttered in a low, harsh voice, caught her off guard. He only used her full name when he was about to get serious. Well, more serious than usual, anyway.

"Sloan," she answered coolly.

His lips twitched. "You hate it when I call you that."

She did. She really did. It was what Jake had called her, and all reminders of Jake were too much to bear.

"I needed to get your attention." He went quiet for a moment. Then, to her surprise, he breached the ten feet of distance between them and knelt in front of the mattress.

He didn't touch her. Didn't even blink. He simply stared at her with that impenetrable gaze of his.

"What is it?" she said uncertainly.

"You're playing this wrong."

She narrowed her eyes.

"Rylan," he clarified. "You need to stop antagonizing him, sweetheart."

"I can't help it," she grumbled. "He annoys me."

Sloan gave a rare chuckle. "I know. But the harder you push him away, the more he'll push back. The more he'll pursue you." He arched one dark eyebrow. "The whole point was to make him *not* take notice. To make sure he doesn't get suspicious. Which means you have to stop fighting him."

She swallowed. "What, you think I should fuck him?"

His square jaw tensed up. "That's not what I'm saying."

"Then what?"

"Just . . . be nicer."

A genuine laugh popped out of her mouth. "Um, impossible. I'm not a nice person, honey."

"Yes, you are."

The intensity in his gaze brought a flicker of discomfort. And she was even more uncomfortable when he edged forward and lightly stroked her chin with two strong hands.

It was so excruciatingly intimate that she leaned away from his touch and averted her eyes.

Sloan didn't look upset by her withdrawal, only resigned. "Rylan isn't Jake," he said gruffly.

Her shocked gaze snapped up to his. "I know."

"Jake is dead."

"I know."

"We killed him."

"I kn—" This time the response got stuck in her throat. Sloan's blunt, emotionless voice sent a shiver up her spine.

Silence stretched between them. An eternity of it, as Sloan's dark eyes probed hers.

"You still want to go ahead with our plans?" he finally asked.

She nodded without hesitation.

"Then cut back on the aggression. Give Rylan something else to focus on. Something that doesn't involve him chasing you into bed."

"Like what?"

"You'll figure something out." He rose to his full height and straightened his broad shoulders. He was so much taller than Jake had been. There was so much power and restraint rippling from his warrior's body.

"It should have been you," Reese whispered.

Those big shoulders stiffened.

"You should have been the leader, Sloan. Not Jake. Not me."

His dark eyes went veiled. "It's exactly the way it's supposed to be, sweetheart."

Then he ducked into the room next door, leaving her to ponder his cryptic response.

9

Jamie missed her target completely. Epically, in fact, as the bullet hit the corner of the building thirty yards away and caused a chunk of brick to splinter off.

Loud laughter from her opponents rang behind her. Rylan, who was leading the exercise, strode up to her. "What the hell was that, sweetheart?" Looking exasperated, he tossed over his shoulder, "Blue Team! Ignore what your team leader just did! It's not to be replicated!"

"Why am I team leader again?" Jamie grumbled, lowering her rifle.

"Because nobody else wanted to do it."

"*I* don't want to do it."

"Sure you do." Rylan leaned closer and she became distracted by his scent, masculine and heady, a hint of sweat and spice.

But even as she inhaled deeply, there was another scent still lodged in her nose. Lennox, whose familiar smell had surrounded her when his abs were inches from her face two nights ago. When his cock was tunneling in and out of Beckett's mouth. Lennox's scent always held a trace of citrus, which confused her because there weren't exactly any lemon trees in the area. But it was something she'd noticed since they were kids.

"Jamie?"

Crap. She'd spaced out again. "Sorry, what?"

Rylan looked exasperated. "All right. I think it's time for a break." He glanced at the crack she'd left in the brick facade, sighed, then cupped both hands over his mouth and shouted, "Grab some water and re-group, everyone! The next event will start in an hour. Until then, pair up and practice those fighting moves."

Jamie stifled a laugh. They'd already competed in one other "event" this morning—short-range target shooting—and her team had come away with the cov-eted "point." Which meant absolutely nothing, be-cause Rylan and Pike's scoring system didn't make a lick of sense to her.

There were four teams competing in the training tournament, with Jamie, Lennox, Beckett, and Travis serving as team leaders. Jamie's group included a teenager named Sara, who'd beat out Lennox's charge, Randy, to win the shooting competition earlier. The girl had impressed the hell out of Jamie with the way she'd handled that Glock.

Despite the complicated point system, it was obvi-ous the tournament was a resounding success so far. Rylan had posted the schedule of events in the rec hall, and along with keeping track of the scoring, he and Pike were continuing to help the competitors hone their skills. Jamie hadn't heard a single complaint about the rigorous schedule or the backbreaking physical exertion since the tournament began. It seemed that everyone, young and old, was having fun.

Well, maybe not *everyone*. Lennox had that moody look in his eyes again, she realized when she snuck a peek in his direction. She'd done that a lot today, sneaking glances whenever he wasn't looking.

Her mind refused to quit obsessing over what had happened at the loft. What the hell did it mean? Why had Lennox let it happen? He'd never, ever gone there with her before. He'd drawn a line between them years ago, right down the center of their friendship, making sure to keep sexual activity firmly on the other side of that line.

And then he'd gone and trampled right through the barrier he'd erected. He'd whispered filthy instructions to Beckett, his husky voice coaxing Jamie to the most intense orgasm of her life. It had scared her so much that she was now avoiding him.

They'd barely exchanged five words these past two days, but Lennox hadn't once commented on the distance between them. She suspected he was equally uncomfortable about what had happened, but he was expressing that discomfort in a far more hostile way, with sullen looks and the occasional narrowing of his eyes, as if he were trying to burrow into her mind.

"What's going on with you?" Rylan asked, concern creasing his brow.

She lowered the rifle, letting the strap hang loosely from her shoulder. "I haven't been sleeping well," she admitted.

"You should've paid me a late-night visit . . ."

His tone was teasing, but she just rolled her eyes. "Really? Because I've barely seen you since we got here."

Rylan gave a sheepish look. "Yeah . . . I've been busy."

She bristled inwardly. He'd been busy, all right. Busy ogling Reese.

Rylan's infatuation with the Foxworth leader wasn't a big secret, but this time around, his intensity and determination to get into Reese's pants were alarming. Jamie constantly caught him staring at the redhead, and she didn't think he'd gotten laid even once since they arrived in Foxworth.

A loud thump caught her attention and she turned her head to find Kade sprawled on the pavement. He was glaring up at Lennox, who was totally unapologetic about the blow he'd delivered.

"You need to stop telegraphing your attack," Lennox remarked dryly. "I can see every move you're about to make from a mile away."

The men had stripped off their shirts for the sparring session, and Jamie's gaze raked over her best friend's impressive chest. The roped muscles, the tattoos, the hard six-pack. She wanted to lick every inch of his sinewy golden skin . . .

No, damn it. She needed to stop thinking about him in that way. Whatever had happened between them in the loft wasn't going to happen again. She wasn't allowed to be attracted to Lennox again. Last time it only ended with heartache and frustration. Longing after a boy she couldn't have, watching him screw every girl in camp except her. It had hurt.

And the sting of rejection had stuck with her for months. She didn't ever want to feel that way again.

She forcibly wrenched her gaze off Lennox and shifted it to Rylan, whose bare chest was equally enticing. Whose defined biceps flexed as he ran a hand through his hair. It was getting longer, falling into his eyes.

Before she could stop herself, Jamie reached out and gently brushed the golden strands off his forehead. God, she needed Rylan to kiss her and distract her from all these confusing feelings. At least with Rylan she knew where they stood—good friendship spiced up with lust. Nothing more.

"Thanks," he said huskily.

She trailed her fingers along his cheekbone. "How about you come find me later?" she suggested in a voice that sounded breathy to her ears. "Help me fall asleep tonight."

His blue eyes went heavy-lidded. "I can do that."

"Good." Then she leaned in and pressed her mouth to his.

Usually she liked kissing Rylan, but today she found it hard to focus on the teasing strokes of his tongue. And her pulse was surprisingly steady, considering the eagerness with which Rylan was kissing her.

"Son of a bitch, Len! I think you broke my nose!"

Jamie pulled away from the kiss when she heard Kade's pained cry. Beside her, Rylan snorted, but she didn't find the situation nearly as amusing. Her concern doubled when Lennox's gruff voice drifted over to her.

"Jamie, love, we need you."

Where Rylan's kiss had failed, Lennox's words succeeded in making her heart beat a little faster. It was the first time he'd called her *love* since the night with Beckett. Sure, he used that same endearment with every other female, but she liked to think it meant something different with her. Years of history had shaped and strengthened their friendship. It was the single most important relationship in her life, and she knew Lennox felt the same way.

He loved her. And she loved him. Deeply.

Platonically. She forced herself to remember that as she hurried over to the two men.

Shit. There was a lot of blood. Kade had one hand pressed over his nose, but it wasn't stopping the sticky stream from oozing between his fingers and dripping down his chest in bright red rivulets.

Lennox flicked his gaze at her. "You got this?"

"On it." She stepped forward and said, "Let me see, sweetie."

Kade's voice was muffled behind his palm. "Bastard broke my nose."

He sounded so outraged she had to choke down a laugh. They were drawing the attention of the people around them, but Jamie focused solely on Lennox, who didn't look at all sorry about what he'd done.

"You shoulda moved faster," he told Kade.

"Fuck off."

Jamie gently pried Kade's hand away from his face. "Let me have a look."

Someone nudged her, and she turned to find Rylan holding out a T-shirt. She used the soft fabric to dab at Kade's face and mop up the blood, then gingerly touched his nose. His blood stained her fingertips, but it was no longer gushing. The flow had slowed, and it was clear that the bone hadn't been displaced.

"It won't need to be set."

"You sure?" He cursed again. "Because it hurts like a motherfucker."

She dabbed away more blood. "It's broken, but it's a good break. Trust me, just ice it down and let time do all the work. You're lucky it wasn't worse."

"Lucky," Lennox agreed. "You think it hurts now? Would've been worse if she had to set it for you."

Kade took the shirt and pressed it to his nostrils. "How do you know so much about setting a broken nose?"

Jamie jerked a thumb at Lennox. "Because this asshole got into a lot of fights when we were younger. I had to set his nose half a dozen times."

"She knows what she's doing," Lennox said grudgingly.

Now that her hands weren't busy, she once again felt awkward in Lennox's presence. "Go put some ice on it," she told Kade. She lightly squeezed his arm, then walked off to rejoin her team.

Frustration burned in Lennox's throat as he watched Jamie go. Shit. He hated the distance between them. *Hated* it. But he knew it was his own damn fault.

He shouldn't have allowed things to escalate between them the other night. He shouldn't have sat there stroking his dick while he'd issued brusque orders at Beckett.

Damn it, he couldn't get Jamie's moans out of his

head. The sounds she'd made when Beckett was fingering her . . . Every throaty, breathy noise had been imprinted in Lennox's brain.

But now things were weird between them. She couldn't even look him in the eye, and she'd barely spoken to him in two days.

His gaze shifted from Jamie to Kade, who was still scowling at him.

"Sorry," Lennox mumbled. "I got carried away."

Kade sighed. "It's fine. You're right—I need to move faster."

As the other man left to hunt down some ice, Lennox went over to the cistern to wash his hands. Once again, his gaze sought out Jamie, whose blond head was turned as she spoke to one of the women in her group.

He'd known this would happen. He'd shown her a glimpse of the lust he felt for her, and it had scared her away. She'd been locked up in her room every night since then, and he'd been too chickenshit to knock on her door.

But he couldn't avoid her forever. Sooner or later they'd have to talk about shit. Which was why, when Rylan and Pike asked for volunteers for the next event, Lennox spoke up in a sharp voice.

"Jamie and I volunteer."

Her head whirled in his direction, uncertainty flickering in her eyes.

He just smiled.

The members of his team shouted their encouragement as Lennox entered the fighting square Rylan and Pike had set up. Randy slapped his back and said, "You got this, bro," and Lennox grinned in response. He and the kid were becoming fast friends.

Jamie still hadn't moved an inch. She stood with her group, her expression more and more unhappy as she watched Lennox stretch one arm behind his head.

"He called you out, gorgeous," Rylan said in a singsong voice. "Time to represent your team."

She frowned.

"If you forfeit, the Green Team gets the point . . ."

"We'll get the point either way," Lennox taunted. "She's hesitating because she knows I'm gonna win."

Jamie's nostrils flared. Lennox's smirk widened. His best friend was competitive by nature, and he knew his challenge wouldn't go unmet.

Jamie took a quick sip of water, then handed the plastic bottle to the woman beside her. Her team members cheered as she joined Lennox in the ring.

They were completely unmatched in terms of size. At six-two, he towered over her five-four frame, and he had at least eighty pounds on her. But Jamie's size was deceptive. She'd taken Kade down the other day, and in the past she'd gotten Lennox on his ass more times than he'd like to admit. Though it probably had to do with the fact that she knew him so damn well. Jamie always seemed to sense what he was going to do before he did it, and she adjusted her counterattacks based on that.

"You really want to do this?" she muttered.

She still wasn't meeting his eyes, so he grabbed her chin and twisted her face toward him. "You scared, love?"

A sneer curled her lips. "Bring it on, baby."

"Same rules as yesterday," Pike said. "Three rounds, five minutes each. Winner will be judged on skill, or automatically declared if one of you taps out."

Lennox cracked his knuckles and grinned at her.

Jamie retaliated by whipping off her tank top, which left her in a cotton bikini bra. "Don't want to get your blood on my shirt," she said sweetly.

Her teammates hooted.

He was too busy staring at her tits. The perfect swell of cleavage spilling out of the tiny bra.

Rylan's sharp whistle signaled the start of the first round, and Jamie came at him so fast he didn't have time to react. Her fist connected with his jaw with a sharp crack, but Lennox managed to lock her wrist with both hands before she could land another punch. He twisted her arm and spun her around, holding her against his chest in a tight lock.

"Is that all you've got?" he whispered in her ear.

She made an angry sound and jammed her elbow into his gut, with enough force that she was able to wiggle out of the hold and stumble backward. Then she bounced on the balls of her feet, both fists up. Her fighting pose was so fucking cute he had to smile.

They circled each other for a few moments, a slow, almost seductive dance that stirred his groin to life. And then it was go time. In the blink of an eye, they both launched forward, fists flying, forearms coming out to block. Even as Lennox worked to restrain himself, to go easy on her, he couldn't stop the flood of adrenaline that surged through his veins, and it was only fueled by the loud cheers of the crowd around them.

"Kick 'im in the balls!" one of the girls on Jamie's team shouted.

When he trapped her in another armlock, Jamie proved she wasn't above taking her teammate's suggestion. Her knee flew up and connected with his groin. Lennox barked out a curse, the jolt of pain causing him to slam his fist into her abdomen. She flew back, her eyes blazing at him.

"Fucking dick!" she yelled.

Ignoring the pain shooting through his testicles, he flashed a cocky grin. A moment later, Rylan whistled again.

"End of Round One!"

Rylan and Pike promptly bent their heads together to confer before declaring Jamie the winner of that bout.

Lennox rolled his eyes when she stuck out her tongue at him. Little brat.

The second round was more of the same. They each got in a few good blows, until one costly error gave Lennox the upper hand. His sharp uppercut made her stumble, and the nanosecond in which she lost her balance allowed him to kick her legs from under her and send her tumbling to the ground. A second later, Lennox was on top of her, his thighs on either side of her torso, his forearm against her slender throat. He didn't exert enough pressure to squeeze her windpipe, but the dominant pose made it clear that he could.

"Tapping out?" he teased.

"No." Sweat beaded on her forehead as she tried to shove him off her. She batted at him with her fists, but he had her pinned solidly to the ground.

The cheers and whistles from his teammates faded away. All he could focus on was Jamie's beautiful face, the way her perfect mouth twisted in frustration as she realized she couldn't overpower him. He became aware of her thigh muscles quivering beneath the weight of his lower body, the way her breasts heaved as her breathing grew labored. He felt himself hardening but didn't bother disguising the response by shifting his hips. He just let her feel every hard inch of him.

Her blue eyes widened. "Lennox . . ." Soft and questioning.

He realized he was still staring at her, allowing all his naked hunger for her to show in his eyes. The knowledge that he wasn't strong enough to mask his lust spurred him to push his forearm deeper into her throat.

"Tap out," he growled.

Something akin to disappointment flickered in her eyes. Then her arm came out and she tapped her palm on the pavement.

His team roared. Hers booed.

Lennox was unsteady getting to his feet. As Rylan gleefully announced, *"Winner!"* Lennox held out his hand to Jamie, his heart beating erratically.

Her mystified gaze searched his face as she took his hand so he could help her up. She didn't look pissed that he'd won the fight.

Truth be told, he didn't feel as if he'd won a damn thing. He felt as if he'd lost.

"Nice job," Jamie murmured, and something in her tone brought a squeeze of pain to his heart.

She walked over to her teammates without a backward glance. The defeat lodged in his chest only thickened.

Shit. Maybe he needed to follow her lead. Keep avoiding her. Keep pretending that the other night had never happened. He might have screwed up by opening the sex door, but there was an easy fix for that. All he had to do was slam the door shut, lock it up, and throw away the key.

And . . . he spared a rueful glance at his crotch . . . it was probably best if he got laid tonight.

10

"I need to sit down before my ankles explode." Bethany's massive belly bobbed as she awkwardly lowered herself onto the couch next to Jamie, who instantly moved over to make room for the pregnant woman.

Smiling, she glanced at Bethany's bare ankles, which did look a tad swollen. "Aw, sweetie. You need to stop working at the restaurant. You're on your feet too much."

"My feet? You should see my feet," Bethany retorted. "God knows I can't, but I'm told my toes look like sausages." She sighed. "I hate being fat."

Jamie leaned in to kiss her cheek. "You are not fat. You're beautiful."

"Sorry, but the music's too loud. All I heard was *you're* and *fat*." Bethany blinked innocently, which made Jamie laugh.

The music was kind of loud, though. And the rec hall was *packed*. Nearly every Foxworth resident was at the party Rylan was throwing to celebrate the successful first day of the tournament. Jamie had to hand it to him—the idea to turn the training into a competition had really done the trick. Instead of complaining, everyone was teeming with excitement now. She'd even seen half a dozen teenagers in the courtyard earlier practicing their knife-throwing techniques.

Reese was bound to be happy about this. By the time Rylan and Pike were done, the woman would have a highly trained army at her disposal.

"Heard you and Lennox got into it today," Bethany said curiously.

"Not really. It was just a training exercise."

"You sure? Arch said it looked pretty intense."

Jamie didn't remember seeing Bethany's man at the fight. Or around town, for that matter. Arch was one of the men who didn't require any training. He was already as lethal as they came, and was usually assigned to the watchtower at the back gate.

"It was nothing," Jamie insisted. "Really." If by nothing she meant *he was on top of me and hard as a rock.*

God, he'd been impossibly hard. And he hadn't even tried to hide it. Which was only all the more confusing. Lennox was sending so many mixed signals her head was spinning. He seemed determined to push her away, while at the same time desperate to pull her closer.

But it didn't matter. Any sexual involvement between them was not a good idea, especially now that she'd witnessed the kind of damage it could cause. All they'd done the other night was orgasm in the same vicinity and it had led to days of awkwardness. She didn't even want to imagine what would happen to their friendship if they actually had sex.

"If you say so." Bethany sounded unconvinced, but

she was smart enough not to push the issue. Instead she chewed on her bottom lip for a second, then said, "I wanted to ask you something."

"Ask away."

"Hudson . . ." Bethany trailed off.

Jamie's guard instantly shot up. "What about her?"

"I didn't get a chance to spend any time with her when she and Con were here, but I overhead Reese and Sloan talking the other night." Bethany frowned. "Is it true she's Dominik's sister?"

Jamie hesitated. Then nodded.

Which clearly wasn't the desired response, because Bethany's mouth instantly curled into a sneer.

"It's not as bad as it sounds," Jamie said hastily. "Believe me, I wasn't thrilled about it either when I found out, but Hudson isn't like the others in the city. She's not out to get us."

"But her brother is."

"He might not be." Jamie still wasn't convinced of that herself, but she felt she owed it to Hudson to come to her defense. Connor's woman had been nothing but kind to her. "Hudson and Dominik's father used to be in charge of the Enforcers. Did you know that?"

Bethany shook her head. "I'm not too knowledge-able about their military hierarchy."

"There's not much to know. Each colony has a commander who calls the shots, and a head Enforcer who leads the men on the field. Hudson's father was the commander, but after he died, Ferris took over. Since then, the rules have changed. More colony sweeps, increased violence." Jamie shrugged. "According to Hudson, Dominik isn't happy with all the changes. Supposedly he's trying to fix that."

Bethany looked doubtful, and Jamie didn't blame her one bit. "Really? Because the colony sweeps are still going strong."

"I don't know what he's doing or what his plan is," Jamie admitted. "But for what it's worth, he did help Hudson escape from the Enforcer compound. When he had the opportunity to kill Connor, he let him go instead. And he even gave Hudson a satellite phone she can use to contact him. She sent him her coordinates, and so far he's been keeping the sweeps away from her location."

"Lucky her," Bethany said bitterly. "Because he sure as hell isn't keeping any of those assholes away from *here*. Did Reese tell you what happened with Nestor last month? How that dickhead was waving his gun around like a madman, demanding Reese give him Sara?"

Jamie stiffened. "Sara?"

"He wanted to take her on their colony sweep so she could 'service' him and his men. Fucking pervert was lucky Gideon was at the farm that day—"

"Gideon?"

"Sara's father. Gid would have strangled the man with his bare hands. Sloan stepped up, though." Disgust colored Bethany's tone. "The Enforcers are monsters. I honestly can't believe that Dominik, their *leader*, is any different."

Neither could Jamie, but she was willing to give Hudson the benefit of the doubt. For now, anyway.

"Why do you ladies look so serious?" came Arch's deep voice.

The ginger-haired giant approached the sofa and

perched on the edge of it. At six-seven and close to three hundred pounds, the man was imposing as hell, but his expression conveyed nothing but tenderness as he leaned in to stroke Bethany's huge belly.

The sight made Jamie's heart ache. Nobody had ever looked at her like that before. Like she were the sun and moon and everything in between.

"I was telling Jamie about Nestor," Bethany admitted.

Arch's green eyes hardened. "Fucking bastard. Sloan should have killed him."

"The Enforcers would have opened fire if he'd done anything more than knock Nestor out," Bethany said firmly. Arch's hand was still on her stomach, and she covered it with her own. "Sloan did the right thing."

"Strongly disagree."

As the couple began to bicker about what Sloan should or shouldn't have done, Jamie raised her whiskey glass to her lips and took a long swig. The alcohol burned her belly, slowed the flow of her blood. She was already a little drunk, but not drunk enough.

If she was going to officially exorcise her attraction to Lennox, she needed to be much, much drunker.

She glanced around the room, her gaze sweeping over the rowdy group of men standing around the pool table. The couples in various stages of undress. The sexual escapades being conducted in the shadowy corners of the room. She spotted Rylan leaning against the wall, a bottle in one hand, his blue eyes fixed on the door. She got the grating feeling he was waiting for Reese.

She shifted her gaze in search of Lennox and found him in the back corner. He was sitting in an over-stuffed chair, and he wasn't alone—there was a dark-haired woman in his lap, nibbling on his neck and playing with his hair. Lennox had a hand on her hip, and he was slowly grazing his fingers over the strip of pale flesh where her shirt rode up from the waistband of her jeans.

"Who's that?" Jamie nodded in the direction of the woman and gulped some more whiskey.

Bethany followed her gaze. "Oh, that's Cassie. You've met her before."

Right, she had. The brunette worked in the laundry room; Jamie remembered handing off her sheets and pillowcases to Cassie during her last visit.

"She doesn't usually come to parties." Arch grinned when he noticed where Lennox's hand had disappeared.

Almost immediately, Cassie's spine arched erotically as Lennox fondled her breasts under her shirt.

Jamie experienced an unfamiliar prickle in her chest. Shit. Was that jealousy?

"I guess Len used his powers of persuasion to get her here," Arch remarked.

The man was persuasive, all right. Jamie would never forget the sound of his deep voice commanding her to come on Beckett's fingers.

As an ache formed between her legs, she tore her gaze off her best friend and shifted it back to Rylan. Fuck it, she decided. Sitting here with Bethany and Arch was nice and all, but she was too wound up. She needed some action. She needed an orgasm that would rock her body so hard she forgot her own name.

Setting her jaw, she reached for the bottle on the table and poured another glass of whiskey. Bethany watched with a wide grin as Jamie chugged the contents of the glass in one gulp.

"Easy, darling," Arch murmured.

But she didn't want easy. She wanted hard. A good, hard dicking that would clear her mind of Lennox.

Jamie waggled her eyebrows at the couple. "Sorry, guys, but I'm abandoning you now. I see something I want."

She was a little unsteady getting to her feet. Crap. Maybe chugging that whiskey was a mistake. Reese's booze was much stronger than the stuff back at Connor's camp.

Leaving Bethany and Arch on the couch, she made her way to Rylan, whose gaze zeroed in on her cleavage as she approached. She'd worn a skintight red minidress tonight, the one that Lennox teased her was nothing but a rag. Probably true, considering that it barely covered her breasts and thighs. She'd paired the dress with high heels that made her legs look a lot longer than they were, and the appreciation she saw in Rylan's eyes made her happy about her wardrobe choice.

"Hey."

Rylan set his bottle on the little ledge behind him. "Hey," he answered in a husky voice.

That was the only exchange of conversation she allowed before looping her arms around his corded neck and kissing the living shit out of him.

He responded eagerly, groaning into her mouth as his big hands captured her covered breasts. When his tongue slipped through her parted lips, she tasted the alcohol on it, along with the heady flavor of his arousal.

"Christ. You feel good." Rylan rubbed his lower body against hers. Then, before she could blink, he hauled her up and cupped her ass, pressing her back into the wall. Jamie wrapped her legs around his waist, her breath hitching when he started grinding his clothed erection against her core.

Heavy-lidded blue eyes raked over her flushed face, and he rocked his hips harder, his erection thickening. Damn it, she didn't want to be teased. She wanted him *in* her. She needed him to stoke the fire that had been consuming her ever since Lennox ignited that first spark the other night.

Her hands clawed at his zipper. He reached down to help her out, and they were a second away from undoing his pants when Rylan froze. Then his head turned sharply toward the door.

As Jamie peered over his shoulder, the arousal inside her fizzled like a candle in the rain. Reese had entered the room. Wonderful.

The redhead didn't glance their way. In fact, she seemed oblivious to their presence as she went to talk to Beckett. Rylan, however, was wholly tuned in to *her* presence. So much so that his breathing, which had been labored seconds before, was calm and even now. His heart, which had been hammering against Jamie's breasts, was now beating steadily.

She felt him withdraw from her before he'd even

set her on her feet. The absent expression he wore made her want to scream.

"Sorry, gorgeous," he murmured regretfully. "We're gonna have to finish this later."

The soft kiss he brushed over her cheek didn't even begin to soothe the sting of rejection. She gaped at his retreating back as he headed over to Reese. Whatever he whispered in the redhead's ear caused her to stiffen, but Reese didn't object when he led her to the door.

Jamie's cheeks burned as she watched the two of them leave the rec hall. Whether Rylan had whisked Reese away for sexual reasons didn't matter. He couldn't have made his intentions clearer if he'd spray-painted them on the walls—he wanted Reese. His priority was Reese.

He doesn't care about you.

Jamie had never felt more pathetic in her life as the bitter truth sank in. Rylan didn't have feelings for her. He was attracted to her. He enjoyed screwing her. But he would never be able to give her what she really wanted.

The realization should have devastated her. In fact, she stood there for five whole seconds, waiting for tears to prick her eyelids. They didn't.

She was embarrassed, yes. Hurt, maybe a little. But devastated? No.

Still, the hurt and embarrassment weren't exactly welcome, but she squared her shoulders and forced Rylan's rejection to roll off her back. She didn't need him. She could snap her fingers and another man would appear like an apparition, begging to make her feel good. Well, maybe not Lennox. Lennox was too busy making someone else feel good.

For some inexplicable reason, the burn of humiliation Rylan had evoked didn't sting as much as the thought of Lennox and Cassie fucking in the corner.

Jamie shook her head. She didn't need that drama in her life either.

What she needed was another glass of whiskey.

Rylan felt like a total ass for deserting Jamie so abruptly. He liked the woman a helluva lot. She made him laugh, and *damn*, she turned him on like nobody's business. His cock was still rock-hard, his body yelling at him for depriving it of the release it craved.

But right now there were matters far more important than sex. For the first time since he'd arrived in Foxworth, Reese was alone. Yep, her ever-present shadow, Sloan, was nowhere to be seen.

Rylan would be damned if he passed up on such a golden opportunity.

As they stepped outside, he was immediately hit by a gust of cool air. The late summer they'd been enjoying had finally decided to abandon them. All the trees lining Main Street now boasted leaves that were turning various shades of red, orange, and brown. The air was crisper. The sky cloudier.

Fall was Rylan's least favorite season, mostly because it led to winter. And winter in the free land? Fucking sucked. Though it was definitely more tolerable now that he lived in a camp with working fireplaces and a generator. Before that, he'd spent his winters shivering his balls off. Sometimes he'd been lucky enough to find a place with a working generator, but that was a luxury, not a given.

"What's so important you had to drag me out here?" Reese demanded.

He met her annoyed gaze head-on. Connor had told him to use every trick in the book, so tonight he was opting for a different approach. "I thought it was time we talked. Straight up, no bullshit."

"I didn't realize we were bullshitting each other." Her tone was dry.

"You're always bullshitting me, Reese." He liked the way her name sounded on his lips. He suspected he'd like the way she *felt* on his lips too. Or beneath him as he fucked her blind. He swallowed, pushing aside the wicked images. "Whatever you're planning, Connor and I can help you."

She looked amused. "I'm not planning anything."

"Again with the bullshitting."

She responded with a smirk. "I don't know what you think is going on here, Rylan, but I was up-front with Connor. My people are weak. I need them to be strong. End of story."

He chuckled. "Baby, there's much, much more to the story. I'm insulted that you think I don't know that."

She didn't answer. She just stared at him with that veiled expression he loathed.

His first instinct was to push her, force her to talk, but he knew that would backfire. He'd grown up on a farm where he'd dealt with plenty of stubborn animals, including a willful terror of a horse that would refuse to get in her stall most nights. Rylan had discovered that a gentler approach was more successful in coaxing the difficult mare to do his bidding.

Connor would have bulldozed Reese into talking, but Rylan would continue to bide his time.

"Fine, we'll keep playing this game, gorgeous. Just know that the offer is on the table. If you need assistance, we're here for you. Outlaws have to stand together, right?"

She rolled her eyes. "One for all and all for one, huh?"

"Nice motto."

"It's not mine. Someone wrote it in a book a long time ago."

"Yeah? Never read it."

"You should. Wouldn't hurt to broaden your horizons, honey."

"I'm not interested in fiction. Just fact. Just what's in front of me."

And right now what was in front of him was a woman he wanted so badly that his dick was in a constant state of rigid agony.

He stared at her lips, lush and red and without a hint of makeup. Her skin was naturally beautiful too, smooth and creamy. But those lips . . . they were his favorite thing about her. They were capable of doing so many sexy things. Plumping when she was deep in thought, tightening when she was displeased, parting when she was aroused.

Before he could stop himself, he reached out and touched her mouth. The slight trembling of her bottom lip was the only sign she gave that his touch affected her.

"I want to kiss you so fucking bad," he rasped.

Reese didn't even blink. She also didn't slap his hand away, so he took that as permission to keep going. He traced the seam of her lips with his index finger while his gaze drank in the sight of her. She was a beautiful woman, with her big brown eyes, delicate features, and soft mouth. If he'd seen her from afar, he would've thought she was an innocent. Sweet and pure. But he knew better. He knew her tongue was sharper than his favorite hunting knife. He knew she was as open with her sexuality as he was with his.

"I want to feel your mouth against mine. I want to lick my way inside."

She still didn't answer. The moonlight brought out the brighter red highlights in her copper hair, making the long strands glint enticingly.

"I want to suck on your tongue," he muttered.

Silence. She continued to watch him, and he continued to rub the pad of his finger over her lips. Jesus, he wanted to taste her.

After what felt like hours, her lips quirked beneath his fingers, curving into a mocking smile. "Are you done?"

Frustration squeezed his chest. Gritting his teeth, he let his hand drop to his side. "Yeah." He cleared his throat. "I guess I am."

"I think you've had enough."

Jamie let out an indignant squeak when Lennox swiped the half-empty whiskey bottle from her hand. She hadn't even seen him approach, which was a testament to the superb job the alcohol was doing.

"Where's your friend?" she asked, trying to snatch the bottle back.

Ignoring her, Lennox marched forward a few paces and deposited the bottle in the hand of Nash, who looked over in surprise, chuckled, then turned back to the curvy woman he was talking to.

"What friend?" Lennox stalked back to her.

"Chassie. No, Cassie. The chick you were screwing around with."

"She went to bed."

"Alone?" Sarcasm crept in. "Aw, are you losing your touch, baby?"

Lennox shrugged, which drew her attention to his shoulders. He had beautiful shoulders. It was a silly thought, but it was true. His shoulders were so deliciously broad. And his arms . . . utter perfection. Strong, muscled, covered with ink. Jamie's entire body felt weak as she imagined those arms pinning her down as he pounded into her with his cock.

A wave of lust nearly knocked her off her feet, causing her to grab onto one of those firm arms in order to steady herself.

"You're drunk," Lennox muttered. "You should go to bed."

"I'm fine."

"You can barely stand."

"I can stand just fine."

His expression became stormy. "You almost fell over."

"That wasn't because of the whiskey. I . . ." Her mouth snapped shut. No. She wasn't giving him another opportunity to reject her. She already had another man's rejection weighing her down tonight.

As if he'd read her mind, Lennox's voice lost its

hard edges. "He does care about you, love. In his own way."

She clenched her teeth. "I know."

"Do you?" he said thoughtfully.

"I'm not as clueless as you think, Len. Of course he cares about me. Just not in the way I'd like him to." She laughed scornfully. "But hey, at least he's not scared to admit he wants to screw me. He doesn't hide the lust he feels, or run from it."

"The fuck does that mean?"

"You know exactly what it means." The frustration of the past two days came pouring out like water from a broken pipe. She wanted to scream at him, but they were surrounded by people, so her voice came out as a hiss instead. "What was that the other night, Len? Were you bored? Drunk?" Another harsh laugh was ripped from her throat. "Too drunk to realize it was me?"

His gray eyes flashed.

"That's it, right? It wasn't my pussy you were panting over. It was some other woman's." She smacked her palm in the center of his chest and he flinched. "You're an asshole, Lennox. I've always known that. I've tolerated it, laughed about it. But you went too far the other night. You don't want me? Fine. But don't play with me like that. At least pretend to give a shit about my feelings—"

He struck like a deadly snake, grabbing a hunk of her hair and yanking her backward. His hand cupped the back of her head before her skull could slam into the wall, but his grip remained stronger than steel.

"*Pretend* to give a shit about you?" he spat out. "Guess what, honey? You're *all* I care about."

Her heartbeat accelerated.

"Every move I make is directly driven by my feelings for you." His fingers tightened in her hair, his chest pressed right up against hers, a solid, immovable object. "When I make a decision, you think it's *my* safety I take into consideration? It's fucking *yours*. I don't take a goddamn breath without considering how it would affect you."

Jamie was stunned. And scared. And so turned on she couldn't breathe.

"I knew exactly who I was with." He shoved one large hand between their bodies and curled it over her. "This pussy? It was mine that night."

His big body began to shake uncontrollably. Jamie didn't know if it was from anger or lust, but it was goddamn beautiful. His eyes glittered like storm clouds releasing flashes of lightning. His pulse hammered in his throat. His hot breath incinerated her cheek.

"It's been mine for years," he hissed out, cupping her so hard she squeaked in pain. "I could've taken it whenever I damn well pleased."

The ache between her legs was so acute she nearly toppled over. Luckily there was nowhere for her to fall. Lennox's hard body was trapping her against the wall, and she could feel his chest trembling as if he was struggling for control.

She'd seen him like this before. It happened when he got frustrated, when he was faced with a problem he couldn't fix, an obstacle he couldn't overcome. The frustration would soon transform into rage or lust, depending on how he harnessed it. Depending on what he chose as an outlet for the aggression—his fists or his cock.

"Goddamn *mine*," he repeated, and in that moment she knew he'd made his choice.

His mouth crushed hers, swallowing her moan of surprise. It was a brutal kiss, violent and forceful and not at all how she'd imagined it would be when she was younger. She'd fantasized about gentle lips and a sweet tongue, but Lennox delivered something entirely different.

He took greedy pulls on her tongue, not allowing her to come up for air. He suffocated her with his kiss until she was dizzy, until her lungs burned for oxygen and her frantic heartbeat was all she could hear.

And then his mouth disappeared. Jamie blinked, and suddenly he was on his knees in front of her.

Her legs snapped shut for some odd reason. The look in his eyes terrified her. It was dark and feral and gleaming with unadulterated need.

Lennox's fingers locked around her closed thighs like steel bands. "Give me what's mine," he growled.

Her heart nearly burst out of her chest. She gazed down at him, throat tight, nipples tingling, core throbbing.

"You want me to take it, is that it?" His voice was low and silky. "Because I can. I can pry these sexy legs apart and fucking take it." His thumbs scraped the tender flesh of her inner thighs. "But I won't, because you're going to give it to me."

Jamie swallowed repeatedly, but her mouth remained drier than dust. Although they were hidden away for the most part, tucked in a shadowy corner of the rec center, she was wholly aware that people were watching them. She made out Beckett's intrigued face, Bethany's concerned expression.

"Look at me," Lennox ordered.

Her gaze dropped to the primal, sexed-up man on his knees and she was suddenly reminded of a story her mother had told her a long time ago. About a box full of sins and the curious woman who'd foolishly opened it without considering the consequences. Well, Jamie had done the same damn thing. She'd goaded Lennox into opening this door, but she hadn't been prepared for this. For *him*.

This wasn't Lennox, her best friend. This was a terrifying, seductive stranger.

"Give me what I want, Jamie."

Her legs parted as if controlled by a higher power. She couldn't have kept them locked if she'd tried. She wasn't wearing underwear, and Lennox's hot gaze immediately zeroed in on her bare sex. He licked his lips and she shivered.

Then he grabbed the bottom of her dress and whipped it all the way up to her waist so that every inch of her was exposed. "Wider," he rasped.

Jamie widened her stance.

His eyes burned brighter.

She knew he could see how drenched she was. That he could feel how slippery her inner thighs were.

"You think I don't want you?" He was mocking her now. "You don't know shit, Jamie. You don't know how long I've fantasized about this."

He traced her folds with one finger, rubbing the

moisture clinging to her inner lips. Then that wicked finger trailed lower, breaching her opening with its tip.

She jerked from the shot of pleasure that hurtled into her.

"Open your eyes," he barked.

Her eyelids flew open. She hadn't realized she'd closed them, but Lennox clearly wasn't happy that she had.

"I want you to watch who's doing this to you." The words were rough, seductive. "Watch as I lick you. As I shove my tongue inside you and fuck you with it."

Oh. My. God.

Never in her wildest dreams had she imagined those filthy words coming out of her best friend's mouth. The thrill of it sent another gush of moisture to her pussy, and Lennox chuckled when he felt her arousal coating his finger.

"Yeah, that's it. Get nice and wet for me, love."

Her wide eyes stayed focused on him. On his mouth, as it slowly descended over her clit, as his lips gently rubbed over the aching bud. Shock waves rippled through her. Oh hell, that felt good. And then his tongue came out and it felt even better. Hot and insistent, but torturously slow as he lavished soft licks on her clit, then dragged his tongue up and down her slit.

Her breathing grew shallow. Her legs started to shake. Chuckling against her core, Lennox brought one hand to her waist and curled his fingers over it, holding her steady. His other hand stroked her thigh in the same languid tempo his tongue was using on her clit.

God, it wasn't enough. Her hips started to move. She was helpless to stop it, because the light friction was becoming unbearable. She needed more, damn it.

Lennox growled. "Fuck yeah. Rub your pussy all over my face."

She thought she heard herself moan. It was hard to tell because her heart was thudding louder than the bass line pounding from the speakers. She couldn't believe Lennox was doing this to her. She couldn't believe how incredible it felt.

Everything about him was turning her on. The hungry noises rumbling in his throat. The furrow in his forehead as he concentrated on pleasuring her. The enormous bulge in his pants. God, that cock. She wanted it. She felt needy and empty and he was the only one who could make it all better.

"I need your cock," she begged. "Please, Lennox, I need it."

"No." The husky response vibrated in her core, and then he buried his face in her pussy and sucked hard on her clit.

"Oh God. *Yes*." Jamie fisted her hands in his hair and rocked harder against his greedy mouth.

"That's it, baby. Grind down. Let me feel you."

She was shamelessly riding his face now, but it still wasn't enough. She cried out when his tongue lapped at her opening. A moment later, he pushed it inside her, releasing a savage groan as he lodged his tongue deep.

"Jesus," he muttered after he'd licked his way out. "So sweet."

So this was what an out-of-body experience was

like. Her surroundings, her entire fucking world, blurred at the edges as pure, mindless sensation consumed her body. She had the vague sense that she was trembling, pulling his hair, moving her hips as he speared his tongue into her. Pleasure whipped up and down her spine like bolts of lightning, escaping her mouth in the form of gasped, hoarse moans.

Lennox moaned too. "I'm gonna come just from tonguing you. That's how good you are, baby."

He brought his tongue back to her clit and sucked hard. Then he lifted his head, and she saw that his lips were swollen, glistening. The hand on her thigh squeezed tight, bringing a sting of pain.

"This is what you wanted, right? For me to stop pretending?" His gorgeous eyes shone with intensity as he dragged two fingers down her thigh, skimming her pussy lips. "Well, this is it, love. This is me not pretending."

"Lennox—" she started. Then stopped, because she wasn't sure what she'd wanted to say.

"This pussy is mine tonight." He plunged both fingers into her core. "I'm the only one that gets to lick it, suck it, you hear me? So now fuck my face and show me how much you want it."

Nothing could have prepared her for this. She'd seen him with other women, heard the screams he summoned from them. But seeing and hearing had nothing on actually *feeling* it.

She went on sensation overload as he stroked her inner channel. His fingers curled over the sweet spot there, rubbing hard, while his merciless tongue worked her clit. He didn't stop. Didn't give her a moment to catch her breath. He simply brought her to the brink of sexual madness and then pushed her right over that summit, triggering an explosion of pleasure that blazed through her body.

She came on his face and he drank her up, licked her up, refusing to let her crash down from the high. Her clit was so sensitive she began to squirm, but Lennox didn't retreat. He eased the pressure around the quivering bud and slowed the thrust of his fingers, but his greedy tongue kept swirling, his blunt fingertips kept rubbing that spot deep inside her.

Jamie cried out again, this time with pleasure that bordered on agony. It was too much. Every nerve in her body was hypersensitive now, her pussy swollen and throbbing from the orgasm, yet none of that mattered to the man between her legs. He feasted on her, tormented her, *wrecked* her, until her squirming eventually turned into grinding. Until the pleasure gathered again, building and pulsating before detonating in another blinding rush of ecstasy.

This time she couldn't take it. As the waves of pleasure ebbed, she pulled his hair to yank his lips off her, but the mere act of moving her arms caused her wobbly legs to buckle. Lennox caught her before she could sink to the floor, rising to his feet and locking his strong arms around her waist.

He kissed her again, and she tasted herself on his lips. She tasted his arousal too. Felt it pressing against her core, the long, solid ridge of his erection.

"I want you inside me," she whispered.

Lennox made a tortured sound. Every muscle in his face went taut, his gray eyes conveying both reluctance and hunger.

Their gazes locked. The other voices in the room faded away into nothingness. Jamie wasn't sure if anyone was still watching them. She didn't care, because nobody else existed to her right now. Nobody but Lennox.

The man she'd known forever, but who she was meeting for the first time tonight.

11

He'd crossed the line. No, he'd eviscerated the line. Thrown gasoline on it, lit a match, and set it on fire. But Lennox didn't fucking care, because the fire was inside him now. Burning so hot it had reduced his normally good judgment to ashes.

He didn't remember walking out of the rec hall. Or walking to the building where he and Jamie were crashing. Or walking upstairs. And into their sleeping quarters. Apparently there'd been a lot of walking involved, but he didn't remember taking a single goddamn step.

Yet here they were, alone in his room, with Jamie's dress on the floor.

He'd fantasized about this moment for years. Jerked off to it on many a cold, lonely night. But none of the dirty scenarios his mind had conjured up in the past held a candle to the real thing. Jamie's naked body stretched on the bed, her golden hair fanned out on the pillows, her pussy glistening.

"I can't believe I waited this long." He was surprised he was able to speak with all the gravel in his mouth. God knew he couldn't seem to formulate any coherent thoughts other than *Take her, take her now.*

"Waiting sucks." Arching an eyebrow, she lifted one knee and offered herself up to his gaze. "So don't make me wait."

His chuckle came out strangled. With surprisingly steady hands, considering that his heartbeat was erratic as fuck, Lennox began to strip. His belt buckle jingled as his jeans hit the floor. His shirt disappeared somewhere under the bed.

Once he was fully naked, he sat at the edge of the mattress and grazed a finger up her bare leg. Her skin was so damn soft. When he reached her inner thigh, she shivered, but not as hard as when he ran his finger along her slit. Her pussy was still swollen from the orgasms he'd given her. Still wet too, soaking his fingertips when he teased her entrance.

"Lennox," she begged.

He moistened his dry bottom lip. "What do you want, love?"

"You."

She sat up abruptly and locked her arms around his neck, tugging him down on top of her, and then they were kissing again, a fervent joining of mouths that sucked the breath from his lungs. He couldn't stop kissing her. It was too good. She tasted like expensive whiskey and sexy woman, and he greedily drank in her flavor before finally coming up for air.

Tilting his head, he buried his nose in her hair and inhaled the scent of her shampoo, the coconut stuff that was stocked in all the cabins back at Connor's camp. Her skin smelled just as sweet, a heady fragrance that was uniquely Jamie.

He kissed her neck, sweeping his tongue over her silky flesh while his hands skimmed every sexy curve of her body. Her hands weren't idle either. One slid between them and curled around his cock, giving it a firm pump that made him see stars. He was harder than steel, all the blood in his body pulsing in his dick and turning his brain to mush.

The next thing he knew, he was flat on his back and Jamie was kissing his chest. His stomach. His hips. Everywhere. Her warm lips explored every inch of his torso, and the noises she was making, the tiny purrs and breathy moans and feminine growls ... he'd never heard those desperate sounds leave her mouth before.

Her pink tongue came out to tease one of his nipples, licking and toying with it until it was a tight, painful bud. "I've wanted to do this for so long, Len."

He couldn't fight the burst of satisfaction that went off inside him. He knew she was drunk. That she'd probably regret every word in the morning. But he didn't care. He'd wanted this too. Her rosebud lips all over him. Her eager tongue. Her frantic hands.

"How long?" he rasped.

Her cheeks reddened. "Since I was sixteen years old."

Lennox offered a knowing look. "Since the night you watched me jerk off." He reached down and gripped his aching cock, pumping it enticingly. "Right?"

Her flush deepened. "You knew I was there?"

"Of course I knew. Why do you think I took so long to finish?"

Now she looked outraged. "You were teasing me on purpose?"

"Fuck yeah." He rubbed his thumb around his cock head, slowly, lazily, drawing out the erotic caress. He'd done the same thing all those years ago. Teasing both her and himself, stroking his cock as if it were the first time he'd ever had his hand on it.

Jamie swatted his fingers away. "You should have asked me to join you. I knew some tricks, even back then."

A surge of anticipation raced through his blood. "Yeah? Show me."

Smiling, she lowered her head and lavished a soft lick on the head of his cock. Her blond hair fell like a curtain over his thighs, tickling his skin while her tongue tickled his dick.

Jesus. He'd waited so many years to feel this woman's mouth on him. He wanted to push inside and choke her with his goddamn dick, mark her, *own* her. But she was taking her time, teasing him with tiny, barely there licks that unleashed a string of expletives from his mouth.

"Suck me," he ordered.

"No."

He thrust a hand in her hair and gave a sharp tug. "*Suck me.*"

"No." Then she twisted her head toward his wrist and sank her teeth into it.

The jolt of pain caused him to release her, but his fingers didn't go far. They dipped down to her throat and curled around it. He felt her pulse throbbing, saw the excitement shining in her eyes as he gave a slight squeeze. Jamie had always liked it rough. He'd seen her with other men and—nope, he wasn't going there.

He banished the memories when an unexpected streak of jealousy jolted through him. It was odd, because he'd never been jealous of her previous lovers before. He'd never cared—

You cared.

The mocking voice in his head reared up. It was true. He *had* cared. But it hadn't mattered, damn it. He'd been determined to protect their friendship, which meant he couldn't touch her. He would've been a total ass if he'd denied her the pleasure other men could give her.

"What are you going to do if I keep saying no?" she asked, defiance gleaming in her blue eyes.

Lennox dragged his tongue over his lips. He knew exactly what she wanted him to say. So he said it.

"I'm going to hold you down and shove my cock down your throat."

She moaned.

"You'd like that," he said with a chuckle.

"Mmm-hmmm. But maybe we can save that for another time." She closed her lips around him and sucked hard.

His hips snapped up when her mouth slid down nearly to the base of him. "That's it, love. Take it all."

She slowly licked her way back to his tip . . . then sucked down again in one fast motion. Sweet Lord. She'd set a mind-blowing tempo. The wet, lazy path of her tongue climbing up to his cock head, followed by the rapid descent of her mouth as she swallowed him. His dick brushed the back of her throat each time, and the hot suction and greedy little licks made his balls tighten in agony.

He kept his eyes open, watching as she blew him,

as she took hungry pulls on his dick. Her small hands stroked his abs, his thighs, his sac. His gaze rested on her tits, swaying seductively as she bent over him. He couldn't see her pussy, though. Damn it. He wanted to know if she was wet. If sucking him was turning her on.

"I'm craving your pussy, baby," he murmured. "Bring it up here."

She lifted her head, and a devilish smile curved her swollen lips. Then she twisted around and wiggled her ass up to his face, positioning her knees on either side of his head. Lennox groaned when he gazed up and saw paradise.

He gripped her ass cheeks with both hands, bringing her closer to his mouth so he could drag his tongue along her wet slit. Jamie whimpered, then resumed her single-minded task of sucking his brains right out of his dick.

He was in heaven. Her sweet pussy in his face, her hot mouth on his dick . . . absolute heaven.

"Jesus, baby, you taste so amazing," he muttered against her folds. "A dying man would rise from the grave if he had you on his tongue." In response, she whimpered and rubbed her clit against his lips, and he choked out a curse. "Fucking hell."

His hips rose to meet each deep stroke of her mouth, the pleasure in his body twisting and growing and prickling across his skin. Why had he waited so long to do this? Why had he deprived himself of it? Of *her*?

"Lennox." His name left her lips on a breath, hot against his shaft, as she started to grind on top of him.

Her clit pulsed on his tongue, her juices soaking

his face as he lapped her up. He kneaded her firm ass cheeks, then trailed one finger down the crease to tease the tight ring of muscle there.

Jamie jerked and moaned around his cock.

A smile stretched his lips. Oh yeah, ass play was bound to make her come on his face again. He'd seen the way she reacted when other men—

There are no other men. Just you.

Just him. It had always been him for her. He knew that now, and he suspected Jamie did as well.

As his cock throbbed and swelled in her eager mouth, Lennox stroked her ass with the tip of his finger and worked his tongue over her clit. Jamie was squirming now, trying to press against his finger.

"Lennox," she begged, and the sound traveled through his shaft and seized his balls.

With a growl, he breached her sensitive opening. He pushed his finger inside at the same time his mouth latched tightly around her clit. Jamie went off like a rocket. Her mouth disappeared from his dick as she let out a blissful cry and shuddered in release.

She was still moaning in abandon when he flipped her over. Her head hit the pillows, golden hair tousled and falling in her eyes, her legs parting for him even as she continued to tremble from the climax. Lennox dove over the side of the bed for his pants, finding a condom and sheathing himself in five seconds flat.

"Goddamn it, I need to be inside you," he burst out.

Her answer was another moan.

Shit, he couldn't go slow. He couldn't be gentle. Couldn't think straight. He knelt between her open thighs and drove his cock deep. The tight clutch of her pussy was goddamn incredible.

"Gonna be rough," he mumbled, surprised he could even formulate a real sentence. "Need it too bad."

"Then take it," she pleaded, raising her ass off the mattress to deepen the intimate contact.

The shock of pleasure that rippled through him sent him falling forward. He captured her mouth in a hard kiss as his hips flexed, as he pounded into her with everything he had. He was no longer in control. Each punishing thrust triggered another alarm bell in his head, a plea to slow down, a warning that he was hurting her, but Jamie's wild moans eased his concerns.

She dug her nails into his ass and met him thrust for thrust, drawing him in and squeezing him tight every time he retreated, as if trying to trap him inside. Their bodies slapped together, sweat slicking their chests as he filled her, over and over again, hard and fast and mercilessly deep.

When he came, it was in an explosion of pleasure that shut down his brain and seared his skin. The orgasm lasted minutes, hours. He was absolutely wrecked, completely drained, when he finally sagged against her. Jamie held him. Her lips brushed over his shoulder. Her hands stroked up and down his sweaty back.

He could feel her erratic heartbeat fluttering against his pec. The moisture still soaking the place where they were joined.

Something occurred to him. Something unacceptable. "You didn't come."

She laughed softly. "I got distracted watching you."

His pulse continued to race from that mind-shattering orgasm. "Give me a minute. I'll fuck you again."

That got him another laugh. "You've already given me three orgasms tonight."

"Not enough," he mumbled, then withdrew from her tight sheath so he could ditch the condom. He was still semihard, and already getting harder as he swept his gaze over her bare tits and saw the rosy flush on her pale skin.

Lennox rolled over on his back and closed his eyes, needing another minute to catch his breath. To come to terms with the fact that he was going to fuck his best friend all night long.

He'd just accepted that terrifying and thrilling truth when Jamie whispered, "What does this mean, Lennox?"

He opened his eyes. Then closed them again as a sigh rose in his chest. "I don't know."

12

Lennox was gone when Jamie woke up the next morning. She fought a rush of disappointment, then an even bigger rush of dread, because his absence had triggered an unwelcome thought.

Were things about to get awkward between them?

God, she really hoped not. She couldn't stomach the thought of Lennox shutting down on her again, avoiding her again. But her worries were erased when she rolled over and found a crumpled note on Lennox's pillow.

She smoothed out the paper, smiling when she glimpsed his familiar handwriting.

Promised Randy I'd meet up with him before tournament for extra training. See you there. —L.

She was pretty sure she was the only person on the planet who could have read that note, because Lennox's masculine scribbles were damn near illegible.

Sometimes it scared her how well they knew each other. She could list every single one of Lennox's likes and dislikes. His favorite food—toast, of all things, though that was probably because bread was a rare commodity in the free land. She knew his drink of choice was tequila, and that his favorite weapon was the old bolt-action rifle that had belonged to his dad. She knew he hated carrots with a passion and preferred the coast to the mountains. That he hated taking walks unless it was raining out.

Last night she'd gotten to know a whole different side of him. She'd been introduced to a rough, demanding man whose sexuality rippled off him in waves, a man who was insatiable in bed and could go all night without so much as a smoke break.

He'd been incredible.

A shiver ran through her as she climbed off the mattress. The delicious soreness between her legs made her smile. Hell, even her nipples were sore. She'd never been fucked that hard—or that good—in her life. She had no idea if they would do it again, but holy hell, she wanted to.

Her favorite thing about the building they were staying in was the bathroom. Whoever had worked here all those decades ago must have lived in his office, because the bathroom had a spacious shower stall, which allowed her to take advantage of her favorite thing about the town itself: readily available hot water.

After a quick shower, she brushed her wet hair and pulled it back in a ponytail. For clothing she threw on leggings and a loose striped shirt, an outfit that would be easier to fight in. She hadn't checked to see what "events" there were today, but she wanted to be prepared in case sparring was on the schedule.

When she walked outside, she discovered that Rylan and Pike had set up big pieces of plywood in the town square and beyond it, some as far as three and four hundred yards away. Looked like they were playing with guns today.

Since her team members hadn't arrived yet, she drifted over to say hello to Beckett, who took one look at her and said, "So you two finally screwed. Years in the making, huh?"

Jamie played dumb. "I have no idea what you're talking about."

"Uh-huh. Sure." His dimples popped out as he grinned. "So, how was it?"

She paused. Sighed. Then said, "Fan-fucking-tastic."

Beckett hooted, which captured the attention of the man they were discussing. Lennox had been talking to Randy, but now his head shifted toward her, and the look in his eyes almost knocked her over. Oh, they weren't done, all right. His gaze held so much heat she could feel flames prickling her skin.

Lennox licked his lips. Slowly. Thoroughly. As if he was imagining licking something else. Her thighs clenched so hard she had to break the eye contact. Fortunately her group arrived before she did something crazy, like march over, undo Lennox's pants, and ride him in front of everyone.

"Hey, Jamie." Sara walked up to her.

The girl was smiling, but it was a reserved smile. Highly cautious. Jamie liked her, but she wished Sara would let down her guard more often.

Jamie glanced around. "Where's your dad?" For once, Sara's father was out of sight.

"At the farm, helping Scott and Anna." An unexpected twinkle lit the girl's dark eyes. "See? He's not always breathing down my neck. Oh, and he lets me feed myself and tie my own shoelaces sometimes."

Jamie snickered, then reached out and touched the girl's arm. "Hey, it's nice to have someone looking out for you. Trust me, you're lucky your dad is here."

Sara was a perceptive girl, and her expression instantly softened. "Your parents are dead?"

Jamie nodded and swallowed a lump of sorrow. She had adored her parents, especially her mother, who'd been tough as nails. Sometimes Jamie still couldn't believe her mom had died of *pneumonia*. The woman who'd come out victorious in every battle she'd ever fought hadn't been able to conquer one stupid illness. It was so damn sad. Her dad had been tough too, but also very gentle. God, he'd told the silliest jokes around the campfire.

Losing them both had been like a knife to Jamie's heart. She probably wouldn't have survived it if it weren't for Lennox. He'd been there for her during the grieving process, same way she'd been there for him when he lost his own parents.

"I'm sorry," Sara said quietly.

"Me too." She cleared her throat of the massive lump inside it. "Come on, let's go see what Rylan and Pike have in store for us today."

As it turned out, the day's target practice would be a group effort. Each team had to select five shooters to fire at three targets of varying distances. The team with the most direct hits would get the coveted point.

Jamie studied her team. "Okay . . . obviously my girl Sara over here," she said with a decisive nod.

The teenager beamed as she quickly stepped to Jamie's side.

"And . . . um . . ." Jamie scanned the faces. "Porter and Walt."

The two thirty-something men who were good with a rifle moved forward.

"And . . . how about Tina?" Her gaze rested on the twenty-year-old with mocha skin and big dark eyes. Tina had kept to herself so far, and Jamie was determined to draw her out of her shell.

Once all the shooters had been picked, everyone lined up to the spot Rylan indicated and studied their first target. Jamie was busy studying the other teams. Lennox's group included Randy and three guys she didn't recognize. Beckett's team featured their star shooter, Sam, the woman Pike had been impressed with since day one. And Travis had taken a risk and chosen team members who were all under the age of nineteen.

"All right, Green Team. First shooter," Rylan announced.

Randy stepped up and hefted the rifle on his skinny shoulder. A silence fell over the town square as he slowly lined up his shot. One squeeze of the trigger and the kid sent a bullet straight into his target. It didn't hit the center, but the far left corner, which summoned a curse from Randy's lips.

Lennox, however, patted him on the back and said, "Nice shot."

"It sucked," Randy grumbled.

Jamie found it hard to pay attention to the next two shooters—she was too distracted by the sight of Lennox's ass, tight and firm beneath his snug cargo pants. She'd dug her nails into that ass numerous times last night. When she'd run her finger down the crease, she clearly remembered a violent shudder overtaking his body. She wondered if he liked ass play . . .

God, there were so many dirty things she still needed to learn about him. She couldn't fucking wait.

Lennox caught her staring, and his gray eyes smoldered, resting on her breasts. Her nipples stood as if on command, puckering under his sultry gaze.

"Blue Team!" Rylan barked.

Jamie's head snapped up. Still distracted, she looked at her people. "Um . . . Porter, you're up first."

As the bearded man aimed his rifle, she heard Lennox chuckling. He knew exactly where her mind had drifted, and his mocking laughter irked, because *ha*, like he hadn't been thinking the same damn thing.

After everyone had taken their turn with the first target, Travis's team of young guns was in the lead thanks to their impressively accurate shots. Lennox's team was in second place, followed by Beckett's, while Jamie's group trailed behind.

The second round caused a huge shift in the rankings, as the farther distance was trickier, requiring the novice shooters to take factors like wind and gravity into account. After the last shot was fired, Lennox's team moved up to occupy the first slot. Jamie's group was in second, and the spectator members of her team cheered wildly for their shooter comrades when Rylan announced the standings.

"Even the smallest change in distance will change the way your rifle shoots," Rylan reminded one of Travis's teenagers, a boy who'd demanded to know why he could hit all the short targets but not the long ones. "It's not just a difference of millimeters—it could mean adjusting your aim half a meter, maybe more."

As Rylan answered more questions, Lennox sidled up to her. "You should give up now," he taunted. "You're not beating us."

His deep voice sent a shiver through her. When she remembered the way he'd issued wicked commands at her, the shiver turned into a full-blown shudder.

"You might do better if you weren't so distracted. What's on your mind, love?" he asked innocently, but his knowing smile told her he was playing with her again.

She glowered at him. Oh, hell no. He wasn't allowed to pretend she was the only one who was hot and bothered thinking about last night. And he definitely wasn't allowed to win this event, because then he'd lord his victory over her all day.

It was time to ramp up the pressure.

As the third and final round commenced, Jamie wasted no time putting her new plan in motion. The plan was simple: drive Lennox wild.

She moved forward to take her turn, loosely holding her rifle in one hand. She donned a contemplative expression, slipped one finger into her mouth, and pretended to examine the target in the distance. Then she winked at Lennox and curled her tongue around the tip of her finger.

When she heard his strangled curse, she stifled a laugh and fired her rifle. The bullet hit the target dead center, splintering a hole right through the plywood.

Pleased with herself, she lowered her gun and smirked at Lennox, whose eyes were more than a little glazed.

"You're up, Len," Rylan announced.

"Hold on," Jamie called, coming to Lennox's side. "Team leader conference."

Lennox looked as though he was gritting his teeth. "What is it?"

She stroked his bare arm, and a muscle ticked noticeably in his jaw. "It's getting windier," she told him. "Just wanted to make sure you account for that before you shoot."

"Well aware of the wind."

Her fingers danced along his biceps. "Don't forget to aim above the target," she said helpfully.

His breath hitched when she stroked her way up his corded neck to his mouth. "No shit," he ground out.

She teased his lips with her fingertips. "And remember to breathe."

The intensity in his eyes was overwhelming. Jesus. He might as well have been fucking her, the way he was looking at her.

With a saccharine smile, she moved her hand off his mouth, smacked it on his ass, and sauntered off.

She wasn't surprised when Lennox missed the target completely. To the very vocal dismay of his team.

"That was a disgrace," Jamie informed him when he stalked up to her.

"You don't play fair, love."

"So?"

He narrowed his eyes at her. "Do I need to challenge you to a duel?"

"Swords or pistols?" She tilted her head. "Actually, forget the duel. I'd rather have a good old-fashioned Wild West gunfight."

"Wild West?" Randy asked curiously.

They both turned toward the kid. Jamie noticed Lennox's expression was resigned. "You don't know about the Wild West?" he prompted.

Randy shook his head.

"Me neither," another teenage boy admitted.

"Same," Sara spoke up, walking over to them.

"It was one of the most badass periods in history," Lennox told them. "Cowboys and Indians, saloons, poker games that usually ended in gunfights. Pretty much a time with no rules and lots of violence."

"Sort of like now?" Sara said dryly.

Lennox sighed. "Yeah, sort of like now."

Rylan broke up the history lesson by signaling the final shooters to take their places, and once the third round was over, Jamie's team was declared the winner of the event. Her charges broke out in victorious cheers. Sara surprised her with a huge hug. Even Tina was grinning from ear to ear, which made Jamie's sabotage of Lennox taste all the sweeter. She was thrilled to see the two very reserved girls having a good time.

Rylan clapped his hands together. "All right, everyone. Grab something to eat and meet back here in an hour for the next event."

"More target shooting?" one of the kids whined.

"Yep, but double the distance this time. This is what separates the boys from the men." Rylan glanced at Jamie. "Damn good shooting this morning, gorgeous."

The compliment made her swell with pride. She turned to gloat at Lennox, but her mouth slammed shut when she saw his face.

"I'm starving. Let's go." His rough tone of voice told her they weren't going to the restaurant or the help-yourself kitchen across the street.

He didn't touch her. He didn't look at her. For all he knew she wasn't even following him, but of course she was. She'd go anywhere Lennox led her right now, just to see his eyes burn with arousal again.

They ducked into a narrow alley situated between two storefronts, and Jamie didn't even have time to take a breath before his mouth was on hers. He hadn't lied—he *was* starving, devouring her mouth with single-minded purpose while his big hands deftly slipped under her waistband.

He tugged her leggings and panties down, but not off. The stretchy fabric remained pooled at her ankles as Lennox spun her around and pushed her forward. Her palms fell flat against the brick wall, bracing her for what was about to happen. She heard voices, footsteps echoing from the sidewalk, but she ignored them. Or maybe they faded away. Her entire being centered on the incessant pulsing between her legs, yet when she felt Lennox's hands clamp onto her ass, she instinctively closed her legs.

"Oh no, you don't," he rasped. "You don't get to close your legs on me, Jamie. You're going to take this, you hear me? You've been teasing me all morning and now I'm giving you what your body has been begging for."

Jesus, she'd unleashed a beast. She'd let him out

of his cage last night, and there was no locking him back up. Lennox was in charge now.

She squeaked when he yanked her legs apart and cupped her from behind. Heat flooded her core and spread outward, until every square inch of skin was tingling wildly.

"So wet," he muttered, rubbing his palm over her. But he still tested her readiness with his fingers, pushing one inside her, then two, as her inner muscles clenched around them.

She heard his belt jangle. The hiss of his zipper. A crinkling of plastic as he sheathed himself. When she tried to twist her head toward him, he shoved it back so she was facing the wall.

"Look straight ahead, love. You're not going to see what I'm doing to you. You're going to feel it."

She felt it, all right, as Lennox drove into her so hard her forehead smacked the wall. His cock filled her completely, stretched her, thrilled her. Clearly he was not to be tested today, and she couldn't have stopped this if she'd tried—nor did she want to. She pushed her ass back, accepting each punishing thrust, begging for it with the frantic motions of her body.

Her orgasm crashed to the surface far quicker than she'd anticipated, catching her by total surprise. A helpless moan slipped out as her pussy contracted around him, a wave of pleasure sweeping her away. Lennox was coming too, she realized. He pumped into her from behind, his strokes jerky, erratic.

His shallow breathing tickled her ear. He rested

his head on her shoulder, still trembling behind her. "Fucking hell, Jamie."

"Wh-what?" It was hard to talk.

"I'm nowhere near done with you. I just came like a motherfucker and I'm ready to explode all over again."

She knew how he felt. Her sex was already throbbing again, the sensitive muscles rippling around his cock, which remained rock-hard inside her. He groaned, but didn't withdraw, and although she knew it probably wasn't smart to use the same condom, she was too turned on to protest when he started thrusting again.

His fingers dug into her waist as he fucked her to another orgasm that left her breathless, and when he finally pulled out a few minutes later, she was a limp, sated mess. Her hair had fallen out of its ponytail, wild and tangled. The strap of her tank top was torn—she had no idea how that even happened—and her pussy felt deliciously ravaged.

Despite the aftershocks of pleasure rippling inside her, the same doubts she'd harbored last night crept in. "Goddamn it, Len," she choked out. "What does this mean?"

"I still don't know." He sounded beyond frustrated.

She hastily pulled up her pants. He did the same, then flicked the condom into a nearby Dumpster.

They stood there staring at each other for several long beats. Then they spoke at the same time.

"We're friends—"

"Our friendship—"

Awkward laughter echoed between them.

"You first," he said gruffly.

She pressed her lips together, searching for the right words. "Our friendship is important to me. I don't want to jeopardize it by getting into a relationship."

"Me neither."

She gulped. "But I don't want to stop what we're doing."

"Me neither."

"So . . . what now?"

He ran a hand through his messy dark hair. "Don't know," he muttered again.

They released simultaneous sighs and leaned against the wall, side by side. His presence was so familiar, so comforting. She'd known this man since they were children. And while normally she could read his mind, right now she had no clue what he was thinking or feeling. What he wanted from her. What she wanted from *him*.

She'd always had a clear vision for her future. She'd longed for the same three things since she was a kid—a home she felt safe in, a man she was in love with, and a child they would raise together.

And you can't have that with Lennox?

The question lingered in her mind and left her feeling perplexed. It was difficult to explain, even to herself, why it couldn't happen. She just knew, deep in her bones, that letting herself fall in love with Lennox would destroy everything they had.

Or build on it.

Or that. But the fear that stabbed into her heart at the thought of losing her best friend was too strong to ignore.

Lennox must have felt the same way, because he cursed softly. "We keep it separate," he said.

She wrinkled her forehead. "What do you mean?"

"We're friends. We'll always be friends. That can't and won't change."

Jamie nodded slowly.

"So when we fuck, our friendship doesn't enter the picture. We're just two horny people who want to get off with each other. We don't bring our history into it. We don't bring our feelings into it." His tone was steadfast. "When we're in bed, we're not the Lennox and Jamie who have known each other forever. We don't discuss our plans or reminisce about the past. We don't do anything but make each other come. When our clothes are on, we're Lennox and Jamie again."

She gave another nod.

"It'll just be sex," he maintained.

"Len—"

His hands were suddenly on her face, cupping her chin with an odd combination of tenderness and force. "I won't lose you, love," he said fiercely. "You know me—I'm terrible with women. I boss them around and piss them off. I get bored so fast it makes their heads spin. I don't stay with anyone for more than a few months."

She did know that, and maybe that was why she was so certain a relationship with Lennox could never work out.

In the back of her mind, a desperate voice insisted that Lennox could never grow tired of her. He was still by her side, after all, even after so many years.

But the idea that he might leave her one day was

too much to bear. If abiding by his rules meant keeping this man in her life, then she'd agree to anything he asked.

"Just sex," she echoed, but she remained doubtful. "Do you really think we can keep things separate?"

Lennox answered in a grim voice. "We don't have any other choice."

13

The second week of training was under way when Reese finally decided to drop by and observe one of the events. After all, she *had* promised Sloan she'd try to be nicer to Rylan.

But she got the feeling Rylan could see right through her. Ever since she showed up, he'd been eyeing her as if he expected her to attack him at any second.

She didn't blame him. She'd been nothing but bitchy to the guy. Most times he deserved it—he could be so unbelievably annoying sometimes—but there were times when he didn't deserve the attitude she gave him. She knew that, and yet whenever Rylan was around, it seemed she was in a constant state of *bitch*.

As she observed the shooting competition, she discovered that Rylan and Pike had worked wonders these past two weeks. Teenagers who'd never even held a gun were now shooting bottles right off the ledge where the targets had been set up.

She couldn't contain a burst of satisfaction. A storm was brewing in the free land, and she needed her people trained and ready when it came time to take action. Even the kids.

Other people might have vacillated, questioned whether or not they were doing the right thing by instilling violent instincts in these children. Not her, though.

Her whole life had been gearing up to this point. Years of barely checked rage and meticulous planning had brought her here. Cozying up to the Enforcers, allying herself with outlaws like Tamara, not to mention Garrett and his northern community, Mick in the south, Brynn on the coast. She'd started putting the pieces in place when she was twelve years old, far younger than the kids who were currently firing weapons and kicking the shit out of each other all around her.

"Let's take a break, guys." Rylan clapped his hands, then approached the raised ledge where Reese had taken up residence.

He stopped when his bare chest was inches from her face. The man had an impressive amount of muscle. And his skin still bore his summer tan. Or maybe he had a naturally golden skin tone. None of his tattoos were in color, she noticed as she swept her gaze over his chest. They were all done in black ink, some beginning to fade, others still crisp and defined. There was a lot of text, scrawled quotes she'd never taken the time to read because she didn't want to know more about this man than she already did.

"Enjoying the show?" he drawled.

She pretended he wasn't referring to the way she'd checked out his chest. "They're looking good. You guys are excellent teachers."

"I'm glad you're happy with our progress." He smirked. "Care to tell me the reason for it?"

"I already did. I need my people to be able to defend themselves and each other."

"Still sticking to that story, huh?"

Lord, he was like a dog with a bone. No, he was like that stray dog that used to scamper around the camp she'd lived in before discovering Foxworth. Stealing scraps, begging, causing trouble, and the moment someone caught on to his tricks, he'd sit like an angel and peer up with big innocent eyes. Roll over and beg for you to pat his belly.

The comparison made her chuckle.

"What?" Rylan watched her suspiciously.

"I was just thinking how you remind me of this stray puppy at my old camp."

He didn't appear to be insulted. Instead his eyes gleamed mischievously as he said, "Woof."

Reese couldn't stop the smile that tugged on her lips. She immediately scolded herself for it, but it was too late. Rylan had already seen it.

"Was that a smile? Holy shit. I didn't realize your mouth was capable of doing that." He paused, tilting his head playfully. "You know, I could make you smile a lot more if you spent a little time with me . . ."

"I think Pike is calling you over." He wasn't, but her remark achieved its purpose. Rylan glanced toward his friend, and when he glanced back, Reese had banished all traces of humor from her face.

Rylan sighed. "You're so goddamn difficult, Reese." He stalked off, visible frustration tightening his shoulders.

The smile broke free again. She enjoyed pissing

him off. Which was probably why this be-nice-to-Rylan plan was so fricking challenging for her.

"Aw, take pity on him already, will you?" Jamie strode up with two water bottles, handing one to Reese as she hopped up on the ledge. "I've never seen him chase after someone this hard."

"I've never seen him chase anyone, period," Reese said dryly. "I'm not sure why he's even bothering with me, seeing as how women flock to him with no effort on his part."

Jamie grinned. "With good reason. He's a spectacular lay."

Reese couldn't help being intrigued. And when she decided to voice the question on her tongue, she told herself it was for information purposes only. She'd seen Rylan in action, but the woman next to her had actually *experienced* him. "All right, I'll bite. What makes him so spectacular?"

"The piercing, for one." Jamie's blue eyes took on a dreamy quality. "Have you ever fucked a man with a pierced cock?"

Reese shook her head.

"Well, it feels incredible, hits this spot inside you that makes you lose your mind." The blonde offered a tiny smile. "Plus, he likes it rough, which is always fun. And he's not bad with his tongue either."

"I'm still not seeing the spectacular part."

Jamie looked thoughtful. "Honestly? I think it's just *him*. His enthusiasm, his lust for life. It's downright contagious. And he loves women—no, he worships them, and he truly cares if they get off. I've been with a lot of men who didn't give a shit if I was enjoying it."

"Tell me about it." Before Jake, there had been some real assholes in her bed. Most of the time she hadn't cared, because the sex had only been a tool for her. She'd learned at a young age that sex equaled power. Which meant that sacrifices—often in the form of orgasms—had to be made. Even so, it had certainly been a nice change to meet a man who actually cared about her pleasure.

"You should give him a chance. Or in the very least, a test run." Jamie wiggled her eyebrows. "If he doesn't make you come at least three times, I'll eat my hat right in front of you."

Reese had to laugh. "Nah, I'll pass. Plenty of other men around if I have an itch that needs scratching. Like your buddy Lennox. Now, *there's* a man who knows the meaning of multiple orgasms."

To her surprise, Jamie blushed. Then she averted her eyes.

"Did something happen I'm not aware of?" Reese asked slowly. "Did you and Len get into an argument? Are you not friends anymore?"

"No, we're still friends." Jamie mumbled something else under her breath. Something that distinctly sounded like "and we fuck now too."

"I'm sorry, did you say you're fucking now? Since when?" In the three years she'd known them, Jamie and Lennox had been purely platonic.

"Since four nights ago," Jamie confessed.

"Was that really the first time you two had sex? After all these years?"

"Yep."

"Why did you wait so long?"

"Because he never seemed interested in it. And I valued his friendship too much to push him." Jamie sighed. "Lennox doesn't do relationships. He fucks and runs—that's how it's always been with him. The moment someone gets too close, he bails."

Reese pondered that. "Does that mean you're ready to lose him as a friend?"

"I won't lose him." Jamie's reply was swift and firm. "We agreed to keep our friendship out of the bedroom. If we're naked, we're just two strangers. No feelings, no history."

Reese snickered. "Yeah. Good luck with that."

"It'll work," Jamie protested.

She doubted it. Maybe she was a cynical bitch— okay, fine, she *was* a cynical bitch, period. And she knew without a doubt that the kind of history Jamie and Lennox had wouldn't just disappear once their clothes were off. It would bleed into every sexual encounter. And if love entered the picture? Forget it. The two of them were screwed.

"Things are absolutely going to change if you're sleeping together," Reese said gently. "You know that, right?"

"Not necessarily. You've slept with Lennox and it hasn't changed *your* friendship."

"Len and I have never been, nor will we ever be, as close as you two are. He's my friend, sure, but there's no chance of me ever falling in love with him."

"How can you be so sure of that?"

"Because he's not my type. We have a good time in bed, but that's as far as it will ever go." Reese smiled. "He's one hundred percent *your* type, though."

Jamie's eyes narrowed. "How would you know what my type is?"

"I've known you for three years, honey. I've watched you for three years. Lennox is exactly the kind of man you want. He *is* the man you want." Reese shrugged. "You need to be prepared that the relationship you had before is going to change. Sex always changes things."

Jamie was worrying her bottom lip with her teeth now. Reese felt bad about upsetting her, but she wasn't one to mince words. Besides, it was better to prepare Jamie for the worst than to coddle her. Better that the woman knew precisely what was in store for her rather than be completely blindsided when her entire world was turned upside down.

Because sex had a disturbing way of stirring shit up. Reese had learned that the hard way.

"Why are we doing this again?" Jamie asked later that evening. She was highly amused as she watched Lennox pick the lock at the entrance of the sprawling one-story building.

"Because Reese has something against history," was his distracted reply.

Okay, then.

Grinning, Jamie took a step back to peer at the sign above their heads. The white concrete was crumbling in some places, but she could still make out most of the letters that spelled out FOXWORTH PUBLIC LIBRARY.

Decades' worth of rain, snow, and other weather damage, along with total lack of upkeep, had eroded both the sign and the building. The path leading to the front steps had grass growing between the cracks in the pavement, and some of the weeds on either side of the front doors were taller than Jamie.

Lennox was using a slender metal hook to maneuver the inner workings of the lock. The lock-pick kit was one of the most valuable treasures they'd procured during their years of scavenging. Jamie had found it at a hardware store in a western city that was almost completely destroyed by the bombs that fell during the war. Some place called Boise.

Gosh, she'd loved the years she and Lennox had spent driving through what used to be America. The places they'd visited had the most interesting names, far more exciting than "the Colonies." She always joked to Lennox that if she'd lived in the world before the war, she would've chosen to reside in Hippo, Kentucky.

"You know, we do have books in Foxworth." Beckett had been smoking a cigarette near the Jeep, but now he joined them on the library steps. "I've got a whole stack of 'em in my garage."

"Textbooks?" Lennox countered. He popped his current tool in his mouth and used another one to poke at the lock's cylinders.

"No, but I have some pretty cool fiction books. There's a bunch by this author named King. Really creepy shit." Beckett shivered.

Jamie laughed, but Lennox was too focused on breaking into the library to show any amusement. When the lock finally clicked, he gave a satisfied grunt, then rose to his feet and pushed the door handle.

"Randy and the other kids have zero knowledge about the history of our world," he said, sounding annoyed. "They don't even know prewar geography. And the other day I was talking to that kid Ethan about basic types of government, and he was staring at me like I was speaking French. And then when I said that, he asked me what *French* was."

Jamie frowned, surprised by that last bit. She and Lennox had grown up with people who'd believed in the importance of a well-rounded education, so she was well aware that languages other than English had once been spoken in the world. Hundreds of them, in fact. When the council had taken control, they hadn't just eliminated religion, class, and politics, but also decided there should be only one global language, and they'd chosen English. Anyone who'd survived the war and didn't know the language had been forced to learn it.

"Reese and the others only teach them stuff that's pertinent to the world as it is now." The sneer on Lennox's face revealed that he didn't support that philosophy.

Beckett countered with "Because now is all that matters. Who cares about how the globe was split up before the war? We live in the Colonies now."

"It's important to know where you come from," Lennox said firmly.

He opened the door and the three of them stepped inside, where darkness instantly engulfed them. They flicked on their flashlights. Three pale yellow beams lit up the space, illuminating a small lobby area. All the computers on the large circular desk were covered by ten layers of dust.

"This way." Lennox shone the light on an arched doorway to the left.

The second they crossed the threshold, the familiar scent of books triggered a wave of nostalgia that transported Jamie right back to her childhood. Her and Lennox's parents had accumulated hundreds of books over the years. Oftentimes they had to leave them behind when they abandoned camp, but they'd always found new ones along the way, a new collection to build on.

She breathed in the musty smell of well-read pages, tracing her fingers along the dusty spines of the books in the first aisle. A little metal tag told her she was in the self-help section. She moved her flashlight over the titles and snickered at the first one she saw. The loud sound bounced off the walls and echoed beneath the high ceiling of the library.

"What's so funny?" Beckett came up beside her.

She pointed the light at a book called *A Man's Guide to the Secrets of the Female Mind*.

He snorted. "This author is clearly a fraud. Everyone knows the female mind will remain a mystery until the end of time."

As the two of them wandered down the aisle chuckling over various self-help titles, Lennox's faint voice called out to them in the darkness. "Over here. Beck, bring the duffel."

They found him in the world history section. Beckett unzipped the large canvas bag while Lennox began pulling out books and tossing them over.

Nearly thirty tomes had made it into the bag before Beckett looked at Jamie and asked, "Is he always this intense? I didn't realize he had such a hard-on for textbooks."

An indulgent smile lifted her mouth. Of all the kids in their childhood camp, Lennox was the one who'd been the most captivated by the history lessons. Far more interested than she'd been, though she'd attended each lesson just to be near him.

"Learning gives him a boner," she said frankly.

Lennox overheard that and chuckled, but didn't slow down his quest. They hit the geography aisle next, where he relieved the shelves of several heavy atlases while Jamie ducked into the neighboring aisle and perused the medicine books there. She knew Hudson had worked as a nurse in the city, so she grabbed a few titles she thought might interest the woman. Then she stumbled on an even luckier find— a book full of home remedies, and one about the healing attributes of plants that grew in the Colorado area.

She promptly threw them in the bag, which was getting heavier by the minute.

Jamie tracked Lennox down to the language section. "I think you have enough."

"A few more," he said absently.

Her flashlight illuminated the hard cut of his jaw, which was covered in dark beard growth because he hadn't shaved in a couple of days. His stubble had scratched her thighs this morning when he woke her up by burying his face between her legs. The naughty memory made her body ache.

Before she could stop herself, she wrapped both arms around him from behind, then slid her hands down to his groin. The book he'd been inspecting was all but forgotten. Groaning softly, Lennox eased his hips forward, and she could feel him hardening beneath her palms.

God, she couldn't think straight with his tight ass pressed against her and his lemony scent infusing her senses. When she stood up on her tiptoes and kissed his neck, he groaned again and thrust his growing erection into her hands.

"Guys, listen to this."

They broke apart when Beckett appeared with a paperback novel in his hand. He had his flashlight pointed to one of the pages and he sounded gleeful as he began to read. "'You want more of this big cock, you dirty little slut?'" Beckett raised his voice to a higher pitch. "Gina moaned in delight. 'Yes. God yes. Please, Drake, give it to me. I've been such a bad girl.'"

Jamie snorted, while Lennox let out a soft whistle. "Damn," he remarked. "No wonder the council monitors everything that's being published these days. That's some raunchy shit."

"What's it called?" Jamie asked curiously.

"On Her Knees." Beckett barked out a laugh, then flipped some more pages and stopped on another passage. "'That's it, you dirty little slut, swallow every last drop.'" He glanced pensively at Jamie. "Again with the 'dirty little slut.' Should I be calling women that when I'm in bed with them?"

"Only if you want your balls chopped off."

"What's the matter, love?" Lennox pulled her toward him. "It doesn't turn you on?"

"Nope."

"Really? But what if we want you to be our dirty little slut?"

Beckett moved up behind her, and suddenly she was sandwiched between the two men. "Or how about we'll be the dirty sluts?" he suggested, his breath hot on her ear. Then he drew the lobe in his mouth and sucked.

Heat sizzled down to her core. With Lennox's erection pressing in her stomach and Beckett's rubbing against her ass, she was trapped between two walls of pure masculinity, and loving every second of it.

"Does that mean I get to be in charge?" she asked.

Lennox chuckled. "You're always in charge. We both know that."

Beckett kneaded her ass cheeks. Lennox undid the button of her jeans. Both men clicked off their flashlights, and then hers was yanked out of her hand and turned off too. Darkness surrounded them. No windows on this side of the library, which meant no moonlight, just pitch-black. But there was something insanely erotic about not being able to see them.

"What do you say, Beck? Should we show her how dirty we can be?" Lennox's deep voice echoed in the aisle.

Beckett was already working her jeans and panties down her hips. "Shoes," he murmured.

She kicked off her sneakers. A second later she was naked from the waist down and Beckett was on his knees behind her, nuzzling her ass with his cheek.

She heard a rustle of movement. The heat of Lennox's body disappeared. He was sinking to his knees too.

"Spread," he whispered.

Jamie parted her thighs and jerked when a hot, rough tongue rasped over her clit. Beckett's teeth sank into her ass at the same time, and the prick of pain combined with the jolt of pleasure triggered a helpless moan.

Holy hell.

No, not hell. *Heaven*. With Beckett nibbling on her tender flesh and Lennox flicking his tongue on her clit, moving it around in teasing circles, she was in absolute heaven. One long finger slid down her crease toward her pussy, and pleasure shot through her when Beckett pushed that finger inside her. There was nothing more exhilarating than having two men completely dedicated to *her* pleasure.

"You taste so sweet," Lennox muttered. "I could eat you for days, baby."

He wrapped his lips around her clit and sucked. Beckett added another finger and thrust deep.

Jamie's mind grew foggy, her entire being focused on the pulsing between her legs. She whimpered, rocking her hips against Lennox's face while at the same time trying to push back against Beckett's probing fingers.

"Good, love?" Lennox mumbled.

"So good," she mumbled in response.

He peppered kisses on her thighs, her stomach, her hips, before licking his way back to her core. She couldn't see a damn thing. All she could do was feel. Each stroke of Lennox's tongue. Each thrust of Beckett's fingers.

When she suddenly felt a warm tongue between

her ass cheeks, she jerked hard against Lennox's mouth.

He lifted his head with a laugh. "Whatcha doing back there, Beck?"

Beckett gave an answering chuckle. "Just having some fun."

Jamie's pulse careened when he resumed tormenting her ass, his tongue touching that puckered ring of muscle. Holy shit. She was going to self-combust. The nerve endings were so sensitive there. Her body was on sensation overload.

As Lennox continued to tend to her clit, Beckett's fingers slid back into her pussy while his tongue penetrated another erotic zone, spearing her hard.

The orgasm started in her fingers and toes. Tingling wildly, dancing along her skin, then igniting in a shock of pleasure between her legs before shooting outward again. She moaned as the waves cascaded through her. It was so damn intense, and the two men rode it out with her, the hungry noises they were making intensifying the rush, prolonging the climax until she was a droopy, whimpering mess.

By the time she recovered, they were both laughing, husky sounds laced with pure male satisfaction.

She heard another rustling, a click, and then light hit her eyes, nearly blinding her.

"I think she enjoyed that," Lennox told Beckett.

The other man brought his wet fingers to his mouth and sucked them dry.

Jamie was still shaking as she bent over to retrieve her flashlight. She switched it on and swept the light over their groins. They were both visibly hard.

"My turn to return the favor?" she teased.

To her surprise, Lennox shook his head. "That'll have to wait until we get back to camp. We've already been here too long—we need to get going."

She knew her disappointment showed in her eyes, but Lennox remained firm. He picked up her discarded pants and handed them over. "Get dressed, love."

She obeyed, because arguing with him always got her nowhere.

They were just walking into the lobby when Beckett's flashlight caught something in the hallway behind the main desk. Something that brought excitement to both men's voices.

A fully stocked vending machine.

"Holy shit!"

"Fuck yeah!"

Her sexual tormenters had turned into little boys, racing over to the machine and pointing their flashlights at the glass to peer happily at the candy behind it.

"How has this thing not been cleaned out already?" Jamie wondered aloud.

"I guess nobody cared enough about reading good books to come to the library," Lennox replied with a snort. "Beck, you got something we can use to break this glass?"

"Just my gun."

"No. I don't want it firing by accident. Track something else down."

As Beck disappeared down the hallway, Jamie heaved the duffel bag over one shoulder. "I'll take this down to the car and dump the books so we can fill it with your loot."

"Thanks." Lennox was staring longingly at the chocolate bars in the machine.

Laughing to herself, Jamie hurried out to the Jeep. She emptied the bag and left the books in the backseat, then popped back into the library, where she discovered Beckett wielding a huge ax with a bright red handle. He must have found it in one of those break-in-case-of-emergency glass cabinets, because there was also a fire extinguisher sitting at his feet. She instantly picked it up—the extinguisher could be useful for Graham's kitchen.

"I'm taking this to the car," she said as the men prepared to break the glass. "I'll wait out there for you."

That got Lennox's attention. His head turned sharply in her direction. "Stay in the Jeep, love. Don't go anywhere."

"Yes, sir."

"I mean it. Stay put, stay alert, and keep your gun out."

She nodded, then went outside again and leaned against the passenger door of the Jeep.

Aside from the overgrown foliage, the area seemed to be untouched by the war. Jamie had been to towns where entire buildings were nothing but skeletons, where the bombs had turned sidewalks and roads into gaping, charred craters. The coastal cities were even scarier. Most were underwater, but she and Lennox had visited ones that had somehow managed to remain standing. Barely, anyway—half the time they'd had to drive in the opposite direction because the roads were now rivers, some as deep as ten feet.

But towns like these, which showed so few signs

of the war ... she could imagine actual civilization here. People driving their cars or walking to work. Mothers pushing baby strollers down the sidewalk. Friends chatting over coffee at an outdoor café.

Her gaze shifted to the row of white town houses across the street. Water damage had marred the exteriors and rusted the small second-floor balconies, but it was easy to imagine how the houses had looked all those decades ago. And with the neighborhood so quiet and untouched, it was easy to believe that some treasures might have been left behind in those houses.

Gun in hand, she moved away from the Jeep and crossed the street. She figured she had a few minutes to investigate at least one house, so she popped into the first one in the row. The front door was unlocked, and the interior smelled musty when she stepped inside.

Damn, the house was cute. The front hallway was small but it led to a spacious living area with a dining nook in the corner and a kitchen with dusty appliances. A brisk examination of the white cabinets revealed that someone had already raided the place for food.

The upstairs had been spared, she discovered a minute later. The medicine cabinets were empty, but the walk-in closet in the master bedroom was full of men's suits and pretty dresses. One in particular caught Jamie's eye, a short white dress with a gaping neckline and silky fabric that felt lovely between her fingers.

She tugged it off the hanger and tucked it into her shoulder bag, then wandered over to an oak dresser to rummage through the black velvet jewelry box atop it. She found a gorgeous pearl necklace and a diamond bracelet that sparkled under her flashlight. Both promptly went into her bag.

The raid took all of five minutes, and Jamie left the house through the patio door in the kitchen rather than the front entrance. It wouldn't hurt to check if there were cans of gasoline or other useful supplies in the backyard.

But she realized her error the second she stepped outside. The yards behind the houses weren't fenced off—it was one long stretch of overgrown grass.

She heard their voices before she saw them. Smelled the smoke before she registered the campfire.

The seven men gathered around the crackling orange flames swiveled their head in shock.

Almost immediately, the shock turned to suspicion. And then interest. Heated, undisguised interest.

Shit.

Shit, shit, shit.

She'd stumbled onto a camp of bandits.

14

"Well, lookee here," one of the bandits drawled. "Aren't you a pretty little thing?"

Jamie's gun snapped up, her pulse racing as the men rose to their feet.

Despite their various heights and builds, they all had one thing in common: they were garbage people, with tattered clothing, unkempt hair and beards, and greedy eyes. Instead of forming communities and trying to keep the peace, bandits operated on a *take* mentality. They stole from other outlaws. They raped their women. They killed without remorse.

Their existence had always made Jamie furious. There *had* to be some sort of rules in this world, some semblance of civility, some shred of humanity. But men like these were savages. They only cared about themselves. Their next meal, their survival, their cocks . . .

"Aw, put that gun down, sweetheart," a man with a bushy red beard coaxed. He looked delighted to see her standing there. "We're not going to hurt you."

"No," another one agreed. When he flashed a smile, she noticed that three of his front teeth were missing. "We just want to be friends."

"Don't come any closer," she hissed when two of them stepped toward her.

They didn't listen. They kept approaching.

She clicked off the safety and cocked her gun. The pair of them froze, but they were still smiling.

"Do you even know how to shoot that thing, honey?" Red Beard asked with a chuckle.

"Damn right I do. And I'll shoot your goddamn balls off if you come near me."

She lowered her aim to his groin, carefully edging backward. Her heart was pounding even louder now, because there was no fear thickening the air. Not on their parts, anyway. They seemed entertained by the fact that she was pointing a gun at them. And the hunger in their expressions was unmistakable.

"Aaron," she heard one of them murmur.

And then a bandit with a shaved head lunged forward.

Jamie didn't hesitate. She whipped her gun toward him and fired a shot. The bullet hit him in the chest, and the stocky man hit the grass with an agonized shout.

All hell broke loose before the crack of the gunshot even faded away. Without glancing at their fallen comrade, the other men attacked like a swarm of angry hornets. Jamie fired again, but she couldn't hit six men at once, damn it. She shot one in the shoulder and another one in the leg before the gun was wrenched out of her hand and she was falling to the ground.

A heavy body landed on top of her, two meaty hands going for her throat. She batted at her attacker with one fist while her other hand slid down to her waistband. "Get the *hell* off me!" she roared as she fumbled to unsheathe her knife. Fuck. Her fingers were slippery from fear and sweat.

Still pounding her fist against the man's jaw, she managed to clasp the handle and pull the knife out. One upward slice and the blade was lodged in the side of the bandit's neck. A wave of blood gushed out, soaking her face.

Spitting out the coppery drops, she rolled out from under the dead man, but the others were faster than her. In a heartbeat she was flat on her back again. Her knife was kicked away, and suddenly two men were pinning down her arms while a third straddled her thighs. It was Red Beard, wearing a feral expression, his spittle splashing her face as he growled at her. "You little *bitch*!"

Jamie spat right back at him. He reared in indignation, then crashed his fist into her jaw. She was momentarily stunned, black dots swimming in her vision and a woozy sensation fogging her brain. She fought to stay conscious. Fought the tight lock on her arms. But the men were too strong. And God, they reeked. Of booze, of sweat, of desperation.

"I get her next," one of them muttered.

Red Beard reached for her waistband. She felt his hardness digging into her belly, and nausea bubbled in her throat when he rubbed his erection against her.

The lifeless body of the first man she'd shot was sprawled not even five feet away from them, but Red Beard and his pals didn't seem to care. Which was a disgusting testament to the way these men lived. They didn't give a shit about anyone but themselves. The lump on the grass might as well have been a tree or a bush, instead of their traveling companion.

Jamie battled a wave of panic when Red Beard unsnapped her jeans. His buddies were holding her down and no amount of struggling could release her from their iron grips.

Lennox.

She clung to the certainty that Lennox and Beckett would be walking out of the library at any second. Jamie opened her mouth and started screaming. Loud, ear-piercing shrieks that would alert Lennox to her presence, but which quickly got her another sharp blow to the face.

"Shut the fuck up," Red Beard snapped.

A hand clamped over her mouth—his friend's dirty hand. The odor of grime and soot filled her nostrils, nearly causing her to vomit.

"I'm not even gonna make this good for you," the man on top of her muttered as he tried to work her jeans down. "You lost that chance, honey. Now I'm gonna make it hurt. I'm gonna tear you open with my cock, you hear me? I'm gonna fuck you until you're bleeding and bruised and—"

His head exploded.

Jamie screeched in horror as his head *literally exploded*. One second he had a face. Wild red eyes, a narrow forehead, a mouth that was moving. The next, he was nothing but a cloud of blood and brains that spattered all over her.

Suddenly she was free, but still too stunned to move. It was the sound of gunshots blasting in the air that sent her stumbling to her feet. She heard footsteps, then saw two more bodies hit the ground. Panicked yells came from the bandits, more footsteps, and a blur in her peripheral vision as a large body sprinted away.

She turned her head to see Lennox and Beckett racing toward her, guns drawn, eyes glittering ferociously. Relief swamped her body like a flash flood.

"Beck!" Lennox shouted.

The next thing she knew, Beckett was running after the two bandits who'd taken off in a breakneck run.

Jamie wiped her face with one shaky hand, but that just succeeded in smearing Red Beard's blood into her mouth and eyes. Her hair was soaked with it, sticking to her forehead and neck.

She jerked when she felt a strong hand on her chin. "Jamie. *Jamie.*"

Lennox's voice penetrated the fog. She blinked and registered his familiar gray eyes.

"Are you okay?" he demanded. "Are you hurt?"

"I'm fine," she whispered.

"They didn't hurt you?" His hands were running up and down her body now, checking her for injuries. He growled when he found that her jeans were undone.

She swallowed. "Tried to."

Another growl rumbled in his throat, and then he was gone, marching toward the last surviving bandit. The man had been shot in the leg, and he was groaning wildly as he tried to crawl away.

Without a shred of hesitation, Lennox pointed his gun and fired. Jamie flinched as she watched another man's head explode. Then she swept her distraught gaze over the grassy area. She saw the body of the man she'd killed, and three more bodies courtesy of Beckett and Lennox.

Hopefully Beckett would take care of the remaining two, but when she heard the roar of motorcycle engines and the screech of tires in the distance, her hopes plummeted.

Beckett returned less than a minute later, frustration darkening his eyes. "Fuckers took off," he spat out. "They had their Harleys stashed at the side of the house." He glanced at Lennox. "Should we go after them?"

Lennox cursed, then thought it over. "No. The cowards will be long gone before we even make it to the Jeep. They won't show their faces back here."

Jamie knew he was right. Bandits were opportunists, only stealing and pillaging when it was advantageous to them, when they were confident they could get away with it. Now that they knew there were outlaws in the area who were armed and well trained, they'd scurry away like the spineless rats they were.

"Were those the same ones who attacked Foxworth?" Lennox asked the other man.

Beckett shook his head. "Nah. Never seen these ones before."

Lennox lowered his weapon and sneered at the bloody, motionless bodies on the grass. "Beck," he said.

The man waited for him to continue.

"Go wait in the car."

Beckett must have heard the same ominous note in Lennox's voice that Jamie did, because he disappeared without another word.

Jamie swallowed the lump of fear that rose in her

throat. Lennox's eyes were blazing with red-hot fury. And it was directed at her.

"Len," she started.

He silenced her with a harsh look. "Do you see what he did there?"

Confusion washed over her. "Who?"

"Beckett." His features were drawn so tight his entire face was transformed. A hard, vicious mask that made her palms go damp. "I told him to wait in the car." He slanted his head. "And you know what he's going to do?"

Jamie gulped again.

"He's going to *wait in the fucking car*!"

Before she could respond, he gripped her chin again and jerked her head upward so she was looking him in the eye.

"What the *hell* were you thinking going off by yourself?"

She was too weak to push him off her. She thought of the pretty white dress and the sparkling pearls and diamonds in her bag, and shame seeped into her bones. Lennox was right. She'd taken her quiet, peaceful surroundings for granted. She'd broken the first rule of outlaw life—allowing herself to believe there wasn't any danger.

"I—I was raiding the house," she stammered.

"You were raiding the house." He echoed her in a monotone, but his gray eyes were as dark as thunderclouds, flashing with emotion. "You were raiding the house."

"Lennox." Annoyance climbed up her throat. She got it. She'd screwed up. But the two of them had gone on raids and supply runs hundreds of times before.

They'd split up before, run into bandits countless of times, but he'd never reacted with this degree of anger.

Lennox went silent. His jaw ticked.

Then he lost it.

"You could have been killed! They were going to rape you, damn it!" His fingers tightened in her hair. "The next time I give you an order, you fucking obey me, you understand?"

"*Obey* you?" Her irritation morphed into a lightning bolt of anger that matched the one blazing in his eyes. "You are *not* in charge of my life, Lennox! I don't follow your orders!"

"Like hell you don't. The only reason you're alive is because I've always been there to take care of you."

Her jaw dropped. "That's bullshit. We're a team. We've always made decisions *together*. We give orders *together*. Or was I wrong about that? Has it been you this whole time?" She was spitting mad now. "*You've* been in charge and I've just been cowering behind you like a frightened two-year-old?"

"I told you to wait in the car!"

"And I chose to raid the house! That was *my* risk to take."

"Was it worth it?" he snapped back. "Because those bastards would have *raped* you if Beck and I hadn't shown up."

His hands dropped to her shoulders, shaking her so violently that she slammed her palms on his broad chest and shoved him away. "I screwed up!" she burst out. "Okay? I didn't clear the area before I went inside the house, and that's on me. I fucking get that."

"It wouldn't have happened if you'd listened to me!"

"Well, I didn't." When he advanced on her, she gave him another hard shove. "What are you going to do about it, Len? Spank me? You're not my father, and you don't get to tell me what to do."

"Maybe I should," he hissed out. "Because clearly you've forgotten how to use your goddamn brain. Maybe you *need* someone telling you what to do if these are the kinds of stupid decisions you're going to make."

They were breathing hard, and with the dropping temperature she could see each puff of air that escaped their mouths. Lennox looked ready to murder her. She felt the same way, so close to throttling him that her hands were tingling. He'd never treated her this way before. Like a child. No, like an *imbecile*. He actually had the nerve to call her *stupid*? To stick out his big manly chest and act as if she couldn't walk down the street without holding his hand?

God, Reese had been right. Things *were* changing. Lennox never would have dreamed of talking to her like this before.

And she didn't fucking like it.

"You need to be careful about what you say next," Jamie said, her voice deceptively soft. "Because I'm this close to strangling you right now, Lennox."

"You want to strangle *me*?" Disbelief passed through his eyes. "Do you realize what it felt like to hear those gunshots? To run out here and find you on the ground with some sick fuck between your legs? Do you realize how close you came to dying?"

"Yes." She clenched her teeth. "And I'm grateful that you and Beckett came along when you did—"

"You're *grateful*?"

"—but that doesn't give you the right to shout at me and call me stupid."

"I didn't call you stupid. I called your actions stupid."

"Same thing."

Silence fell over them as they stared at each other. Jamie took a breath, trying to calm her erratic heartbeat, to cool the hot rush of fury still boiling in her blood.

"We should go," she muttered. "Beckett's waiting."

She stalked past him before he could make a snide remark about how *Beckett* knew the meaning of waiting when she clearly didn't. God, she couldn't even look at him. She knew she'd screwed up, but she hadn't deserved his hurtful attack. She hadn't fucking deserved it.

They were supposed to be equals. She'd thought they were, but he'd made her feel like a piece of dirt under his shoes. And right now she needed to get as far away from him as possible before she did or said something she would regret.

The drive back to Foxworth was riddled with tension. Beckett didn't say a word, wisely understanding that something had gone down between them, and Jamie was grateful for his silence. She and Lennox hadn't spoken either, but she knew he was still pissed off at her, because his mouth stayed locked in a tense line until the moment he drove through the town gates and parked the Jeep in the courtyard.

The three of them hopped out, their boots silently hitting the dirt. Ignoring the stack of books in the backseat, Lennox mumbled something about needing to tell Reese about the appearance of more bandits in the area, and stalked off. Beckett trailed after him.

Jamie went to the law office instead of tagging along. She was still pissed off too. At Lennox. At herself. At fucking everything. She needed a shower and a drink, in that order. The first one was easy to cross off the list, but after she'd washed all the blood and dirt off her body and headed outside again, she hesitated on the sidewalk. The thought of chatting with anyone who might be at the restaurant was about as appealing as having Lennox rage at her again.

She went to the kitchen instead, which was really just another restaurant, but this one was used only to store food in the huge walk-in freezers and refrigerators. She grabbed a beer from one of the fridges, ignoring the rows of liquor bottles on the shelves across the room. Anything stronger than beer would go right to her head and bring on an adrenaline crash she didn't feel like enduring.

She'd thought she was alone in the dark restaurant, so when a deep voice said, "Hey," she jumped nearly two feet in the air. Kade was seated at a table in the shadowy corner of the room. He held a beer bottle in both hands, watching her with wary eyes.

"Hey," she answered in a wobbly voice. "I didn't see you there."

"Everything all right?"

"Nope."

That made him chuckle. He rapped his knuckles on the tabletop. "Want to sit down?"

Not really. She felt like pacing the room until she managed to dispel the negative energy coursing through her. She still wanted to rip Lennox's throat out for the way he'd talked to her.

But since she couldn't exactly murder her best friend, she forced herself to sit across from Kade and gripped the beer bottle tight enough to turn her knuckles white.

"What happened?" Kade asked.

She took a small sip. "We ran into bandits on the road."

Concern immediately filled his dark eyes. "They give you any trouble?"

"Yeah. It got pretty bad for a moment there. But Lennox and Beck came to my rescue." She couldn't stop a twinge of sarcasm at the end.

"You say that like it's a bad thing," he said dryly.

She swallowed some more beer, her heart squeezing as she remembered Lennox's enraged face. "He yelled at me," she confessed.

Kade looked as though he was trying not to laugh. "Lennox?"

Jamie nodded unhappily. "It was bad. He totally lost it, Kade. Like, *lost it*. I've never seen him like that before."

"He was worried about you. And probably scared shitless about what could have happened if he hadn't shown up."

"He's allowed to be scared. But he's not allowed to treat me like I'm an idiot. We've been traveling together for years. He knows I can take care of myself."

"Sounds like you couldn't tonight," Kade hedged in. "You said so yourself—you needed rescuing."

"Maybe, but the way he reacted . . ." The anger returned, simmering in her belly. "We've gotten each other out of jams before. Trust me, this isn't the first time I've screwed up, and God knows he's screwed up before too. But we've always backed each other up, because that's what we do. We're there for each other." A helpless feeling clogged her throat. "Tonight he acted like I'm the weak link in our relationship. Like it's up to him and him alone to give orders and make decisions. Like he's the one who's always protected *me* and I've never done the same for him. Which is complete bullshit."

Even with the lights off, she could see the thoughtful gleam in Kade's dark eyes. "I heard you guys are sleeping together now."

She bristled. "So?"

"But you weren't before?"

"No." Why did she get the feeling she was about to hear the same speech that Reese had given her earlier?

"It's different when a man is having sex with someone," Kade began.

Yep, there it was. Another bullshit speech about how everything would change.

He saw her skeptical expression and added, "Seriously, honey. It's a whole other level of protective instincts. Possessiveness. It's like this basic, primal urge suddenly comes out and makes a man extra determined to protect the woman in his bed."

"Why?" She asked more out of annoyance than curiosity, because sex had nothing to do with whether or not a woman could take care of herself.

Kade shrugged. "Maybe it's because he's seen her at her most vulnerable? Sex is intimate. You're naked, exposed. There's a certain degree of trust involved."

He raised his bottle to his lips. "I don't know. It's hard to explain. Bottom line—sex turns guys into cavemen."

"Yeah, well, he still had no right to call me stupid," Jamie muttered.

Kade whistled. "Shit. Lennox called you stupid? He must've *really* been worried about you."

That didn't appease her. Lennox had every reason to be worried, but there was no excuse for the way he'd handled himself.

"If it makes you feel any better, I get the same bullshit from Xan."

Kade's confession sparked her curiosity, especially when she recognized the implication. "Wait . . . are you saying the two of you are sleeping together?" She'd seen Kade and Xander share women before, but she'd never witnessed them going at it solo.

"No," he answered, chuckling softly. "We're not. But I was in a similar situation as you were tonight when Connor and the guys found me two years ago. I was getting the shit kicked out of me by bandits— they fucked me up pretty good—and I don't think Xander has been able to erase that first impression of me, all bloody and beaten."

"How many men were there? Attacking you, I mean?"

"Three." He gave another chuckle, rueful this time. "I was literally out of the city for two days when it happened. I had no idea what life was like out here. I knew some Enforcers who'd had contact with out-laws, and they always described you guys as fierce but incredibly loyal to each other. I hadn't realized bandits existed, men who didn't give a shit about anyone but themselves. So I wasn't prepared, and I suffered for it." He shrugged. "But that put a brand of weakness on me. They still think I'm weak."

"They don't think you're weak," she objected.

"Of course they do. Connor sent me here for more training, for fuck's sake," Kade said with a laugh. "It's different with Xan, though. He doesn't just try to teach me how to defend myself. He somehow got it in his head that he needs to watch over me."

"He cares about you."

"Lennox cares about you," Kade countered.

They fell silent as they sipped their beers again. She knew Kade was right—Lennox did care about her. But he'd made her feel . . . *inferior* tonight. And weak. He'd made it sound as if he'd been carrying her all these years, when she'd truly believed they were carrying each other.

She didn't like that. No, she *hated* it. Hated thinking that Lennox viewed her as helpless or lacking. That they weren't a team, but a leader and his obedient follower.

She swallowed another gulp of beer. The bitter liquid slid down to her stomach, joining the unbearable knot of bitterness already lodged there.

"suffered for it," he shrugged. "But that was a world of worry ago in fact. They still in place now?"

"You don't think you'd know?" she observed.

"Or at least they don't matter. Neither here nor there for public sales," Kade said with a laugh.

"If you travel with X in those, I'd say it's likely to teach me how to defend myself. He sure knew got it in his head that he needs to protect me."

"He cares about you."

"He cares a lot about you," Kade countered.

They fell silent as they approached their house again. She let her face warm up. I don't really care about him, but Kade made her reel . . . I don't. Not tonight. And I won't. Kade made it sound as if it had been betraying her all those years when she'd silently believed they were different from others.

She didn't like that. No, she hated it. Hated thinking that I only viewed Kade as hopeless at tasking. That they weren't a team, but she fell and his reach on following.

She swallowed another gulp of beer. The bitter liquid slid down to her stomach, turning the unease that knot of bitterness slowly loosen there.

15

Lennox's meeting with Reese was brief. The Foxworth leader wasn't pleased that a second group of
bandits had drifted this close to her town, but other
than send a few men to make sure the assholes were
really gone, there wasn't much more she could do.
And she agreed with Lennox that she didn't expect
them to return.

After he left Reese's building, he went on an
immediate hunt for Jamie. She wasn't in their rooms,
the restaurant, or the loft, which left one other place
he needed to check—the rec hall.

Sure enough, he spotted her the moment he walked
inside. She was sitting alone in the corner, a bottle
of beer resting on her knee. Lennox took one look at
her cloudy, stay-the-hell-away-from-me expression and
knew she was still pissed.

He might have overreacted earlier. Just a tad.

More than a tad, asshole.

Regret floated through him as he thought about
his behavior. The second he and Beckett were alone
earlier, the man had told him in no uncertain terms

that he needed to apologize to Jamie. Apparently Beck had heard Lennox shouting all the way from the Jeep, and he'd given Lennox a sympathetic pat on the shoulder when they were leaving Reese's apartment. Even Beck knew that it would take a shit ton of groveling to earn Jamie's forgiveness.

Lennox stifled a sigh and approached Jamie the way one might approach an animal with a thorn in its paw. He knew she was hurting, but he also knew that she'd lash out if he gave her even the slightest provocation.

He sat beside her on the couch. "Hey," he said gruffly.

She sipped her beer and stared straight ahead.

"Come on, love," he urged. "Talk to me."

"Oh, we *talk* to each other now?" Sarcasm dripped from her voice. "I thought our relationship just involved you yelling at me."

A sliver of guilt pricked his gut. He shouldn't have yelled at her. But he'd been so fucking scared. His heart had been ripped from his chest when he saw her on the ground like that, vulnerable and afraid and at the mercy of those scavengers. They'd had their filthy hands on her, damn it. Even now a rush of visceral rage burned his throat as he remembered it. As he envisioned what those bastards would've done to her if he and Beckett hadn't heard the gunshots.

Truth was, it was his fault. He'd checked the area around the library, but not the houses. He'd been too eager to break in and find some books, and, once they were inside, too focused on making Jamie come to be as vigilant as he normally was. And then he'd let her go outside by herself because he was too busy trying to score some *candy*.

Jesus. What kind of protector was he? How had he allowed such trivial distractions to get the better of him?

"I'm sorry," he told her.

Jamie didn't respond.

"I shouldn't have yelled at you, baby. I shouldn't have called you stupid."

"No shit." The hurt in her voice made his heart clench. "I'm *not* stupid, Len."

"I know that." He touched her cheek, and cursed when she stiffened. "Please, love. Don't tense up on me. Let me make this right."

"It's not going to happen tonight." Her blue eyes continued to flash with anger. "I'm still pissed off at you. There's too much aggression inside me right now."

"Then let's release it."

The suggestion brought a scowl to her lips, but Lennox didn't dismiss the idea as quickly as she did. He knew Jamie well. When she was mad, she lost her temper and struck out at whoever was around her. But when she was *hurt*? She bottled it up. She let it gnaw at her insides because she hadn't quite mastered the talent of channeling all the volatile energy.

He would help her channel it. When he felt like this, he either fought or fucked. Since they'd already seen too much violence tonight, it looked like he'd have to coax Jamie to do the latter.

"I'm serious," he said when she made a derisive sound. "Let's release all that aggression, love. It's nothing a few orgasms won't help."

She gaped at him. "You think orgasms are going to make it better? I want to *hit* you right now, Len."

Shit. She really was wound up. He might need to call in some backup.

Lennox scanned the room until his gaze stopped on Beckett, who wore his trademark lazy grin as he chatted with Arch and Bethany. No, Beck would be too playful. The fire in Jamie's eyes required a different kind of stoking than what Beck could offer.

He shifted his gaze and spotted Sloan talking to Nash. Which was an odd display, since Lennox had never seen the man do anything but lean against the wall and watch Reese. Either way, he doubted Sloan would be interested in what Lennox had in mind.

And fuck, the thought of Sloan or Beckett or any other man touching Jamie tonight, after already witnessing those goddamn bandits pawing at her . . . it made his blood boil.

He forced the protective urges aside. "Who do you want?" he asked hoarsely. His gaze moved again, then landed on the one man he knew who would not mind the violence. "How about Pike? He'll let you claw at him all night."

A furious sound escaped her mouth as she shot to her feet. "You're unbelievable. You really think a threesome is the answer? *That's* your apology?"

She stormed off before he could answer. Lennox cursed and hurried after her, but she was already out the door and his pleas for her to stop went unheeded. As frustration surged in his blood, he chased her down the street and into their building, but she was quick when she wanted to be, and he didn't catch up to her until she'd reached her bedroom. When she tried to slam the door on him, he muscled his way inside and growled in frustration.

"Damn it, Jamie!"

"Damn *you*, Lennox!" Her cheeks were bright red. "Leave me alone. It's late. I want to go to sleep."

"Not until we talk."

"Again with the talking bullshit? Because it sounded back there like you were in the mood for a gang bang." She blew out an angry breath.

"I just want you to let out your anger," he said through clenched teeth. "I know you, love. You're going to keep it all inside and it'll make you crazy."

"Yeah, well, I don't need *Pike* to help me with that. I don't want him or anyone else tonight."

"Not even me?" His chest squeezed at the thought that he might have blown it with her for good. He swallowed, forcing himself to ask, "Are you saying we're done?"

His fear must have been written on his face, because her expression immediately softened. "No, we're not done." She grumbled out a curse. "But I don't want to be around you right now. I'm too wound up. I want to hurt you."

Clearly his dick was a masochist, because it stirred at that. "Then hurt me," Lennox said softly.

"Lennox." She sounded exasperated.

"I mean it." He moved closer and pinched her chin with his fingers. "Hurt me, love. I fucking deserve it. I shouldn't have lost it on you earlier and I deserve to be punished for it."

When she didn't respond, he started ripping his clothes off. His belt was yanked out of the buckle. His jeans and boots hit the floor. His shirt snagged against the arm of the chair. Then he stood naked in front of her, and despite the tension still crackling between them, it was impossible for his dick not to get hard when Jamie's eyes were on him. When her body was this close to his.

"Punish me," he commanded.

"You're being ridiculous again."

He grabbed her hand and brought it to his chest, then forcibly raked her fingernails over his skin. The sting of pain was surprisingly welcome. Shit. Maybe they both needed the violence tonight.

"For fuck's sake, Len!" Jamie jerked her hand away, but didn't smack him with it.

Her expression had transformed from annoyance to arousal. The air all around them thickened as her blue eyes roamed his naked body. She stared at his jutting erection. Her tongue came out to swipe her bottom lip. Then a curious smile tipped her mouth and she placed her hand on his chest again.

He flinched when her nails clawed down his abs. Harder than before. Deep enough to leave faint dots of blood.

"You're an asshole, Lennox." She didn't sound angry. Just thoughtful.

"I know," he said hoarsely.

One fingernail scraped his nipple and he tensed, waiting for her to bring the pain. But rather than pinch or scratch that hardened bud, she captured his bottom lip with her teeth instead. She bit down hard, making him curse wildly. She'd drawn more blood.

"More," he rasped, licking at the blood dripping from the corner of his mouth. "Make me hurt, love."

A wicked gleam entered her eyes. She reached

down and circled her fingers around his cock. She clutched him so tightly it triggered a jolt of pain. But also pleasure. Her rough grip made his balls ache. Filled him with anticipation.

Still squeezing the daylights out of his cock, she leaned in to kiss him, then whispered, "Get on the fucking bed."

He was on the mattress so fast he experienced a wave of vertigo from the rapid shift from upright to horizontal.

Jamie approached the foot of the bed. Without a word, she started removing every scrap of clothing, assaulting his vision with flashes of smooth skin and perfect curves. His hungry gaze tracked the motion of her naked body as she walked over to the canvas bag across the room. Her tits swayed sensually as she bent over to unzip the bag.

When her hand emerged with a coil of thin cable, Lennox's mouth went dry.

A moment later, she was crawling up his body to straddle his thighs. The cable hung loosely from her fingers, and she scraped the end of it over his bare stomach. "Hands above your head," she murmured.

He was quick to obey. And he said nothing as she bound his wrists together, then secured them to the bed frame. She'd tied the cables tighter than she needed to, because even if he'd had the use of his arms, he wouldn't be going anywhere. But he knew it was part of his punishment. She *wanted* the wires to dig into his wrists, and Lennox knew it was going to hurt like a bitch once his blood flow was obstructed. But he didn't care. He'd hurt her tonight.

Pleased with her work, Jamie straightened up. She

reached for his cock again and dragged her nails down the hard length. "You were a bad boy tonight, Len."

"So bad," he agreed.

"You want me to punish you, but this feels like a reward." She stroked his shaft, then lowered her head to rub her cheek over his engorged tip. "Doesn't seem fair, does it? You freak out on me and I punish you by taking this big cock in my mouth?"

He moaned when her tongue flicked over his slit and lapped at the precome pooled there.

"But I guess there's something to be said for sexual torture, right?" She lifted her head and smiled at him.

The dark gleam in her eyes sent his pulse careening. Shit. She wasn't going down the path he'd expected her to take—slap him, bite him, ride him until they were both limp. Evidently she had other ideas, and now his heart was beating even faster, because he didn't like surprises.

Jamie moved her other hand to his balls, toying absently with the tight sac as she pumped his dick. "I can do whatever I want to you, baby." She met his eyes. "And you're not going to stop me, are you?"

"No." He swallowed hard. "I won't."

"Good." Then she dipped down again and sucked him.

His hips jerked off the mattress, instinctively seeking more contact, trying to delve deep into her hot mouth. That only caused her to retreat. She kissed her way to his balls and began tormenting him, licking and nibbling and driving him bat-shit crazy. His eyes slammed closed as he lost himself in each new burst of pleasure that went off inside him. When he heard a sucking noise, his eyes flew open to find Jamie had popped one finger in her mouth. She got it nice and wet, her heated gaze fixed on him. Then she trailed that finger down the crease of his ass, and his entire body stiffened.

"You can't stop me, can you?" she mocked.

His breath got stuck in his lungs, making his voice shake. "No."

Laughing softly, she used the tip of her finger to toy with the delicate skin right beneath his sac. An unexpected shock of heat rippled through his cock. He moaned in surprise, and she laughed again, then wrapped her lips around his cock head at the same time she pushed her finger into his ass.

Holy shit.

"Jamie . . . ," he said helplessly.

She wasn't listening. Her mouth had swallowed him up, wicked tongue swirling around his tip while she rubbed his tight passage, hitting a spot that had him crying out. Sweet Lord. What was she doing to him? And why did it feel so fucking good?

Lennox trembled uncontrollably as she worked him with her mouth and her finger. The headboard vibrated as he fought against the cables around his wrists. He wanted to touch her. Wanted to shove his hands in her hair and pound into her mouth. He couldn't get loose, though, and soon he was too weak to keep trying. His dick was pulsing with excitement, and every time her finger breached his sensitive hole, he found himself bearing down on it.

Jesus, he was close. His spine was tingling. His balls ached as they'd never ached before. His ass was on fire, goddamn it, and for some reason he welcomed the burn.

He groaned in dismay when she suddenly released him. She was laughing again, but her expression grew serious when their eyes locked.

"We're a team," she said firmly.

Her finger pushed in deep, and he grunted in pleasure.

"Say it, Lennox. We're a team."

"We're a team," he croaked.

With a satisfied look, she dipped her head and sucked him all the way down to the root. Then she scraped her teeth over his cock head and gave a gentle bite, and he came so hard that his mind imploded. Wild shudders overtook his body as he shot down her throat, as he squeezed his ass cheeks and bore down harder on her finger.

He was gasping for air by the time she released him, his wrists frantically banging the bed frame. "Untie me," he begged. "I need to touch you."

"No." Her tone was firm, her eyes taunting him. "That's your punishment, Len. You don't get to touch me. You don't get to make me come." Her hand slipped between her legs. "I want you to see how well I can take care of myself."

He couldn't breathe again. His gaze was glued to the seductive movement of her palm as she rubbed it over her core. Son of a bitch. She was right. This *was* punishment. It was torture. His fingers were buzzing, and not because of the lack of blood reaching them. He was desperate to touch her. Every sexy inch of her.

But she denied him. She stretched out next to him,

lifting one knee up so he had a perfect view. One finger delicately stroked her clit, pink and swollen and so damn appetizing his mouth filled with saliva. And even though she'd just milked him dry, his cock was throbbing again.

He'd lied to her the other day. Partly, anyway. He *did* get easily bored of women. But he could never tire of Jamie. Even thinking it was completely absurd.

Jamie kept him on his toes. She excited him as no other woman ever had. Keeping their friendship out of the bedroom was the only way he could think of to preserve it. That distance was necessary. It had kept him in line all these years, allowed him to focus on taking care of her. Sex would've been too big a distraction. Hell, it *was* a distraction. A team of armed Enforcers could've swarmed this bedroom right now and Lennox wouldn't have even noticed. He was too busy devouring Jamie's gorgeous pussy with his eyes.

"Me," she murmured as she stroked herself. "I'm doing this." She slipped a finger inside, and the wet noises accompanying each gentle thrust told him she was soaked. "I'm making myself wet." Her index finger moved faster over her clit. "*I'm* making myself come."

And then she did, her beautiful features tightening with pleasure as her body convulsed beside him. It was sheer agony lying there and being unable to touch her. Not having his fingers inside her, his tongue on her, licking up every ounce of her arousal.

When the orgasm faded, she sat up with a dreamy smile, then offered him a fleeting taste by rubbing her wet fingertips over his lips.

Lennox growled when she drew her hand away. "More."

"No." She climbed off the bed.

"Where are you going?"

"Back to the rec hall to finish my beer." Her grin widened. "I'll be back in a few hours to untie you."

"Jamie—" But she was already scooping up her discarded clothing and ducking out of the room.

A strangled expletive flew out of his mouth as he stared at the empty doorway. Fucking hell.

Payback really was a bitch.

16

"You doing all right, sweetie?" Jamie couldn't fight her concern when she entered the restaurant and found Bethany at the counter, clasping her left hand over her lower back. Her right hand was in the sink, covered with suds as water cascaded from the faucet. There didn't seem to be anything seriously wrong, but Jamie didn't like the pained look in the woman's eyes.

"My back is killing me," Bethany groaned. "And Arch is at the farm today, so I didn't get my afternoon back rub."

Jamie had to laugh. "Well, I suck at massages, but I'm damn good at washing dishes." She pointed to a stool. "Sit. I'll take over."

Eyes full of gratitude, Bethany dried her hands on a rag and collapsed onto a stool while Jamie took her place at the sink. "Thanks, sweetie."

"You need to stop working," Jamie announced as she picked up a dirty plate from the stack and ran it under the tap.

"And then what? Sit around on my ass all day?"

Bethany grumbled. "Reese has rules. If you live in Foxworth, you need to contribute."

"I'm pretty sure Reese would make an exception for a woman who's almost seven months pregnant."

"But then I'll go crazy with boredom." Bethany groaned again, still rubbing her back. "What are you doing here, anyway? Isn't there training today?"

"Nope. It's our day off."

Bethany chuckled. "I popped into the rec hall last night and snuck a peek at the scoreboard Rylan tacked up. Lennox is beating you, huh?"

She sighed. "Yep." On the bright side, she'd managed to push Beckett's team out of second place. Travis had moved up too, putting Beckett in last place. Which was probably why she'd just spotted him and his teenage charges setting up to practice their long-distance targets on their one day off.

The farther distances were the most difficult for the younger shooters because it meant adjusting for factors like wind and bullet speed. Jamie's favorite team member, Sara—yep, she was totally picking favorites—seemed to have no problems, though. The girl was a natural sharpshooter.

"We start on moving targets tomorrow," she told Bethany, "so my team might be able to take the lead. I took Sara and Tina to the old high school yesterday and you should've seen them. I was tossing bottles in the air and they were shooting them right out of the sky."

"Wow, you actually lured Tina out of her room? I'm pretty sure that might be considered a miracle."

Jamie thought about the quiet girl, and smiled. "She's super shy, huh?"

"Not shy. Cautious." Bethany's expression became grave. "She lost both her parents a few years ago. Sloan and Arch found her wandering alone in the woods, but she refused to tell them what happened to her. Actually, she refused to speak, period. For two whole days. At one point they thought she might not know how to talk."

"But she eventually told them?"

The woman nodded. "Arch wore her down with jokes and gentleness, and Tina told him everything. Turns out her entire camp had turned against her folks. They were the leaders, and people were unhappy with some of their choices, so they killed them. Shot them both in the head right in front of Tina."

Jamie cursed. "God."

"She's been here for two years, but I honestly don't think she trusts a single one of us. I think she's scared we'll turn on her the way everyone turned on her parents."

A deep crack formed in Jamie's heart. There was so much mistrust in the free land, so much violence. And the threats didn't just come from the Global Council, but from *each other*.

There were still times when she wondered what it would be like to live in West City. Having unrestricted access to food and shelter. Enforcers patrolling the streets to keep everyone safe. Sure, citizens were forced to stay behind the city walls, but maybe that wasn't too high a price to pay. At least they were safe there.

They're not safe.

Her delusional train of thought was instantly

derailed. Of course the city wasn't safe. If it were, then people like Kade and Hudson wouldn't be escaping it.

"I'm glad the kids are having fun," Bethany admitted. "The mood around here was kind of bleak before you guys showed up. Everyone was so paranoid that the Enforcers would come back and try to take some of the girls."

"Reese would never let that happen." Jamie set the plate on the drying rack and reached for another.

"Neither would Arch. That man would die before letting one of our girls become an Enforcer sex slave. He's insanely protective of everyone here."

Jamie went quiet, her mind drifting back to the night at the library. It had been a week since her fight with Lennox. The sex afterward had been hot as hell, and he'd been extra sweet to her since then, but she still couldn't shake her uneasiness. How would he react if they ran into trouble again? Would he yell at her again? Bark orders at her again? Make her feel like the biggest idiot on the planet again? Or would he be able to control his fear and overprotective instincts?

"Does Arch ever tell you what to do?" she asked slowly.

Bethany snorted. "All the damn time."

"I'm sure." Jamie gave a strained laugh. "I mean it in a different way, though. Like . . ." She bit her lip and dropped her gaze to the soapy water in the sink. "Does he ever treat you like he's better than you?"

"*Better* than me?"

"Maybe better isn't the right word. Smarter, I guess. Stronger. More capable." She awkwardly met the other woman's eyes.

"Why? Is that how Lennox treats you?" Bethany demanded.

"No." Jamie was quick to defend him, which was ironic, considering that she'd raised the issue. "I mean, not usually. But he did last week. We got into a huge fight about it."

"He's always been overprotective when it comes to you," Bethany pointed out.

"I know, but this was different. He acted like he owned me. Like his word was law. Like he was going to bend me over his knee and spank me like a child for not following his orders." She tamped down her rising anger. "It was . . . demeaning."

Bethany clearly didn't like that. At all. "I'm going to kick his ass," she hissed out.

Jamie laughed. "No ass-kicking necessary. We worked it out. I mean, at least I think we did." Another confession slipped out. "But the way he acted that night really upset me. I didn't like it."

"I don't blame you." Bethany ran a soothing hand over her protruding belly. "Arch is overprotective, sure. Even more so since he knocked me up. But we're partners and always have been. Even when we disagree, or if I do something he doesn't approve of, he still treats me with respect. He tells me why it pissed him off, I apologize, and we move past it."

Jamie had thought that was how she and Lennox operated too, but the night at the library continued to haunt her.

"Being in love is so tricky sometimes," Bethany added. "You need to learn to compromise. Accept each other's flaws, be patient, respectful, all that crap."

A flicker of fear skittered up Jamie's spine at the words *in love*. She loved Lennox, deeply, but she refused to let herself fall *in* love with him. She was already having a tough time sticking to his stupid rule about putting up a barrier between naked times and friendship times. Introducing love to the fold would only complicate matters even more.

Except . . . well, the encounter with those bandits had happened *after* naked times. They should have been in friendship mode at that point, but Lennox hadn't treated her like the best friend he'd known and trusted all his life. He'd acted like a king rebuking his lowly subject.

Crap. Reese had been right. Sex did screw everything up. She and Lennox had never fought like that before they started sleeping together.

Things were changing between them.

And Jamie had no idea how to stop it.

Lennox entered the garage to find Jamie's gorgeous ass sticking up in the air. Bent over the raised hood of a beat-up Mustang, she was wearing a short blue dress and white sneakers, and her legs were bare, drawing his gaze to her right calf. The L hidden among the flowers tattooed to her skin evoked a rush of male pride.

He liked seeing his initial on her flesh. Her initial was on his arm, but it went so much deeper than the ink. This woman was inside him. Always had been.

"Oh yeah, stay in that position, love. Just. Like. That." Lennox whistled in appreciation as he came up behind her.

Her spine straightened at the sound of his voice,

and then her head flew up and smacked into the metal hood. "Ouch!" She rubbed her forehead and turned to glare at him.

Lennox sighed. "I told you to stay like that."

"You creeped up behind me! It's a natural reflex to go on the defense."

She had a point. She also had a smudge of grease on her chin, which made him smile. This was the first chance he'd had to see her today. He'd been at the farm with Arch and Scott, the man who ran the property for Reese.

Before he'd left this morning, Jamie mentioned she planned on helping Bethany in the restaurant, but she hadn't been there when he popped in. He'd finally tracked her down to Beckett's garage, though he wasn't entirely sure what she was doing messing with Beck's cars.

He gestured to the engine. "Why are you poking around in there?" Jamie had zero knowledge about fixing cars, and they both knew it.

"You don't want to know."

"Ha. Now I'm even more curious. What's up?"

She half sighed, half grumbled. "I was keeping Beck company while he worked on this piece of junk, but it got boring pretty fast, so I was wandering around looking at stuff. And then I accidentally knocked a wrench in here." She pointed an accusing finger at the engine. "Beck said it was my responsibility to fish it out. Apparently that's my punishment for ruining his precious engine. And then he left to get a drink with Travis. Asshole."

Lennox snickered. "Can you see the wrench?" He leaned closer and peered under the hood.

"Yes." Her tone was laced with frustration. "It's right *there*." She picked up a penlight and flashed it at a spot behind the fan belt. "It's stuck between that thingy and the other thingy."

He choked down a laugh. "Huh. Glad to see you're finally picking up the correct terminology for the makeup of a car engine."

She rolled her eyes at him. "It's really stuck in there, Len. I can't get it out."

He decided to take pity on her, grabbing the light from her hand and bending over the engine. By the time his hand emerged with the metal tool, his fingers were covered in grease.

Jamie threw her arms around him after he'd tossed her the wrench. "Don't tell Beckett it was you," she ordered. "Otherwise he'll probably throw it back in and make me get it myself."

"Your secret's safe with me."

They walked over to the barrel on the other side of the cluttered garage, where they washed their hands in comfortable silence.

Lennox was so relieved that things were back to normal between them. This past week had been pretty damn good—lots of hot sex and not a trace of the anger or bitterness that had plagued them after the library excursion. He had his Jamie back, the one who gazed at him like he mattered most in the world to her, rather than the one who'd glared daggers at him after he'd reprimanded her like she was a toddler.

Fuck, he still felt like an ass for doing that. He didn't quite understand it, but his need to protect this woman, to keep her safe, was even greater now. She'd slept in his arms every night this week, and Lennox had often found himself waking up in a panic. Watching her sleep, stroking her hair, making sure she was still breathing.

It made no sense to him, why he was so terrified of something bad happening to her. He wondered if he would've felt the same bone-deep terror if he'd stuck around for more than a few nights with the other women he'd been with. But sticking around wasn't his forte. He'd never let himself get too close to any of the women in his bed. He'd never allowed himself to reach that point where he cared too deeply about them.

His heart inexplicably raced as he watched Jamie dry her hands. They were so small and delicate. He'd seen them shoot a gun with deadly precision. He'd seen them beat the shit out of people. But they were so fucking *small*, damn it.

Gulping hard, he wrapped his arms around her from behind and pressed his cheek to her shoulder.

Her body instantly softened against him. "What's wrong?"

She knew him so well. "Nothing," he lied, then cleared his throat. "You just look so sexy right now." Before he could stop them, his hands slipped under her dress.

Jamie laughed but didn't push him away. "Interesting. I didn't realize grease and car exhaust turned you on."

"*You* turn me on." He nuzzled her neck as he nudged her forward until she was bending over the hood of a nearby pickup truck.

Lifting up her dress, he skimmed his palms over

the sweet curve of her ass. Jesus, his groin fit perfectly against her firm cheeks, as if it had been designed to nestle there.

"Lennox . . ." She moaned his name when he squeezed her buttocks, and a surge of satisfaction injected into his blood.

He was reaching for his belt buckle when heavy footsteps echoed beyond the open metal door. Jamie hastily straightened up and shoved her skirt down. Lennox's hands dropped to his sides.

He instantly recognized the man who burst into the garage—Gideon, Sara's father. Though the man didn't look at all old enough to be the father of a sixteen-year-old. Despite the faint streaks of silver in his jet-black hair, he couldn't have been older than thirty-five.

"I've been looking everywhere for you," the man snapped at Lennox. He didn't even glance at Jamie, who'd flinched at his sharp tone.

Lennox donned a lazy pose. "What can I do for you, Gideon?"

"You want to know what you can do for me?" Hostility lined Gideon's heavy steps as he advanced on them. "Keep that kid away from my daughter!"

Lennox and Jamie exchanged a look. "What kid?" he asked warily.

"Randy! Boy's been sniffing around Sara ever since you and Connor's people showed up here. He never spoke a damn word to her before, and now he's all over her," Gideon fumed. "I've seen the two of you talking—I know you had something to do with this."

Lennox searched his brain for a tactful response. "I've talked to him about his crush, yes."

"*Crush*? He wants to screw my child!"

Jamie spoke up tentatively. "She's sixteen. Hardly a child."

Gideon glared at her in response.

"And I don't think this is about screwing," Lennox added. "Randy really likes her. I've never seen him put his hands on her or treat her with disrespect."

"Yeah? So why is he spending so much time with her outside of training? Extra target practice, going for walks, taking her to the restaurant for lunch. Do you think I was born yesterday? He wants to get in her pants!"

Probably. But Lennox kept the thought to himself. Besides, he wasn't about to judge Randy for possessing the normal base urges that every teenage boy had to deal with. Lennox had fucked his first girl when he was thirteen. Jamie, he knew, had been sixteen, the same age as Randy and Sara.

"I don't want him near her anymore."

Jamie made another stab at peacekeeping. "What's the harm in it? They're just friends. If you feel like they're getting too involved, you can step in, but Randy hasn't done anything to justify this kind of response right now. He's simply being nice and paying attention to her."

"She doesn't need his attention. She doesn't need anyone's attention."

The agonized note in Gideon's voice gave Lennox pause. He glanced at Jamie again, but her concerned gaze was focused solely on Gideon. She stepped forward and gently touched his arm, and though the man winced, he didn't withdraw.

"What's really going on here?" Jamie asked quietly.

"She's a pretty girl," Gideon choked out. "Too pretty, just like her mother was."

Lennox's heart sank like a stone. He had a terrible feeling he knew where this was going.

Gideon raked both hands through his hair and sagged back against the hood of a car. "Her mother and I were eighteen when we had her. We were too goddamn young, but from the moment Sara was born, we did everything we could to protect her. Her safety was our main concern. Our only fucking concern." His voice cracked. "And then Eliza died . . ."

He went quiet for a moment. When he spoke again, it was in sheer disgust, unchecked fury. "Enforcers," he spat out. "They attacked our camp two years ago. Sara was fourteen."

An anguished sound left Jamie's lips.

Lennox wasn't sure he wanted to hear the rest of the story, but the man in front of them kept talking, his tone growing more and more distraught.

"I was out on a supply run when they came. I wasn't there for my girls. I wasn't there when they raped my wife." His massive chest seemed to droop. "They shot Eliza when she tried to stop them from hurting Sara."

Lennox fought a wave of sorrow. He'd heard similar stories, especially in recent years, as increased violence on the Enforcers' parts was being reported. Hudson claimed they were being given aggression drugs. Lennox didn't give a shit if they were. He knew Jamie was trying to be open-minded about Dominik, but he sure as hell wasn't. Lennox would shoot the bastard in the head if they ever crossed paths.

"They left her on the ground like a piece of trash," Gideon mumbled. "I found her curled up next to her mother's body." A tired breath came out. "I've never forgiven myself for not being there."

Jamie wasted no time wrapping her arms around him. "It wasn't your fault."

"I shouldn't have left them alone."

The whispered response dampened Lennox's palms. He shouldn't have left Jamie alone either. The night at the library. He should have stayed by her side.

Panic coated his throat. Fuck, he wasn't letting her go off alone ever again.

"Sara is everything to me. She's the last surviving piece of her mother." With a curse, Gideon stepped out of Jamie's embrace. "When Reese took us in, she promised me Sara would be safe."

"She *is* safe," Jamie argued.

"Not when there are boys in this camp. I was a teenager once too," he said bitterly. "I couldn't keep it zipped either and it led to Sara being born. My daughter already had her innocence stolen from her. I refuse to let her get hurt again, or to let some asshole kid break her heart."

Lennox cleared his throat. "I'll keep an eye on Randy."

Gideon sneered.

"I mean it—I'll watch him. If I see him getting out

of hand, I'll step in. I promise you that." Lennox hesitated. "But Randy is a good kid. He'd never hurt your daughter."

The endorsement of Randy's character didn't seem to convince Sara's father.

Jamie spoke up again, sounding equally hesitant. "And if they do decide they like each other romantically, I think you need to be open to that. Sara went through a rough time, but she's a survivor—anyone can see that. If there's even the slightest chance of her finding love and comfort in this world from a man who isn't her father, it wouldn't be fair to deprive her of that."

Gideon's shoulders sagged. For a second, Lennox thought they'd gotten through to him, until that broad torso went rigid again and his jaw twitched in anger.

"Just keep him away from my kid, you hear me?"

Then he stomped out of the garage.

17

The following day, Lennox made a conscious effort to keep a closer watch on Randy during training, but either Gideon had also paid a visit to the boy yesterday or Randy was clairvoyant, because he didn't so much as look in Sara's direction all day. When Sara's shot won the evening's final event for Jamie's team, Randy didn't even congratulate her, as he usually did when she kicked his ass.

Lennox, however, did walk over to pat Sara on the back, because that had been a damn good shot. They were aiming for moving targets now, which were a helluva lot more formidable than static ones. He knew Jamie had been working with some of the younger girls in her spare time, and it was absolutely showing in their technique.

Jamie's technique, of course, was damn near flawless. She'd always been impressively proficient with a gun, far better than Lennox was, at least when they were kids. These days they were evenly matched, which was why their teams were neck and neck in the tournament, with Beckett and Travis trailing behind.

"Lennox."

He turned to find Reese waving him over. Sloan was nowhere in sight, which was the first thing Lennox commented on when he reached her.

"Where's your shadow?"

"He drove out to the farm to help Scott and Anna. One of our goats is sick."

"Shit. Something serious? Can he infect the other animals?"

"I don't think so, but we quarantined her just in case. It's a she—Scott thinks she might be pregnant." Reese made a dismissive gesture with her hand. "Anyway, I needed to talk to you."

Lennox nodded. "What's up?"

"In private," she added, her gaze drifting to the group behind him.

"All right, then. Lead the way."

He caught Jamie's eye as he followed Reese down the sidewalk. When he noticed a frown appear on Jamie's mouth, he gave her a reassuring look and continued after the Foxworth leader. It wasn't until they were halfway to Reese's building that something occurred to him. That maybe Jamie hadn't been displeased about the conversation he and Reese were going to have, but about something else entirely . . .

But no, she wouldn't be jealous, would she? He didn't plan on screwing Reese, for fuck's sake. And even if he did, Jamie had seen him with other women before. He'd seen her with other men. Hell, they'd hooked up with Beckett in the library.

Except . . . he suddenly envisioned Jamie going off

with another man—and not inviting *him*—and a streak of jealousy burned a path up his spine.

Shit. Maybe their days of threesomes were in the past. Well, unless he figured out a way to share her without chopping off the fingers of any man who touched her.

He shelved the troubling thoughts as he entered Reese's living quarters. She bypassed the bedrooms and led him into a small office tucked off the main room. There were long desks spanning three of the walls, the wooden desktops laden with laptops and stacks of paper.

Lennox spotted the satellite phone Connor had given her sitting on top of a tall filing cabinet. Xander had managed to hack into the city's satellite system in order to make the phones operational, and Lennox couldn't deny they were major assets. With so much distance between certain outlaw groups, keeping in touch had always required making long treks to deliver messages, and often getting there too late to deliver the news. His parents had told him that about a decade after the war, someone had tried reestablishing a postal system as a way to send letters and communicate, but it had been too dangerous out on the road for the postmen. Most of the time they were captured by Enforcers before they reached their destinations.

"Okay, so fill me in. What's going on?" He glanced at the maps and papers littering the office, but saw nothing that shed light on what Reese could want from him.

"Before we start, I need your word that this stays between us," she said sternly.

"Done."

"I mean it, Len. You can't discuss this with anyone. Not Jamie, not Beck. No one."

He was even more intrigued. But he already had an inkling of what Reese was going to tell him, and if it was what he thought it was, then he didn't want Jamie involved anyway. Not yet, at least.

"It stays between us," he promised.

Reese nodded. She unclipped the key ring on her belt and knelt down to unlock one of the cabinets. As the drawer slid open, she stuck her hand inside and extracted a thick roll of paper. She didn't say a word as she pulled the elastic band off the long roll and slowly spread the sheets out on the desk.

Lennox came up beside her and studied the sheets. They had the consistency of tissue paper rather than heavier stock, and the blue lines neatly printed on the white background were beginning to fade.

"I see," he said.

"That's it? No other reaction?"

A smile tugged on his mouth. "It's not much of a shock, love. In fact, I was wondering when you were finally going to bring me into the loop."

Her eyes narrowed. "You knew? How?"

Lennox shrugged. "Garrett paid a visit to the old place about six months ago. He may have let something slip."

Reese's expression went cloudy. "For fuck's sake. That damn man can't keep his mouth shut when he's drinking. I hope he didn't announce it to the whole house."

"Nah, it was just me and him." He chuckled. "And yes, he was drunk."

Reese pursed her lips. "I might need to rethink how much responsibility I'm willing to give him."

Lennox leaned on the edge of the desk and searched her face. "So I guess that means you've already hit up the other camps? Brynn? Mick?"

She nodded. "Vaughn too. Oh, and Tam, of course. They're all on board."

"This is a dangerous plan you're setting in motion." He glanced at the papers on the desk, battling an uneasy feeling. "Very dangerous."

"It needs to be done."

Her tone was deadly. Hell, *she* was deadly. Lennox had heard the rumors about what had happened to Foxworth's last leader. And if they were true, then that meant Reese, with the help of Sloan, had murdered a man in cold blood in order to steal the leadership from him.

Lennox had never asked her about it, though. Truthfully the answer didn't matter. Reese was in a position of authority now; how she'd gotten it was inconsequential to him. He trusted her regardless.

He sensed her shrewd brown eyes boring into his face. "You know what I want from you, Len. Are you going to give it to me?"

He turned to look at her again, but he didn't respond right away. He'd survived this long because he didn't make rash decisions. Because he avoided *exactly* these kinds of risky situations.

"I don't know," he finally said.

Her nostrils flared. Clearly that wasn't what she'd wanted to hear. "Yes or no, Lennox."

He laughed. "Do you require an answer right this second? Because if those are my only two options, then it's a no. But if you're willing to wait and let me think this through, you might get a different answer."

Although she didn't look happy with that, she was smart enough to know when to back off. "Fine," she relented. "Take some time to think about it."

"When do you plan on going forward?"

"After Rylan and the others go back to Connor."

"And you're not approaching Con with this?" That surprised him. Connor was ruthless, and definitely a man you wanted in your corner.

"Not yet." Reese gestured to the papers on the desk. "I want to see how this goes first."

"Gotcha." He gave a brisk nod. "We done here?"

"Yeah," she said, scowling deeply.

Lennox leaned in and kissed her cheek. "Ah, don't get all grumpy on me, Reese. It's not a no, okay? But if you push me, it will be."

He left her to chew on that, and when he emerged from the building a minute later, he was startled to find Jamie waiting on the stoop. The uneasiness returned, but he tried to hide it by flashing a lazy grin.

"Hey, love. Should we get some dinner?" He took off walking before she could object.

Jamie hurried after him, her combat boots thudding against the sidewalk. "Lennox."

He spared her a quick look. "Hopefully Graham will fix us up some burgers. Soon our days of eating beef will be a thing of the past."

"*Lennox.*"

Her severe tone made him stop. Smothering a curse, he reluctantly shifted around to meet her aggravated gaze. "Yeah?"

"What did Reese want?" she demanded.

"Nothing."

"Bullshit. What did she want?"

The lie flowed smoothly from his lips. "We were brainstorming how we can get our hands on more sat phones. Reese thinks they could be useful to keep in touch with some of the other camp leaders. Like Brynn—it's a bitch to send any messages to the coast with all the flooding there."

Jamie planted one hand on her hip and stared at him for several eerily silent seconds, until he was valiantly fighting not to fidget. He succeeded in keeping still, but not in erasing the suspicion from Jamie's eyes. The woman knew him too well.

"You're lying to me." She inched closer. Slowly, menacingly. "What did Reese want?"

Lennox managed to swallow his groan. The sigh, he couldn't contain. It shuddered out in a long, tired breath. "It's better if you don't know."

He wasn't surprised when a flare of anger lit up her eyes. "Are you kidding me?"

"I mean it, love. It's for your own protection."

Her eyebrows shot up. "What the hell are the two of you planning?"

"Nothing."

"Bull—"

"I'm not bullshitting you," Lennox interjected. "At the moment, I'm not involved in any plan. But Reese gave me some things to think about, all right?"

"No, *not* all right. You can't keep me in the dark. If you have something to think about, we can think about it together."

"Reese asked me not to tell you." The statement was supposed to be a last-ditch attempt to get her to back off, but ooooh, shit, did it backfire on him.

Big-time.

Disbelief and fury formed a lethal cocktail that burned so bright in Jamie's eyes he felt the volatile heat singeing the air. She didn't speak for a moment. Then she opened her mouth and addressed him in the coldest voice he'd ever heard from her. "Reese asked you to keep a secret from me." Her jaw twitched. "And you agreed."

"Because it's not something you need to be involved in right now," he protested. "Let me wrap my head around it first and I'll—"

Her palm struck his cheek before he could finish that sentence.

Lennox's head flew back, not just from the blow, but from astonishment. He didn't need more than one finger to count the number of times Jamie had hit him in anger. They were teenagers the only other time it happened. He'd beat up one of her boyfriends for bragging about her to the other boys, and afterward she'd slapped him hard enough to leave a bruise and ordered him to stop interfering in her love life. Christ, she'd been spitting mad back then.

And she was spitting mad now. He bore the proof of that on his cheek, which was still stinging.

"What happened to everything you said after the library?" Her accusatory gaze cut into him. "You promised that we were a team, *partners*, and now you're keeping secrets from me?"

He felt powerless again. "I don't want you involved, damn it. The less you know, the safer you'll be. Fuck,

Jamie, you know what the Enforcers do to make people talk. I'm just trying to protect you if shit goes
south."

"I don't need you to patronize me, Lennox. And I
don't see you trying to protect Reese, do I?" Her bitterness poisoned the air between them. "What, *she's*
strong enough to handle this big secret of yours?
What if *she* gets captured? You think Reese won't
talk, but *I* will? Why? Because I'm weaker than her?
Because you trust her more?"

Oh, shit. He hadn't even considered how belittling
it was to imply—unintentionally—that Reese was
more capable than Jamie.

Fucking hell. He'd messed up again. Even worse
this time.

As remorse clung to his throat, he opened his
mouth, ready to tell her everything Reese was up to.
But Jamie didn't give him the chance.

She was too busy storming away.

Secrets.

He was keeping *secrets* from her now?

Jamie could barely see straight as she burst through
the door of Beckett and Travis's loft. She half expected
Lennox to barrel in after her, but clearly he was
smarter than he looked, because he'd chosen not to
follow her.

Good. She didn't want to talk to him. And she
definitely didn't need him showing up and offering
to let her "punish" him again—no way would she
be sucking his cock this time around. She'd bite the
damn thing right off.

She'd thought they'd worked past all the bullshit,

but evidently she'd been wrong. Here he was again, protecting her from ... from what? What were he and Reese cooking up?

Hurt and indignation sliced into her. And jealousy, damn it. It made her want to scream that he could confide in *Reese* but not her. He'd never, ever chosen another woman over her before.

"Beck!" she called out. "I need you to calm me down!"

She desperately searched the room for Beckett, her closest friend aside from Lennox. Beckett had a warm, soothing energy about him. She needed that right now.

But the only person in the loft was Rylan, whom she didn't even notice until he cleared his throat. She spun around in surprise and spotted him on the couch, balancing a glass of clear liquid on his jean-clad knee.

His lips quirked when their gazes met. "Beck and Trav are in the garage. But why don't you come over here and sit down, gorgeous? Let's see if I can calm you down."

Weary, she joined him on the couch but sat all the way on the other end from him. She wasn't in the mood to be hit on by Rylan right now. Which was ironic, because she'd been infatuated with him up until three weeks ago. But his perfect face and strong body weren't doing it for her anymore, not since the night he'd deserted her in the rec hall. The night she'd slept with Lennox ...

It suddenly dawned on her that it wasn't just Rylan who didn't hold her interest anymore. It was everyone. Travis, Kade, Beckett ... Sure, Beck had been there in the library, but so had Lennox. Jamie was startled to realize that if Lennox hadn't been present, she probably wouldn't have let Beckett touch her.

"Talk to me, Jamie. What's wrong?" Rylan prodded when her silence dragged on.

She debated how much to tell him, then decided, to hell with it. She needed to talk and he was the only one there. "Lennox is keeping secrets from me."

"Ah. I see."

"Everything is changing between us." She couldn't keep the note of anxiety from her voice. "He's been treating me differently ever since we started sleeping together. Acting like I can't take care of myself, like he's the only one strong enough to handle the danger. And now he and Reese are whispering about who knows what and—"

"Reese?" Rylan said sharply. "She's involved in this?"

Jamie nodded. "She asked to meet with Lennox in private and he's refusing to tell me what they discussed. Because Reese asked him not to." A bitter taste filled her mouth again.

"You have no idea what it was about?" Rylan's blue eyes took on an intense light.

"No, but obviously it's dangerous enough that Lennox doesn't want me knowing about it. He said the less I know, the better." Sarcasm oozed into her tone. "He's protecting me."

"You can't fault him for that."

"Yes, I can."

She snatched the glass from Rylan's hand and took an angry sip. Then regretted it instantly, because he was drinking vodka. Damn it. She hated vodka. It always burned her insides, and not in a good way.

"We've been through a ton of dangerous shit together, and all of a sudden he thinks I'm too weak to handle it?" Fuck, she resented Lennox right now. She never thought she would be feeling that way about her best friend.

"Did you tell him?"

She blinked. "Tell him what?"

"How much it hurts you when he implies that you're weak?" Rylan offered a meaningful look. "Or did you start yelling and get all red in the face and lose your temper the way you always do?"

She bit her lip.

"Jamie?"

"I slapped him," she said sheepishly.

Rylan threw his head back and laughed. "Of course you did." One more chuckle, and then his tone grew serious again. "Look, I love how hotheaded you can be, and that you speak your mind and never back down from a fight. But that isn't always conducive to healthy communication. What does Lennox do when you yell at him?"

"He yells back." Jamie couldn't help grinning. That was her favorite thing about Lennox—he never backed down either.

But Rylan had a point. Lately they were so terrible at communicating. Her temper was suddenly on the shortest fuse possible, because Lennox's irrational behavior was pushing buttons she hadn't realized existed. She'd known she wanted a partner, but she hadn't recognized how important it was for her to feel like an *equal*.

The notion that she and Lennox might not be on

equal ground was demoralizing. It had triggered inse-
curities she hadn't expected, and it weighed harder
and harder on her shoulders every time he acted as
though he was more capable than her. And yet instead
of rationally explaining why it hurt her, she kept lash-
ing out at him.

Jamie let out a groan. "I should talk to him."

"No shit." Rylan snickered. "And you're welcome."

She met his smug blue eyes. "What am I thanking you for?"

"For talking you off a ledge. For making you see
that you're a stubborn motherfucker who needs to
stop slapping her man and start telling him when
he's hurt her feelings."

As another smile sprang to her lips, she slid closer
and threw her arms around his neck. "Thank you."
She brushed a kiss on his cheek, and when he playfully
tweaked her hair, all the resentment she'd been harbor-
ing over his rejection faded away. She might not want
to sleep with him anymore, but Rylan was a good man
and she was damn grateful for his friendship.

"You're welcome," he said, then tugged her to her
feet. "Come on, let's go find Lennox so you can kiss
and make up." He paused, going serious again. "And
if you manage to get it out of him—what he and
Reese are up to, I mean—you need to tell me, Jamie."

Normally she would have said no, because when
Lennox spoke to her in confidence, it was something
she'd take right to the grave. But the reminder that
he'd chosen Reese as a confidante today, and not her,
had her feeling vindictive enough that she nodded
and said, "I will."

* * *

Lennox crept away from the doorway. The sight of Jamie in Rylan's arms was branded in his mind, throbbing painfully in his heart. He'd slipped out of the loft just as her lips had moved toward Rylan's face, because he hadn't been able to stomach it. He hadn't wanted to see their mouths meet.

Her mouth belonged to *him*, damn it.

But maybe it didn't. Maybe this was his own damn fault for not laying out some more ground rules before they'd fallen into bed together. A rule like *she wasn't fucking allowed to kiss anyone else if he wasn't around*. Or hell, even when he *was* around. Their days of sharing were over. He knew that now.

But it didn't matter, because she was probably naked on that couch with Rylan right about now, and it was all Lennox's fault. He'd driven her there by keeping secrets from her. And Jamie was right—that wasn't something he did. If Reese's plan wasn't so goddamn risky, Jamie was the first person he would've discussed it with. He'd thought he was being smart by keeping her out of it, but clearly that had been a mistake.

Still, had she really needed to run straight into another man's arms?

A bolt of resentment whipped up his spine. Jamie didn't usually act out of spite. The fact that she'd gone to *Rylan* was like another slap to the face. A proverbial one this time, but it hurt just as much as the physical slap she'd given him before.

He stalked down the sidewalk, not quite sure where he was going. When he heard a female voice, he jumped in alarm, so distracted he couldn't even draw his gun in time. Luckily it was only Reese. She stood at the door of her building, watching him with worried eyes.

"Everything okay?" she called.

"Fine," he ground out.

Her laughter floated toward him. "You're such a bad liar, Lennox." She held out her hand. "Why don't you come up and tell me all about it? Sloan just left, so we'll have some privacy."

He had no desire to talk to Reese about Jamie. He couldn't even make sense of his feelings in his own head, let alone vocalize them.

It's not that hard, bro. You're in love with her.

The thought was like a bucket of icy water to the face. He'd always known it, but hearing his subconscious voice the words shocked the hell out of him.

Fuck, or maybe he *hadn't* known it. At least not the "in love" part. Love, sure. Of course he loved Jamie. She was his entire life and he'd do whatever he needed to make sure she stayed out of harm's way.

It had been so much simpler when he lusted after her from afar. Wanting her but not being able to have her was an easier emotion to control. Now that he had her, he was distracted all the time. She consumed his thoughts. Tested his focus with her addictive sexuality. This morning he hadn't even wanted to get out of bed—a bomb could have gone off and he would've been content to lie there in Jamie's arms while they both went up in flames.

He loved her too much, damn it. He didn't know how to handle it, and he was sick to death of all the changes challenging their relationship.

"Lennox?"

His frustration deepened as he glanced at Reese. There were more changes in play than his confusing emotions about his best friend. What Reese was planning . . . either it was going to work or it would get every single one of them killed.

"You know what? We do need to talk," he said curtly. "If you want me to seriously consider this proposal of yours, I need to know every detail. Talk me through it, Reese. Every last detail."

She nodded and held out her hand.

Lennox climbed the steps and took her outstretched palm, gripping it tight as he followed her into the building.

18

Rylan cursed under his breath when he saw Jamie's entire face collapse. The two of them had just stepped outside, and it didn't take a genius to figure out what had upset her. He'd caught only a fleeting glimpse himself, but there was no way to misinterpret what he'd seen. Reese leading Lennox by the hand into her apartment

"Jamie," he said softly.

Her head jerked toward him, her expression stricken. And in that moment, he knew he'd missed something very important in the year he'd known her.

She was in love with Lennox.

Shit, how had he failed to see that? Maybe because he'd been too busy getting off with her. Or watching her get off with other men.

Never with Lennox, though, but that spoke volumes now that he thought about it. Two people as close as Jamie and Lennox should've been boning from the moment they figured out how to use their equipment. But something had held them back. Rylan suspected that something was love, and he didn't fucking blame them. Love messed everything up. Hell, a part of him wasn't entirely sure it even existed. He'd seen what "love" drove people to do. The unspeakable things they did in the name of it.

Rylan offered a gentle suggestion. "Why don't you talk to him tomorrow? From the looks of it, he and Reese still need to go over their dastardly plans."

He was trying to lighten the mood, but it didn't work. They both knew what Reese and Lennox were doing up there.

"Yeah, I'm sure they're in deep discussion." The chord of pain in her voice was unmistakable.

"Let's go back inside and have another drink."

He reached for her, but she dodged away. "No. I mean, thank you for the offer, but I think I'll go to bed now."

"Jamie—"

She was already hurrying off, her blond hair swinging down her shoulders with each hurried step. He wanted to go after her, but he knew it wasn't his comfort she was seeking, or at least not the kind of comfort he could give her. Women came to him when they needed a good fuck, and that was the way he preferred it.

His mind was weighed down by thoughts of Reese as he strode along the deserted street. He headed in the direction of the building he crashed in, but he didn't feel like being cooped up right now, so he walked right past it.

What the hell was Reese up to? It irked him that she was willing to confide in Lennox, but not him.

He passed the town square. The parking lot where

they were holding their target practices. The old courthouse at the end of the street, and the bell tower that always had a guard posted on it. Behind the tower was a pretty park that Reese's people kept well maintained; Rylan often sat in the small gazebo when he needed to be alone with his thoughts. He'd even stashed a bottle of whiskey there, though he'd hidden it under a loose floorboard so the teenagers in Foxworth couldn't find it and drink themselves stupid.

When he reached the little wooden structure, he realized someone had beaten him to it.

"Got into my stash, huh?" he drawled.

From his perch on one of the benches spanning the interior of the gazebo, Sloan flashed a blank look.

It took a second to realize that the man wasn't drinking whiskey, but tequila. "Ah, my bad," Rylan said. "I thought you found my booze." He knelt at the board closest to the arched opening and pried it open.

When his hand emerged with a half-empty bottle, the other man gave a soft chuckle.

He settled on the bench opposite Sloan, whose long legs were stretched out in front of him in a relaxed pose Rylan had never seen from him. The man's expression remained guarded as usual.

"Why do you do it?" The question popped out before Rylan could stop it.

Sloan frowned. "Do what?"

"Stay with her. Protect her." He truly couldn't comprehend it. "You live and breathe for that woman, Sloan, but I can't for the life of me figure out what you get in return. Your dick's not in the equation, as far as I can tell."

Sloan said nothing.

"Or am I wrong? Are you two screwing like bunnies when nobody is around?"

There was a long silence. Then a muttered "No."

"Then why? What's in for you? Her friendship? Her loyalty?"

He didn't receive an answer, but he hadn't expected to. He didn't know why he'd even bothered trying to make sense of Reese's relationship with Sloan.

Sighing, Rylan changed the subject. "I know she's planning something," he said flatly. "Something big. Something that could get her and everyone else here killed."

"Reese knows what she's doing."

The unexpected response startled him. And it didn't escape him that the man hadn't denied something was going down.

"Whatever it is, we can help. Me, Connor, the others. Xan is a technological wizard—Reese could use someone like him on her side. And Pike is a stone-cold killer. He'll do whatever she asks him to do."

"It's not my call," Sloan said gruffly. "If she chooses to involve you, she will."

"Fine, then talk to her. Convince her that we can be assets to her."

The request got him a shrug. He had no idea if that meant Sloan would talk to Reese on his behalf, or if it was a *fuck you*. He didn't push, though. He didn't know Sloan very well, but he suspected the man wouldn't take kindly to being needled.

Silence fell over the gazebo, but there was no tension, no urgency to fill the quiet with conversation.

Rylan found the other man's presence oddly soothing. He really ought to try to get to know him better. If anything, it would be a way to get closer to Reese. If Sloan liked him, maybe she would too.

But as the silence dragged on, Rylan realized the man was as closed off and enigmatic as his mistress. Those two had secrets. History. That much was clear. Rylan suspected there was pain there too, but he wasn't holding his breath about either of them confiding in him.

He was jerked out of his thoughts when Sloan spoke up in a rough voice.

"What's in it for *you*?"

He wrinkled his forehead. "What do you mean?"

"What do you want from her? Her pussy? Or her trust?" Sloan shrugged again. "Because you have a shot at the first one, and no shot at the second. Reese doesn't trust anyone."

"She trusts you."

Sloan raised the bottle to his lips. "I'm not so sure about that."

Rylan disagreed. Anyone with half a brain could see that Sloan was the only person Reese gave her unconditional loyalty to.

"You're a good guy, Rylan," Sloan said, surprising him yet again. He stood up, loosely gripping the neck of the bottle between his fingers. "I'm sorry I can't help you out."

With that, Sloan walked off. Rylan watched the man's broad back and military stride, and tamped down his growing frustration. He was making absolutely no progress. He'd struck out with Reese, and now with Sloan.

He took a sip of his whiskey, then tucked the bottle at his side and closed his eyes. Yep. He had no fucking clue what his next move would be.

Jamie woke up in a state of confusion. The pillow under her head was scratchy. The blanket was too thin. The heat of Lennox's body wasn't surrounding her like a cozy cocoon. Where the hell was she?

She blinked away the grogginess and discovered that she was on Beckett's couch. Memories of last night came crashing back as she grew more alert. She hadn't gone to her room last night because it would've killed her to sleep alone while Lennox spent the night in Reese's bed. Or worse, if he stumbled back in the wee hours of the morning and crawled into bed with her as if nothing had happened.

Bile coated her throat as she sat up and dragged her hands through her tousled hair. She couldn't believe he'd had sex with Reese.

You don't know that he did.

Yeah, right. Why else would he be holding hands with the woman and following her upstairs? Besides, she knew Lennox. He'd been furious after she slapped him, and Lennox let out his anger in one of two ways—fighting or fucking.

Clearly he'd chosen the latter yesterday.

The urge to scream with rage was so strong she had to press her lips together to stop herself. Beckett and Travis were still asleep in their respective beds, and she didn't want to punish them with such a rude awakening after they'd been so sweet to her last night. They'd wisely left her alone, neither one of them trying to initiate sex, or even conversation.

Beckett had simply handed her a pillow and blanket, and then both men had gone to bed.

She was dreading going back to her room, but she had no choice. She needed to shower and dress for the day's events. But what the hell was she going to say to Lennox when she saw him? Ripping his balls off wasn't an option, unfortunately. She was tempted, though. So fucking tempted. She got sick to her stomach when she pictured him touching another woman. It wouldn't have bothered her before, but it did now, so much that her hands began to shake just imagining him with Reese.

Jamie didn't know if she was disappointed or just more upset when she walked into their living quarters five minutes later and found Lennox's room empty. So he *had* spent the night with Reese.

A growl rumbled low in her throat, then died abruptly when she noticed that his bed had been slept in. Okay. That was better. He'd come home at some point during the night, at least.

Her emotions continued to twist in her stomach as she took a quick shower and changed into her fighting clothes. According to Rylan's schedule, they would be sparring today. Maybe she'd call out Lennox. That way she could beat the shit out of him for sleeping with Reese, but it would be perfectly acceptable because bloodlust was a requirement for the tournament fights. Well, if she was subscribing to Pike's sadistic school of thought.

She paid a visit to the kitchen first, where she happily discovered that someone had baked a dozen trays of bran muffins. She scarfed one down, chugged some water, and then headed for the town square.

Lennox was the first person she saw. He was wearing black cargo pants and a faded gray T-shirt that clung to every sculpted muscle on his chest. He looked so good she felt like slapping him again.

He turned his head when she appeared, and tension seeped into her bones when she glimpsed his expressionless eyes. No. Not entirely expressionless. If she peered deep, she could see the flicker of hurt in those dark gray depths.

What did he have to be hurt about? *She* wasn't the one who'd screwed Reese yesterday.

Lennox approached her with measured steps. "We need to talk," he said in a low voice.

"Damn right we do." Her flat tone matched his.

Their eyes locked.

"You didn't come home last night."

"I slept on Beckett's couch."

That seemed to piss him off for some reason. His nostrils flared, lips curling in displeasure. Which just triggered a burst of indignation, because he wasn't allowed to be mad at her for sleeping on a friend's couch, not after he'd had his hands all over Reese's body last night.

Jamie's already boiling blood damn near scorched her veins to ashes when the she-devil herself strode up. In her black pants and T-shirt, with her copper-colored hair loose around her shoulders, Reese looked gorgeous and more rested than she had a right to be. Her gaze flicked in their direction, but she kept walking toward Pike.

Jamie had to fight every urge not to march over and deck the bitch. She watched as Reese said something to Pike before hopping up on the ledge and surveying the crowd. Well. It looked like the queen was gracing them with her presence today.

Jamie swallowed a lump of anger. "We'll talk later," she muttered to Lennox.

He was equally curt. "Yes. We will."

They went in separate directions to join their teams.

Pretending her whole world wasn't currently off-kilter, she greeted her teammates with forced cheer-fulness. Tina flashed a rare smile in response, but Jamie noticed that Sara's smile was as strained as her own.

"Everything okay, sweetie?" Jamie asked.

"It's fine."

The girl's very obvious lie was a nice distraction from Jamie's internal fantasies about murdering both Lennox and Reese, so she immediately stuck her nose where it probably didn't belong. "No, it's not. What's wrong?"

Sara shrugged, but her gaze flickered at someone behind Jamie's shoulder.

Jamie moved her head in time to see Randy give Sara an awkward wave before turning back to his friend Ethan.

Crap. Evidently Gideon had gotten to Randy and scared the poor boy away.

With a soft sigh, Jamie pulled Sara out of earshot of the others. "Is this about Randy?"

The teenager shook her head. Then she nodded, her cheeks reddening with embarrassment. "I think he's mad at me," she confessed. "But I don't know why."

"Oh, sweetie, he's not mad at you."

"How would you know?" Sara bit her lip. "He's

barely spoken a word to me this whole week. He's totally avoiding me and I don't get it. I thought we were friends."

Jamie stifled another sigh. "I think he's just trying to be . . . respectful," she said as tactfully as she could.

"Respectful? Okay, now I really don't get it."

"Maybe he thought he was coming on too strong." *Or maybe your father made him shit his pants by threatening to kill him if he didn't stay away from you.* "He's a perceptive, kid. He might be trying to give you space."

A wrinkle appeared in Sara's forehead. "Why would he think I need space?"

Jamie didn't want to upset the girl by revealing that her father might have interfered, so she opted for the vague approach. "Teenage boys have a weird sense of logic. Give him some time and I'm sure he'll go back to his normal self."

"I guess." Sara didn't sound convinced.

"Try not to think about it. We're sparring today, and I can't have you distracted, okay?"

Sara nodded, but a deep groove remained etched in her forehead as they headed back to the group.

Rylan stuck two fingers in his mouth and released an ear-piercing whistle, and everyone gathered around as the first round of fights began.

Jamie was in awe of Rylan and Pike for whipping all these people into shape. The teenage Ethan was taking on a man twice his size this morning, yet he was totally holding his own. She watched the kid react with lightning-fast kicks and powerful uppercuts that made her wince. He bobbed and weaved like a champion, using his smaller size to duck under his opponent's fists, then delivered a punch that made everyone whoop.

By the time they stopped for a water break, every team had scored a point. The fights were evenly matched and wildly entertaining, but Jamie was itching for her turn. The tension wreaking havoc on her body refused to dissipate, and it was only made worse by Reese's presence.

Why hadn't she noticed how fucking beautiful the woman was? Well, fine, she had noticed, but for some reason Reese looked even *more* beautiful today. She had the most perfect skin. It was like ivory, and looked so soft and smooth to the touch. And her tits were fabulous. Round, perky mounds that swayed sensually each time she moved.

Jamie wrenched her gaze away, unable to control the annoyance eddying in her stomach. Rylan gestured for her to step forward, and as he scanned the other teams in search of an opponent for her, Jamie couldn't stop the words that burst out of her mouth.

"How about Reese?"

The Foxworth leader's head snapped up in surprise. A second later, her brown eyes narrowed at Jamie.

She met the suspicious gaze head-on, offering a cool one in return. Which brought a flicker of bewilderment to the other woman's eyes.

"Now, that's a match-up I'd like to see," Beckett remarked with a grin.

Rylan didn't sound as delighted as Beck was. "Reese isn't on a team. It won't count for standings."

"I don't care." Jamie flicked a look of challenge at

the redhead. "I figured Reese might enjoy getting in on the fun."

Although the taunt was right there in her voice, it seemed nobody but Reese picked up on it. The woman slid off the ledge and approached them with the grace of a lioness.

"What's this about, honey?" Reese murmured so that only Jamie could hear.

She didn't bother lowering her voice. "I think you know."

It was obvious Reese wasn't used to hearing defiance in her people's voices, because her jaw tightened and her tone had a bite to it now. "All right. I'm in."

Beckett hooted happily.

The sound made Jamie turn her head. Her gaze landed not on Beckett, but Lennox, who was staring at her with visible wariness.

Rather than acknowledge him, she walked into the ring and cracked her knuckles.

Reese did the same, watching Jamie in amusement. "Are we really going to do this?" she asked mockingly.

"Damn right we are." And then she lunged before Rylan had even given them the signal.

All her rage and jealousy toward this woman came pouring out, like the powerful arc of water from the broken fire hydrant she and Lennox had come across once. Her fist caught Reese in the jaw, and though the woman was able to block the second blow, the first one had already done its intended damage. Blood gushed from the corner of Reese's mouth, dripping down her neck. As her eyes blazed, Reese launched a counterattack that left Jamie breathless.

The bitch's fists were like balls of steel. One connected with Jamie's right temple with enough force to make her ears ring. Growling, she retaliated by snapping her knee up into Reese's stomach.

The redhead staggered backward. Jamie took full advantage of the moment by shooting forward to lock one arm around Reese's torso. With her free hand she grabbed a hunk of Reese's hair and pulled hard. She knew it must have hurt, but Reese didn't make a sound. She fought the hold instead, trying to elbow Jamie in the side, but Jamie had two inches on her and red-hot fury on her side.

She gave Reese's hair another violent tug and brought her mouth to the woman's ear. "Next time you ask Lennox to keep a secret from me, I want you to remember this."

Then she twisted the redhead around and smashed her fist in Reese's surprised face. She connected with her eye this time, but Reese was no amateur. She gave as good as she got, clipping Jamie's cheek with a sharp jab, then delivering a blow that split Jamie's eyebrow.

She felt the warm trickle of blood sliding down her face, but the adrenaline coursing through her prevented the pain from registering. She was vaguely aware of the cheers erupting all around them, but they might as well have been coming from ten miles away. The sounds were muffled by the thunderous drumming of her pulse.

She snapped her fists up and unleashed a one-two punch that Reese managed to deflect. When the woman came at her in a counterattack, Jamie utilized a move Lennox had taught her when they were kids and used Reese's forward momentum against her. She flipped the woman right over her shoulder, cackling when Reese found herself flat on her back.

Jamie was on her before she could move, digging her forearm into Reese's throat. She saw the blood on Reese's cheek and mouth, the eye that was starting to swell shut, and satisfaction rose inside her.

"Oh, and one more thing." She dipped her face close to Reese's and hissed, "Keep your fucking hands off him. You feel me?"

She pounded her fist into the redhead's face again, and in the back of her mind she was surprised that nobody was pulling her off. The fight was clearly over. Jamie had clearly won. But Rylan hadn't whistled, and Jamie was still furious enough that she couldn't help getting a few more good licks in there.

She'd just landed another punch when she realized that the woman beneath her was trembling. No, shaking uncontrollably. It took a moment to grasp that Reese was laughing hysterically.

The woman's laughter, which managed to sound melodic even with an elbow lodged against her windpipe, was so perplexing that Jamie released her. Her fist went limp, arm dropping as she warily stared at Reese. "What's so funny?"

"You still"—Reese reached up to wipe the blood from her mouth—"want to tell me there are no feelings involved?"

Jamie's shoulders went rigid.

Reese croaked out another laugh, peering up at her with mocking brown eyes. "Yeah, honey, how's *that* arrangement working out for you?"

19

"What the *fuck* was that?" Lennox stormed into the bedroom after Jamie, but she was too busy stripping off her bloody tank top to pay him any attention.

Rylan had sent her back to her room to change, because not only was her shirt soaked crimson, but it had somehow been torn right in half. And maybe it made her no better than those bloodthirsty bandits, but kicking the shit out of Reese had been the greatest high of Jamie's life.

"Jesus. You're covered in blood," Lennox muttered.

"We were sparring," she said coolly. "That's what happens when you spar. People bleed."

"Really? That's how you want to play it?" He released a string of curses. "You ripped her apart like you were a lion and she was your next meal. I think you broke a couple of her ribs."

"She'll live." Jamie removed her sports bra, which was somehow stained with blood too. Damn it. The red splotches on the white cotton would be impossible to get out. She *loved* that bra.

Lennox's gray eyes rested on her bare breasts.

When she glimpsed the arousal in his gaze, her anger returned in full force. Uh-uh. No way. He wasn't allowed to get turned on by her tits. Not after what he'd done last night.

"Why are you even here?" she demanded as she marched to the bathroom. "Shouldn't you be consoling your precious Reese?"

He followed her in. "What the hell is that supposed to mean?"

Ignoring him, she turned on the tap and began scrubbing her bloodstained hands. She dragged the bar of soap over her knuckles, then used it to dig at the dried blood under her fingernails. The water turned pink as it swirled down the drain.

Lennox hovered in the doorway, and she studied his reflection in the mirror. He looked irritated. And pissed. And confused.

It was the confusion that raised her hackles, because it implied that he had no idea what he'd done wrong.

Jamie whirled around. "You *slept* with her last night."

He stared at her. "No. I didn't."

She faltered, tempted for a moment to believe him. But then she remembered his fingers laced through Reese's. His determined expression as he followed Reese into her building.

"Sure, Lennox. If you say so."

"Are you serious right now? Even if I did sleep with Reese—which I didn't—you're not exactly one to point fingers. You spent the night with Rylan."

It was her turn to feel confused. "No, I didn't."

"Come on, Jamie, I saw you making out with him at Beckett's."

Her jaw fell open. "We didn't make out. And when the hell were you even at Beckett's?"

"I came to apologize after you and I argued." Bitterness colored his tone. "But you were too busy getting *comforted* by Rylan."

She gazed at him in disbelief. "All we did was hug."

He frowned at her.

"It's the truth. I was furious with you and Rylan calmed me down. I gave him a hug and a kiss on the cheek, and then I went to find you so *I* could apologize, and saw you going upstairs with Reese."

They eyed each other for a beat.

"You really didn't—"

"Are you saying you didn't—"

They both stopped, laughing awkwardly.

"I didn't sleep with Rylan."

"I didn't sleep with Reese."

Relief hit her like a gust of wind. She shut off the water and then dried her hands and grabbed the clean tank top she'd draped over the towel rack. Hurriedly slipping it on, she walked back into her room and sat on the edge of the bed. Lennox joined her, keeping a foot of distance between them.

"It didn't used to be a big deal if we were with other people," Jamie said slowly.

"No," he agreed.

"But it is now."

"Yes."

"Why?"

He made a frustrated sound. "I don't know. But I

don't like the idea of you sleeping with anyone but me. Not even if I'm there."

"Me neither," she admitted. "I don't want you to be with anyone else. And I don't want anyone but you."

"Okay. So it's just us from now on." He hesitated. "Or has that ship sailed too?"

"No. It hasn't."

Jamie slid closer and rested her head on his shoulder. He was wearing a flannel shirt that felt so soft beneath her cheek, and it was only another reminder that they were nearing November. She was in a tank top, but she hadn't felt the chill before because she'd been too wired with adrenaline from the fight. She felt it now, though. She knew Reese wouldn't turn the heat on until the temperature outside dropped from tolerably cool to unbearably frigid.

"But if it's only us, then you can't keep secrets from me," she murmured. "If we're not a team, then the ship *will* sail."

Lennox wrapped one arm around her, infusing her with his warmth. "I'm sorry about yesterday. I was a dick."

"Yep."

"But I'm serious, Jamie. Just knowing what Reese is up to could hurt you."

"You should have given me the choice and let me decide whether or not it's a risk I want to take. For all you know, I might have agreed with you and ordered you not to tell me."

He snickered. "Bullshit."

She smiled sheepishly. He was absolutely right. But still. "I'm sorry I slapped you." She touched his cheek where her palm had struck it. It wasn't red or bruised, but she felt as if the imprint of her hand was still there. Yes, he'd been a dick, but she shouldn't have hit him.

Lennox captured her hand and laced their fingers together. "It's okay, love. We both know I provoked you." He paused again. "I'll tell you everything Reese and I talked about. No more secrets from this point on, I promise you that."

She nodded. "No more secrets."

He leaned in and kissed her, and his mouth was so warm and firm and familiar. They'd been physically involved for such a short time, but it was like they'd been doing it forever. Kissing. Touching. Making each other come. Desire soared inside her when his tongue slicked over her bottom lip. She deepened the kiss, chasing his tongue into his mouth and drawing a deep groan from him.

He wrenched his mouth away. "We should talk about Reese—"

Jamie silenced him with another kiss. "Later. We only have an hour break. Let's make good use of it."

She hated being angry with him. She wanted to erase that unwelcome emotion, replace it with something better. Sweeter. Lennox must have felt the same way, because suddenly he was kissing her with an eagerness that stole her breath.

They were naked in no time, tangled together on the bed as his mouth found her nipple and he suckled roughly. She stroked his dark hair and welcomed his lips, his greedy tongue. Pleasure zinged from her distended nipple to her clit, and she hooked a leg around him so his hard length was pressed up between them. Groaning, Lennox moved his hips, and his shaft glided over her core, creating sweet friction against her clit.

There was something different about the way he was touching her. He was gentler. Slower. His hands skimmed her curves and threaded through her hair with infinite tenderness. His kisses were softer, and she drank them in, running her hands down his strong back as his tongue filled her mouth. When he eased his cock inside her, she immediately recognized another significant difference. No barrier. God, his cock was velvety soft and impossibly hard at the same time as his bare length slid deep.

A part of her didn't want to say anything, didn't want to ruin this perfect moment, but she couldn't keep quiet. "Len . . . condom . . ."

His eyes were hazy with pleasure as he peered down at her. "I'll pull out," he whispered.

Jamie's mother had always maintained that pulling out was in no way an effective method of birth control. She could still get pregnant, but God, it felt so fucking good. The heat of him, the way he pulsed inside her. This was reckless, irresponsible behavior that she'd never seen Lennox engage in before, and even though it was stupid, her heart soared with how he threw away the last vestiges of caution and control.

Jamie locked her arms around him and realized she'd been wrong before. The high from the fight was nothing compared to the one she felt now. And damn her to hell, but Reese was right. There *were* feelings involved.

She loved him. So fucking much she couldn't think straight. It didn't matter that he'd acted like a jerk at the library, or that he'd done it again yesterday. Lennox was it for her. He was the only man in this world who made her feel safe and cherished. Who made her heart pound and her body sing.

"So wet. So tight." His tone rang with wonderment. He braced one arm beside her while his free hand cupped her breast. Fondling and squeezing, his thumb flicking over her rigid nipple. His hips continued to move in a slow rocking motion. "I love this pussy, baby. My favorite place in the whole world, being inside you."

She shivered. "Fuck me harder, Len."

"No." He was kissing her neck now, his cock gliding in and out with excruciatingly slow strokes. "Because then you'll make me come and I'll have to pull out." His tongue grazed her earlobe. "And I like it in here too damn much."

He rotated his hips and pushed in deep again, letting her feel every glorious inch of him.

"Close your eyes," he murmured.

She didn't want to. She was enjoying the euphoric look on his face. But she obeyed, her eyelids sliding shut as Lennox's lips tormented her throat with featherlight kisses.

"You like my dick inside you, love?"

"Mmm." She was distracted by his tender mouth, the goose bumps he elicited with each reverent brush of his lips.

Lennox increased the tempo, just slightly, thrusting to the hilt and then withdrawing again. The pressure between her legs was agonizing. She was so wet, and the lack of a condom ensured that Lennox could feel it.

He groaned in her ear. "You're soaking my cock. You're getting close, aren't you?"

"Mmm."

His lips pressed against hers, his tongue sliding past the seam in a greedy plunge. He slammed his cock into her at the same time, and then the weight of his chest disappeared from her breasts as he raised himself up on his elbow. She moaned when his talented fingers found her clit.

"Come for me, love. I want to feel you squeezing my cock before I have to leave this paradise." He gave another deep thrust, but the lazy tempo didn't change.

Eyes shut, Jamie lost herself in every slow stroke, the sweet pressure on her clit. Her orgasm rippled beneath the surface, hot and tingly and desperately close to spilling over. She gasped when it broke free, her inner muscles clamping tightly around his shaft as her body spasmed with pleasure.

"That's it, love." He teased her swollen clit with his fingers and leaned down to kiss her shoulder. "That's a good girl, coming for me like that."

She opened her eyes to find him admiring her. His rugged features were creased with longing and desire, and though he'd stopped moving, her pussy continued to ripple around him.

Moaning softly, Lennox drove his hips forward again. He gave two, three, four rapid thrusts and then he pulled out, his hand encircling his shaft as pleasure swamped his face. He worked his cock in fast pumps, squeezing the head on each upstroke, and when every muscle in his chest tensed up, she knew he was nearing the brink.

"On me," she murmured. "Come all over me, baby."

The request made him growl. His hand slapped faster. He leaned forward, breathing heavily as he jerked his cock until streams of come coated her breasts and stomach.

Jamie ran her finger over her skin and brought a pearly drop to her lips. Smiling, she delicately licked it off her fingertip.

Lennox released a choked groan. "Jesus. That's the hottest thing I've ever seen."

He dragged his finger over the shiny beads of moisture clinging to her belly, then raised his hand to her mouth. She gave another lick, moaning when his salty masculine flavor infused her taste buds.

"My dirty girl," he rasped. "Licking my come off my fingers." He rubbed his fingertips over her lips again and she swept her tongue over them, keeping her gaze locked to his the entire time.

God, he was the sexiest man she'd ever seen. His messy dark hair and metallic gray eyes. His well-honed muscles and gorgeous tats. But she appreciated more than his looks. He was stubborn, like her, but far better at controlling his temper. He was intelligent, but armed with a calculated brutality that he needed in order to survive. He was compassionate. Protective of the people he cared about.

Damn Reese for being right about something else—Lennox *was* her type. He was everything she'd ever wanted in a man.

He stretched his long, powerful body beside her and pulled her into his arms, unfazed that her sticky stomach was glued to his side.

"Just us from now on," he said huskily.

Jamie nodded against his shoulder, her hair falling

over one of his chiseled pecs. She swallowed a lump of emotion. "It's always been just us, Lennox."

Lennox knew she was right. It didn't matter how many people they'd been with in the past. They'd always belonged to each other, and the emotion clogging his throat rendered it impossible to answer. Jamie felt so small and fragile in his arms. Which was a stupid thought to have after he'd just seen her pound the living shit out of another woman.

As his silence lengthened, Jamie finally broke it with a pained whisper. "I can't keep my feelings out of this."

A fissure of dread split open his chest. He'd known this was where they were heading, but he'd hoped to avoid it, at least for a little while longer.

"Len? Did you hear me?"

"I heard you." He gently stroked her hair. It felt so damn silky running between his fingers.

"Lovers when we're in bed and friends when we're out of it . . . it doesn't work for me." She exhaled, and the soft flutter of warmth against his chest made him shiver. "Friendship doesn't work either."

He stiffened at that, trying to sit up. She beat him to it, crossing her bare legs and peering down at him with earnest blue eyes.

"I think it's time to admit we're together. We've always been together, even if we weren't engaging in the physical aspects of a relationship."

Lennox didn't answer. His heart had lodged in his throat. Again, he knew she was right, but he didn't want her to be. He was too scared to admit they were in a relationship. Too terrified to love her more than he already did.

"Do you really think you're going to get tired of me?"

The timid question filled him with alarm. "What?"

"You told me that's what happens to you with other women. You get bored of them and you end it." Determination hardened her eyes. "But we've been at each other's sides for almost twenty years, and it doesn't seem like you've tired of me yet . . ."

She hadn't voiced it as another question, but he knew it was, and he bit the inside of his cheek to stop himself from confessing that he'd been lying through his teeth that day. Tiring of Jamie was impossible. She kept him on his toes. She made him happier than he'd ever been in his life. He loved everything about her. Her strength, her tenacity, even her short fuse of a temper.

What he didn't love was her naive vision of the future. She'd never said it out loud, but Lennox had pieced it together from comments she'd made over the years.

When they'd stumbled on a farmhouse in the Midwest, she sighed and remarked that it was her dream home.

When they'd visited friends in the south and she'd held one of their babies, her eyes shone with adoration.

When she looked at Bethany and Arch, it was with pure, palpable longing.

But those were unattainable dreams. If she was lucky, she might get the house, or the baby, or the fairy-tale love. But she couldn't have them all, and there was no guarantee she'd even be able to keep what she did get. Homes burned down and got shot up by Enforcers, as they'd learned the hard way. Babies died or were ripped out of your arms and taken to the city. And fairy tales didn't exist. Love had the power to destroy you, not heal you.

Lennox slid into a sitting position, unable to tamp down his growing anxiety. "Do you remember when our moms were sick?"

Jamie looked startled. "Of course I do."

"My dad . . . he withered away." His teeth dug deeper into his cheek. "It destroyed him that he couldn't help Mom. That he couldn't protect her from the illness. And after she died and he got sick too, he didn't even try to fight. He just gave up and let himself die."

"I'm not sure what this has to do with us."

He averted his eyes. "I wouldn't survive if I lost you."

"You're not going to lose me." Her tone was firm. Her touch was even firmer as she grasped his chin and forced his gaze back to hers. "Lennox. I think you need to accept that there are some things you simply can't control."

She was wrong. He *could* control this. Control his feelings, regain his focus. Keeping her safe was his main priority, the *only* priority he'd had all these years. But in order to do that, he couldn't allow his love for her to consume him.

"Keeping things separate will only hurt us," Jamie added. "We're not good separate. We're stronger when we're together."

Wrong again. He was *weaker* when he fully opened his heart to her. He got distracted. He made decisions out of panic. He acted irrationally and pissed her off.

"I can't be just your friend if we're sleeping together, Len. If I'm in your bed, then I'm your friend *and* your woman. And if you can't handle that, then I can't be in your bed anymore."

Rather than voice his fears, he nodded. "I can handle it."

"Can you?"

Another nod.

"We're together?" she pushed.

Lennox leaned closer and pressed his mouth to hers. "We're together, love. I promise." He touched her cheek in reassurance, then rose from the bed. "We should head back to the group. The next event is starting soon."

He dressed in a hurry, hoping she couldn't see the lingering fear in his eyes. He hadn't lied to her. They *were* together. And she *was* his woman. She always had been. But he was always going to hold a piece of himself back. It was the only way to keep a clear head.

The only way to keep her alive.

20

They'd been in Foxworth for a month.

Lennox couldn't quite believe it, because to him it felt as if they'd just arrived. And yet here he was, listening to Rylan announce that the awards ceremony celebrating the end of training was being held in the rec hall tonight.

The final event had wrapped up only minutes ago. Lennox's team had been crowned the overall winners of the tournament, but apparently Rylan and Pike had a couple of surprises up their sleeves. The champions would receive the grand prize, but select members of the other teams were going to win steak dinners courtesy of Graham, Foxworth's cook.

Lennox noted the dejected faces around him, mostly belonging to members of the opposing teams. The biggest frown came from Sara, who'd proved she was more than capable with a rifle. He knew she was disappointed that her team hadn't managed to beat out Lennox's in the end, but as he stood there watching, Jamie gave the girl a big hug and declared that Sara was a winner in her eyes. Then she announced she was taking all her female charges to the restaurant for a team dinner.

As the girls trooped off, some of the joy in Randy's eyes faded. The boy stared at Sara's retreating back, and Lennox gave him a sympathetic pat on the shoulder. He'd finally pried the truth out a few days ago—Sara's father had indeed paid Randy a visit, describing in detail what would happen to Randy's tongue, hands, and dick if he talked to, touched, or fucked the man's daughter.

Lennox was hoping some of the initial bravery he'd seen in Randy would make a reappearance, but the kid continued to keep his distance from Sara.

"Come on, let's grab something to eat," Lennox told the teenager. He gestured to Kade, and the three of them trudged toward the kitchen.

After they'd eaten, Randy left to shower and change for the party, leaving Lennox alone with Kade, who leaned back in his chair and propped both hands behind his head. "I can't wait to get back to camp."

Lennox grinned. "Tired of Foxworth already?"

"Too many people here. It reminds me of the city," Kade admitted. "Constantly bumping into someone every time you leave your room."

"Did you live alone? When you were in the city, I mean?" Lennox had heard that once citizens turned eighteen, they were forced to leave their parents' home and assigned new accommodations. But if they had siblings, they were allowed to live with them.

The other man nodded.

"Didn't you have a brother? I thought Xan mentioned that before."

Kade's features went strained. "He had his own accommodations."

"Ah. Okay."

"I spoke to Xander today on the sat phone. They're all eager to have us back."

Kade's brisk change of subject didn't surprise him. It was damn near impossible getting details about the city out of the man. "How are the girls?"

"Piper's driving Xan crazy." Kade chuckled. "Keeps distracting him with blow jobs when he's trying to work."

That made him snort. "Sounds like a nightmare."

"For Xan? Probably. You know how obsessed he is with his computers."

Lennox toyed with the label on his beer bottle, running his fingers over the beads of condensation. "What's the deal with you two anyway? You banging?"

"Why does everyone always ask that?" Kade asked in bewilderment.

"It's not so crazy. You guys are always together. You share women." Lennox shrugged. "Can't blame me for wondering."

Kade donned a thoughtful look. "Would it matter if we were?"

"Fuck no. People love who they love. Who cares if it's two men, or two women, or two men and one women, or two women and—"

"I get the point, bro."

Lennox offered another shrug. "Anyway, I was just curious. I've seen Xan with other guys before, so I wondered."

Kade seemed surprised by that revelation.

"He's bisexual. You didn't know that?"

"No. I didn't."

The man sounded more intrigued than disgusted, which prompted Lennox to drop another bomb on him. "He sucked my dick once."

Kade's jaw fell open. "You shitting me?"

"Nope. It was a while ago, before he hooked up with Connor and the others. He used to visit our place a few times a year."

"Did you enjoy it?"

Lennox rolled his eyes. "A hot mouth on my cock, sucking me dry? No, it was awful." Laughing, he scraped his chair back. "Come on, let's head out. We have the big ceremony. We won, remember?"

Outside, they went their separate ways and Lennox headed straight to his room, where he found Jamie walking around in a towel. He took a moment to admire her sweet curves and flawless skin that was still pink from her shower.

"How was dinner?" he asked.

"Fun. The girls are still bummed that we lost, but they'll get over it, especially once the party starts. They're all really excited about it."

Of course they were. The teenagers in Foxworth had a curfew that was strictly enforced, which meant they were usually in bed once the booze started flowing and the clothes started coming off. Lennox didn't blame Reese for trying to shield their innocent little eyes, but most of them were old enough to know about sex. Hell, most of them were already screwing each other.

"I'm hopping in the shower," he said. "Wait for me and we'll go together?"

She nodded absently as she bent over her duffel. "I'm not even close to being ready."

Her cryptic comment followed him into the shower stall, because it didn't usually take her much time to get dressed. She was feminine as all get out, sure, but she rarely wore makeup and her party attire typically consisted of tight jeans or skimpy dresses.

He didn't linger under the hot spray, just soaped himself up, rinsed himself down, and dried himself off with a scratchy towel. Then he strode naked into the bedroom—and froze when he saw Jamie.

"Jesus," he croaked. "Where'd you find that dress?"

"On a raid." She did a little spin. "You like?"

Like? He fucking *loved*. The white dress was the sexiest thing he'd ever seen her wear, molding perfectly to her curves and stopping right below her knees. The gaping neckline revealed enough cleavage to make him drool, and when she spun around again, he noticed the back was perilously low cut too, nearly grazing the swell of her ass.

"I want you," he growled. "Right now."

She laughed. "Sorry, babe. Not on the agenda right now. Later, maybe."

Maybe? Yeah, right. He was going to be balls deep in her the second the party ended.

Lennox forced himself to stop ogling her, and searched his bag for something presentable to wear. If Jamie was going all out, he probably should too, but it turned out the fanciest shit he owned was a pair of black trousers and a rare long-sleeve without holes in it. Ah well. That'd have to do.

Ten minutes later, they walked hand in hand to the party. He still couldn't stop staring at her. Her hair cascaded down her back like golden strands of silk. And she wore a string of pearls around her neck that disappeared into the sexy valley of her cleavage. Lennox planned on fishing those pearls out of there with his teeth later.

The party was already in full swing when they entered the rec hall. Nearly everyone in Foxworth was in attendance. The large room was packed with bodies, buzzing with voices and laughter.

"Oh my gosh, you look gorgeous!" Jamie gushed when they ran into Sara.

"Beautiful," Lennox agreed.

The teenager blushed, fidgeting with the bottom of her red dress. Both the hem and neckline were modest, but the soft cotton material hugged her curves in an incredibly sensual way. Lennox was surprised Gideon had let her go out in public looking like that.

"Thank you." Sara glanced enviously at the shiny white pearls around Jamie's neck. "You look really pretty. Where did you get that necklace?"

Jamie grinned. "Stole it. Do you like it?"

"I love it," the girl breathed. "I've never seen anything so beautiful in my life."

Lennox's heart squeezed when he saw Jamie's expression soften. He knew exactly what she was going to do before she did it, yet he was still surprised as he watched her unclasp the necklace.

"Lift your hair up, sweetie," she murmured.

Sara's eyes widened as Jamie stepped up behind her. "What are you doing?"

"Completing your outfit. Not that it's possible for

you to look any prettier, but . . ." Jamie deftly secured the pearls around Sara's slender throat, then stepped back to examine her handiwork. "Perfect."

With an almost reverent touch, Sara slowly fingered the pearls. "I can't accept this," she said shyly.

"Too late." With another grin, Jamie smacked a kiss on the teenager's cheek before grabbing Lennox's hand. "Come on, babe, let's get out of here before she tries to give it back."

He chuckled as she dragged him away, but stopped her before she could lead them to Beckett. Planting both hands on her hips, he dipped his head and kissed her. "That was damn nice of you," he whispered against her lips.

"I have my moments."

Then she kissed him back and his surroundings faded away. His cock hardened the moment their tongues met, and if Rylan's voice hadn't interrupted them, he probably would've taken her right there against the wall, to hell with all those teenage eyes.

"Where are my winners?" Rylan shouted. "Get over here, champs!"

Lennox reluctantly released her, a rueful smile playing on his lips. "Duty calls."

"I'll make sure to applaud extra loud for you," she teased.

"You'd better."

He joined his teammates, a group that included Randy, Kade, and the other men and women he'd spent the last month with. The ceremony itself was brief. Rylan must have already hit the bottle, because he delivered a ridiculous speech about triumph and perseverance that made everyone roll their eyes. After Lennox's team took their bows, the individual winners were announced, and Jamie released a deafening whistle when Sara took the prize for her superior target-shooting skills.

Everyone remained in high spirits after Rylan wrapped up the formalities. The music was turned up. The crowd got wilder. Lennox caught several of the teenagers sneaking sips of booze, but he pretended not to notice. They'd worked hard this month. They deserved to get a little drunk and have some fun.

Lennox threaded through the crowd in search of Jamie, finally tracking her to one of the couches, where she was chatting with Bethany. The sight of Bethany's enormous belly triggered a wave of uneasiness. He didn't know how Arch did it. If Jamie was carrying his child, Lennox would be a total basket case. He'd probably never let her leave the house.

"Hey, champ," the pregnant woman greeted him. "Come join us. Jamie was telling me about the time she caught you jacking off on the beach."

He turned to glare at his woman. "Seriously? Why is that a topic of conversation?"

"Because it was hot," Jamie retorted. "And you should be flattered that I'm sitting here raving about your cock."

His lips curved smugly. "I do have a great cock."

Bethany hooted as he settled in beside Jamie. "Prove it," she taunted.

Lennox opened his mouth, but Jamie answered for him. "Sorry, Bethy, but *this*"—she clamped her palm over Lennox's groin—"is for my eyes only."

Her proprietary statement made him harden in her hand. Jamie noticed, and turned to wink at him. *Later,* she mouthed.

Damn fucking right.

"What are you doing out here, gorgeous?"

Reese jumped when she heard Rylan's voice from behind her. She'd been staring at the torches that lined the street, fascinated by the way the flames cast shadows on the sidewalk. Although Foxworth had electricity thanks to the city's power grid, she rarely turned on the streetlights at night. Unless it was raining out, she preferred to light the torches.

She turned around and reluctantly waited for Rylan to join her, hoping he wasn't about to push her for details again. Sloan had filled her in about the chat he'd had with the man, how Rylan had yet again extended an offer of assistance, but she still hadn't decided when to include Connor and his men. Not *if,* because joining up with them was an inevitability. She would be stupid not to take advantage of Connor's skills and resources.

But it wasn't the time yet.

"You should be inside." Rylan frowned, shoving both hands in the pockets of his jeans.

"Why? What do you need?"

"It's not what I need. It's what *you* need." He sounded exasperated. "You asked for this, Reese. You wanted your people to be strong. So now come inside and see how strong they've become. Celebrate with them."

She really didn't feel like it. Despite the positive

energy floating through town today, she'd been carrying around a weight of foreboding since she opened her eyes this morning. She had a bad feeling something terrible was on the horizon, as if there were a sea of black tar slowly creeping up to her gates.

But Rylan had a point. She needed to support her people. That was what a good leader did, right?

"Come on," he prompted.

He took her hand and dragged her toward the front steps of the building, and she let him, because she knew he was right. A dark figure stepped out of the shadows just as they reached the door. Sloan, emerging from whatever corner he'd been holed up in. She wasn't surprised or bothered by that. Sloan's presence was soothing. It enabled her to let down her guard, knowing that he was always there for her.

Loud drum and bass met her ears when they walked inside. Seeing the smiling, happy faces of her people eased some of the pressure in her chest. She accepted the small glass Rylan handed her and slugged back the fiery shot of tequila, welcoming the burn.

In the blink of an eye, Rylan swiped the empty glass from her hand and set it on a nearby edge. "Dance with me," he said.

Reese's gaze instantly sought out Sloan. He was leaning against the wall near the door, his impenetrable gaze fixed on the male hand on her arm. When he gave a slight nod, she allowed Rylan to lead her toward the crowd.

Big hands circled her waist. One of them jostled the radio sticking out of her back pocket, so he slid his palms lower, loosely resting them on her ass. Her body responded to his nearness. To his masculine scent. After a moment of hesitation, she looped her arms around his strong shoulders.

Approval flared in his eyes, and then he yanked her closer so that their bodies were pressed up against each other.

She liked the way he felt, his broad chest crushing her breasts, his thigh thrust between her legs. Maybe she just ought to get it over with. Sleep with him. Use that hard body until they were both limp and mindless. Her panties grew damp at the thought, causing her hips to rock harder.

He buried his face in her neck and she heard him groan softly. The husky sound vibrated through her, floated down to her core and deepened the ache.

"Let me take you to bed," Rylan whispered in her ear.

She swallowed the moisture that suddenly filled her mouth. Rylan lifted his head and she tipped her gaze to meet his eyes. They were the most fascinating shade of blue. Not pale and not dark. They reminded her of the cornflowers that used to sit in those pretty red pots on her mother's windowsill.

He waited for her answer, his gaze fixed on hers as their bodies slowly moved to the music. She supposed this was inevitable too, going to bed with this man. They'd been circling each other for an entire year. Or rather, he'd been circling her, coaxing and prodding and testing her resolve.

"Reese." His voice was low, husky. "I want to fuck you."

"Shut it down."

They both jumped as a sharp voice crackled out of her radio.

In a heartbeat, Reese was out of his arms, tugging the radio from her pocket and clicking it on. "Arch," she snapped. "Talk to me."

"Party's over," was the static-ridden reply. "Send everyone home. Curfew in effect." There was an ominous pause, then, "Enforcers at the gate."

21

Lennox knew something was up when the music abruptly cut off. Animated conversation continued to echo all around him, but he was shooting to his feet long before Sloan's sharp whistle sliced through the air.

"We need everyone back in their quarters!" Reese's second-in-command boomed. "Now."

Lennox had to give the people of Foxworth credit. Nobody questioned the order. Nobody even hesitated. One minute everyone was dancing and drinking and enjoying the party, and the next they were briskly marching toward the exit. There was no pushing or shoving. No one getting trampled in a stampede of panic. Lennox had witnessed this same orderly evacuation during one of his previous visits, and it could only mean one thing.

Enforcers.

"Stay in your rooms," Sloan barked to the crowd. "Consider this a lockdown until further notice."

Lennox reached for Jamie's hand. "Let's go," he urged.

She nodded and followed him to the door. They hurried out of the rec center, but Sloan's voice stopped them as they descended the front steps.

"Lennox, we need you."

Shit. He released Jamie's hand. "Go back to the room, love. I'll be right behind you."

She gazed at him unhappily, ignoring the people streaming past them on the sidewalk. "I'm coming with you."

"No." It was Sloan who expressed the strict sentiment. "We don't let any of our women near those bastards. Women stay indoors." When Jamie's eyes narrowed, the man gave her a contrite look. "This isn't some sexist bullshit on my part, sweetheart. I know you could kick those fuckers' asses to next week, all right? But these reps think they have a claim to all the pussy behind these gates. It's easier to make sure they keep their dicks in their pants if we're not dangling our women in front of them."

Although she still didn't look happy, Jamie's head jerked in a nod. "Gotcha." She turned to Lennox. "Be careful."

She gave him a fleeting kiss before darting off. Lennox could still taste her on his lips as he fell into step with Sloan. "How many?" he asked briskly.

"Six." Sloan adjusted the strap of his rifle without breaking his stride. "Luckily Nestor isn't among them. It's one of the other reps—Charlie, I think."

Lennox had no idea who Charlie was. Or who Nestor was, for that matter, other than being the man Sloan had coldcocked for trying to steal Sara. It was hard to keep track of all the Enforcers that Reese had deals with.

When they reached the courtyard behind the main gate, Reese, Beckett, and Arch were already congregated there, armed with rifles and deadly expressions.

"Where's Ry?" Lennox said warily.

"Out of sight," Sloan answered. "Pike too. We try not to let the fuckers see any new faces. Makes them ask too many questions."

"Then why am I here?"

"Because I want you here," Reese said sharply. "I want you to memorize these faces, Len. You need to be prepared in case they ever find their way to Connor's."

He wanted to point out that Rylan and Pike also lived with Connor, but it didn't surprise him that she'd chosen his presence over theirs. He and Reese had known each other far longer than they'd known the others, and it was clear that Connor and his men hadn't fully earned her trust yet.

Tension seeped into Lennox's bones as they positioned themselves in front of the gate. Arch planted a meaty hand on the handle, then glanced at Reese for confirmation. She nodded. A grinding noise screeched in the air as Arch dragged the heavy metal gate open.

A military truck came into view. Several shadowy figures stood in front of it.

Lennox aimed his handgun at the nearest man, a rush of hatred burning his throat as he registered the familiar uniform. The Enforcers that patrolled West Colony wore black tactical gear with a red stripe down the sides of their trousers and a red-and-white logo over their breast pockets. The logo said something about honor and service, which was bullshit as far as Lennox was concerned, because these men had no honor.

One of the Enforcers stepped forward. He was tall and bulky, with a head of sandy blond hair and a nondescript face that was lined with exhaustion.

"What are you doing here, Charlie? You're supposed to radio ahead," Reese barked when he approached the gate.

"Wasn't planning on stopping here, but we ran into some trouble." The Enforcer nodded at someone Lennox couldn't see.

Two more men stepped forward. The one on the left could barely walk, and was leaning heavily on the other one's shoulder.

"What's wrong with him?" There wasn't a trace of concern in Reese's voice. Only annoyance.

"Concussion, I think. We were heading back to the city after our colony sweep and ran into a few of your outlaw friends," the man said sarcastically.

Lennox's chest went rigid. Shit. Had they found Connor's camp? There weren't any other communities this close to Foxworth.

The Enforcer's nose turned up. "Reeked of booze and filth. Hell, I still can't get their stink out of my nose."

"Not everyone has the luxury of living in Foxworth," Reese said with a shrug.

"I don't think those scavengers live anywhere," Charlie muttered. "Fuckers tried to rob our truck while we were taking a piss break."

Lennox relaxed. Bandits, then. No outlaw would be stupid enough to steal from one measly Enforcer truck.

"Wilson got a good knock on the head fighting one of them off. Started getting woozy and puking in the truck on the drive back, so we figured we'd give him a night to rest before we hit the city." Charlie gestured to the rifle Reese was pointing at him. "Put that shit away. I already told you last month, I have no intention of changing the terms of our deal. Just give us some booze and grub, set us up in our usual quarters, and we'll be outta here at first light."

Reese waved her weapon at the two Enforcers beside him, then the three loitering near the truck. "What about them? They gonna give us any trouble?"

"Only if you give them a reason to." Charlie raised an eyebrow. "So what'll it be, Reese? Deal on or off?"

There was a moment of silence before she grudgingly murmured, "On." Then she turned to Sloan. "Take them to the bell tower. Send someone to bring them some *booze and grub*." Her last words held a mocking note.

Charlie whistled at his men. One of them swiftly slid behind the wheel and started the engine.

A moment later, the truck slowly drove through the gate.

"Len. Baby. You need to stop pacing."

"And do what?" he shot back. "Sit still? Play cards? Relax? I'm not relaxing until those fuckers are gone, Jamie."

Which meant he was in for a long night, because he had no intention of leaving his post. He'd been pacing the floor for the past hour, but always in view of the window. Always monitoring the street below to make sure none of their "visitors" decided to take a late-night stroll.

Lennox understood why Reese did business with them. He wasn't naive enough to believe that Foxworth could exist like this, *thrive* like this, without the arrangements Reese had in place. Dealing with the Enforcers was a necessary evil, a way to ensure the survival of her people.

But goddamn it, she was letting their enemies into their midst. Opening the gate and welcoming a pack of wolves into a town full of lambs. He hated the thought of Jamie even breathing the same air as the Enforcers, let alone sleeping fifty yards away from them.

"This is nothing new," Jamie said from the bed. "Reese has done this hundreds of times before. She gives them a place to stay, they leave Foxworth alone. Just sit down, Lennox."

"No."

He stubbornly turned his gaze back to the window, then blinked in alarm. Either he'd imagined it or he'd just seen someone darting through the square.

His pulse sped up as he moved closer to the windowpane. Reese had ordered someone to extinguish the torches, so all he saw was darkness. No, wait. A flash of red. Was that a woman's dress?

Hadn't Sara been wearing a red dress tonight?

A spark of concern had him spinning around. "I need to go downstairs and check something—"

He stopped talking.

Jamie stood directly in front of him. Bare-ass naked.

"No," she said firmly, "what you need to do is take your pants off."

"I think I saw someone," he protested.

"I think you're panicking," she corrected. Her heavy sigh echoed between them. "I get it. This situation isn't ideal. I don't want them here any more than you do, but we aren't in charge, Len. Reese is, and this is the arrangement she's made with them. Worrying and pacing and pressing your nose to that window all night won't achieve a damn thing. They'll still be here. *We'll* still be here. So let's try to calm down, okay?"

He stalked back to the window and peered out, but he couldn't see anything. There was nobody out there.

He jumped when Jamie's arms encircled his waist from behind. "Lennox. Please." She kissed him between the shoulder blades. "We're stuck in here until dawn." Another kiss. Her hand drifted to his groin. "And since I doubt you're going to let yourself sleep, we might as well try to pass the time in other ways."

His traitorous body responded to her touch. With each stroke of her palm against his crotch, his cock swelled and thickened, until he was fully erect and thrusting into her hand. Fucking hell. This woman was an addiction. He craved her with a fierceness he'd never experienced before.

Groaning, he twisted around and crushed his mouth over hers. When her tongue curled around his, it sent a shock of heat to his balls. He cupped her bare ass with both hands and hauled her up against him, and she hooked her legs around him as he carried her to the bed.

"You turn me into a goddamn animal," he told

her, ripping off his shirt and tossing it away. He lowered himself onto her and rubbed his groin over her pussy, feeling the heat of her searing through his trousers.

Jamie's hands clawed at his zipper, her tits bouncing enticingly as she tried ridding him of his pants. "For fuck's sake, Lennox, help me out."

With a burst of laughter, he undid his pants, but just as he was easing them off his ass, a faint cry wafted in from the open window.

He and Jamie instantly froze.

"Did you hear that?" she demanded.

Damn straight he did. He was already hopping off the bed and doing up his pants. "I told you I saw someone out there," he muttered, angry at himself for letting Jamie distract him with her stupidly gorgeous body. "I think it might have been Sara."

A sharp gasp echoed behind him. "Sara? You mean it looked like a real person?" Jamie sounded distraught. "I thought you were just seeing things in the shadows."

He snatched his gun off the table and turned to find Jamie hurriedly slipping into a pair of jeans. "What are you doing?"

"Coming with you." She threw on a T-shirt, then grabbed her own weapon.

Every fiber of his being wanted to argue with her, order her to stay put, but he knew she wouldn't listen to him. Not if Sara was in trouble. Jamie had taken the girl under her wing from the day they'd met.

"Stay behind me," he ordered. "And if I tell you to run, you run, you hear me?"

"Loud and clear," she said with a nod, and he could

tell she wasn't mocking him. Her expression was too damn somber.

They descended the short flight of stairs to what had once been the lobby of the law office but was now an empty space. Lennox approached the door with Jamie tucked up behind him. He pushed it open.

They heard the female scream the moment they stepped onto the sidewalk.

Shit.

It had come from the town square.

They charged forward with their weapons drawn, and Lennox clicked off the safety at the same time a gunshot cracked in the night air. For a second he thought he'd accidentally discharged his own pistol, or that maybe Jamie had fired hers, but then he saw the dark-clad figure up ahead. The raised arm. The gleaming barrel of a silver Glock.

It was Randy.

Lennox's heartbeat was dangerously fast as he raced toward the teenager. He heard Jamie desperately calling out Sara's name, but there was no answer. A moment later, they both skidded to a stop in front of the statue in the center of the town square.

Lennox's heart lunged into his throat when he spotted Sara huddled at the base of the bronzed horse. She was hugging her knees, her face buried in her arms, and he registered the sounds of soft, barely audible sobs.

A dead Enforcer lay near her feet.

"Sara. Sweetie, get away from him."

Jamie's firm voice broke through the shocked silence. She reached for the teenage girl and yanked her to her feet. Lennox's chest tightened when he realized that Sara's dress was torn. Tears stained her cheeks, and when Jamie opened her arms, Sara threw herself into them, sobbing incoherently as Jamie led her away from the lifeless body on the pavement.

Randy flew up to Lennox, the gun in his hand shaking wildly. "He was hurting her!" the boy blurted out. "I saw them from my window and I grabbed my gun because I knew I had to stop him and I—I . . ." He trailed off. Stunned. Panting.

It was clear both Randy and Sara were in shock, and Lennox didn't push for any more explanation than what Randy had provided. Lennox knew exactly what had happened: the girl had been attacked, and Randy had come to her rescue. There would be plenty of time to sort out the details—later. Right now they had a serious situation on their hands. A dead Enforcer, killed at the hands of an outlaw.

He met Jamie's eyes over Sara's head. The teenager was wrapped around her like a leech, refusing to let go. Goddamn it, where was Sara's father? How had Gideon allowed her to sneak past him when there was an Enforcer unit in town? But that was something that would also need to be addressed later.

"We need to move the body," he said flatly. "And clean up all this blood. And pray like hell that nobody heard the gunshot—"

He spoke too soon.

Footsteps were already thudding all around them. Reese appeared first, a rifle propped on her shoulder and Sloan and Arch on her tail. Kade stumbled into view from Lennox's left, bare-chested and barefoot as if he'd just rolled out of bed. Rylan and Pike converged on the square from opposite sides of the street, the former holding a pistol, the latter an assault rifle.

Lennox's gun snapped up when he registered more footsteps, these ones coming from the direction of the bell tower, where Reese had banished the Enforcers. Four of them were tearing toward the group, boots thumping and weapons drawn.

Reese cursed when she spotted the dead Enforcer, then spared a hasty look at Randy and Sara. "Get them out of here," she ordered Jamie.

"Don't move!"

Before Jamie could usher the kids away, Charlie had his gun pointed at her head.

Lennox resisted the frantic urge to throw himself in front of her. Maybe if Charlie didn't look so calm, he would've done it. But the man's expression, while holding a trace of fury, was utterly controlled. His hand was steady as he trained the weapon on Jamie.

The Enforcer beside him, however, wasn't as skilled at keeping his composure. The man's eyes went wild with outrage when he glimpsed his fallen comrade.

"You bitch! What the *fuck* did you do?" Charlie's man spun toward Reese, gun hand whipping up.

In the same breath, the muzzle of Sloan's pistol soared too. "Come near her and I blow your brains out," Sloan hissed.

The other man was clearly drunk, slurring his speech. "Do it. I'll still get a shot off. I'll kill this little bitch before I even hit the ground."

"Cruz," Charlie said sharply.

He spun toward his commanding officer. "She killed Prescott!"

Reese spoke up in a weary voice. "I'm afraid this is just a little misunderstanding, Charlie."

"A little misunderstanding?" Cruz roared. He pounced again, only to halt when Sloan cocked his gun. Swaying on his feet—damn it, he was definitely wasted—Cruz turned back to Charlie. "You're going to stand here and do *nothing*? You're going to let her get away with this? I told you she couldn't be trusted!"

"Your man attacked one of our girls," Lennox said coldly.

Charlie considered that. "That true?" he asked Reese.

She gave a brisk nod. "It was an act of self-defense." Her tone sharpened. "I warned you what would happen if you messed with my girls again."

Charlie sighed.

Which only enraged his man even further. "You fucking pieces of garbage killed a goddamn *Enforcer*! That's punishable by death in the Colonies!" He jammed his gun in the air, nodding toward Reese. "We need to take her in, sir. Make her pay for this."

The tension thickened, bringing a chill up Lennox's spine. He didn't like that Jamie was here. Sara. Randy. He wanted them gone, damn it. But nobody was moving a muscle. Nobody spoke for an interminably long time, until Arch finally broke the silence.

"Be smart about this, man," he told Cruz.

The Enforcer's wild gaze landed on his dead buddy. The gun wavered in his hand.

"Cruz," Charlie said in a low voice. "Put your gun down."

"Are you kidding me? You're a fucking coward, sir! You're playing nice with these scavengers? They're dirt. They're *nothing*. And they just killed my best friend!"

Lennox stifled a groan. Shit. So this was a personal beef? No way in hell was Cruz going to let this go.

"Listen to your commander, man," Arch said gruffly. "You're outnumbered. And nobody else needs to die tonight."

Almost everyone who met Arch was intimidated by his size, but Cruz wasn't fazed. He took a menacing step forward.

"No, someone does need to die," he spat out. "That's how you outlaws do it out here, no? There're no trials. No justice. It's an eye for an eye, right? This bitch took Prescott's life? Well, I'm gonna fucking take hers!"

It all happened so fast Lennox didn't have time to react. With a growl, Cruz swung his weapon toward Reese's head and fired.

Sloan and Arch rushed forward to shield her.

And Cruz's bullet hit Arch directly in the forehead.

22

Someone was screaming. Screaming so loudly it muffled the rapid burst of gunfire that exploded in the night. It was her, Jamie realized. *She* was screaming. And Arch . . . Arch's body hadn't even hit the ground before gunshots erupted all around her.

She couldn't move. Couldn't breathe. She stared at the red-haired man sprawled at her feet. Her friend. Bethany's lover. Blood oozed from his forehead, and she could swear his lifeless eyes were staring up at her in accusation.

"Jamie."

He was going to be a father . . .

"Jamie!"

Someone yanked her to the side just as the ledge behind her shattered in a flying rush of cement chunks. Kade. He was dragging her out of the line of fire. Because everyone was shooting. Reese. Sloan. Charlie. Jamie's frantic gaze registered a blur of motion, figures diving for cover, bodies hitting the ground.

Lennox. Where the hell was Lennox?

A shock wave of fear knocked her off her feet. No, it was Kade's body. He'd thrown her to the ground behind that stupid horse statue, and his solid chest pressed down on her spine. She heard the sound of cartridges pinging on the pavement, her ears ringing as more shots were fired. She didn't know where the Enforcers were. Didn't know where Lennox was. Didn't know where Sara was.

As panic skittered through her, she raised her head as high as she was comfortable risking. She couldn't see past what was ahead of her, and Kade's heavy weight made it impossible to crane her neck. She managed to wiggle out from under him and spoke in a panicked whisper. "Where's Sara?"

"Jamie—"

She ignored his protest and crawled toward the side of the statue. Her heart was beating a million times a second, but her hand was steady, gun firmly in her grip. She took a breath, then peered out into the square.

Nobody shot at her. But the gunfire was still going strong. A shadowy figure popped up from behind one of the cisterns across the street. There was a burst of light from a gun muzzle, another deafening blast, and then a crash as chunks of brick dislodged from the building behind her and fell to the ground.

Jamie shifted her head and that was when she saw her. Sara. Flat on her stomach next to the dead Enforcer who'd attacked her. Trying to crawl away while bullets whizzed over her head.

Oh God.

"Damn it, Jamie." Kade locked both arms around her as she tried to lunge forward.

"I need to get Sara! She's in shock. And one of those bullets could ricochet off something and hit her, Kade!" When his grip only tightened, she growled in frustration. "Let me go!"

"No." He tugged her back into their safe nook behind the statue, then palmed his pistol at his side. "Stay here and cover me. I'll get her."

"You will?"

"Yes. But you need to cover me, okay?"

She swallowed hard. Her mouth tasted like fear. Adrenaline was racing in her blood. But she managed a nod.

They got into position, Kade crouching beside her. Just as he started to move, a bullet cracked into the bronze horse and the damn thing's leg snapped off, nearly clipping off Jamie's ear.

"You okay?" Kade said urgently.

She shoved her hair off her forehead. "I'm fine."

"You ready?"

She gripped her gun in two hands. "Go," she urged.

Kade darted out, running at a swift crouch, while Jamie rose from her concrete shield and unloaded her clip in the direction of the only threat she was certain of. When the gunfight started, she'd seen Charlie dive behind the stone wall to her right, and now she riddled it with bullets. Pieces of concrete shattered with each shot, showering the ground with white flakes and jagged shards.

From the corner of her eye, she saw that Kade had reached Sara. He scooped the girl into his arms and started heading back.

He was two feet from the statue when a bullet struck him in the side.

Horror flooded Jamie's chest, but although Kade's body jerked from the hit, he kept moving. Seconds later, he threw himself down and dropped Sara into Jamie's arms.

The girl blinked up in confusion. "Jamie?"

"It's okay, sweetie. You're okay." She touched the girl's cheek in reassurance, but goddamn it, it wasn't okay. *Kade* wasn't okay. He'd been shot in the lower abdomen and Jamie felt nauseated when she saw the blood gushing out of the wound.

Kade groaned, collapsing in a sitting position against the back of the statue. "Fuck." An agonized noise left his lips as he pressed his hands to his stomach.

"Stay down," Jamie whispered to Sara, who was now curled up in a ball on the cold ground, oblivious to the gunshots still rocking the air.

Jamie wriggled over to Kade, then ripped off her shirt and balled it up between her shaky fingers. When she pressed the fabric to his side, he flinched in pain. "We need to keep pressure on it," she said quietly.

He nodded. His face was beginning to turn an alarming shade of white.

"*Reese!* Goddamn it, *stop this*!"

Charlie's voice thundered from behind the wall, and Jamie suddenly realized that the square had gone silent. The gunfire had stopped.

She didn't dare peek out again, even though every nerve ending in her body was desperate to find out if Lennox was okay. If Rylan and Pike and Arch—oh God. No, not Arch. Arch was dead.

Nausea squeezed her throat again. She ordered herself not to throw up. To concentrate on pressing the already soaked shirt to Kade's wound.

"I'm coming out, Reese!" Charlie again. He sounded eerily calm. "I'm putting my gun down and walking out right now. I want you to do the same."

There was no answer from Reese, wherever she was. If she was even alive.

Kade gave a soft groan, and Jamie quickly covered his mouth with her palm. "Quiet," she murmured. "I know it hurts, but you have to be quiet." Jesus. He was bleeding profusely. Her hands were sticky with his blood.

Charlie was still talking. "I'm sorry about your man. I really am. Cruz shouldn't have done that." A soft curse. "But he paid for it. I'm looking at his brains right now. Cruz is dead. So are Zeke and Briggs and Prescott. Four of my men are dead, Reese. But I don't want to die tonight."

He waited for a response, but the silence stretched on.

Kade's breathing grew shallower.

"I know you can see me, Reese." Charlie swore in frustration. "I'm unarmed, damn it. I just want to talk, find a way out of this for both of us."

There was a soft rustling. Jamie thought she heard a low male warning, and then Reese's voice rang clearly in the night. "I'm coming out."

Jesus. The woman had balls of steel.

"What's your solution here, Charlie?" Reese's footsteps echoed in the square, her voice getting louder as she neared the statue. "You really want to tell me you're just going to walk away? Pretend like four of your men aren't dead? That you won't come back here and set this whole town on fire?"

Charlie was quick to counter. "And if you kill me, you really think Ferris won't send more men to locate his missing unit? That he won't track us here and then execute you and every single one of your people for killing a troop of Enforcers? At least if you let me go, I can spin the story in a way that benefits us both."

Reese laughed harshly. "You mean a way that benefits *you*."

"*Us*," he insisted.

Reese paused again. Jamie wanted to scream at the woman to make a decision. To do something. *Anything*. Kade needed help, damn it. The bleeding had slowed, but his face was dangerously pale, and his breathing didn't sound so good.

"I'm sorry, Charlie," Reese finally said. "I can't take the risk of you reporting us." Another pause, and then Jamie heard one faint syllable. "Sloan."

A moment later, a deafening shot was fired, followed by a loud thump, as if a body had hit the ground.

Within seconds, the entire area was bustling again. Footsteps, several sets of them, slapped the pavement. Reese was issuing sharp commands at her people. "Sloan, the bell tower. The last Enforcer is still there. He was out cold before, but he might have heard the shots. Beck, get Randy to the infirmary."

Randy? Had he been hurt?

And where the hell was Lennox?

A gust of relief slammed into Jamie's chest when Lennox appeared in front of her. Both his hands clamped around her shoulders, shaking her urgently. "Are you okay?"

"Fine," she assured him.

"So am I," Kade said weakly. "Thanks for asking."

When Lennox's gaze dropped to the other man's

gut, he released a loud curse. "Rylan!" he shouted. "Get over here!"

The blond man rushed over to them, and Jamie hurriedly gave them a report. "He's lost a lot of blood. I felt for an exit wound and didn't find one. The bullet is still inside him."

Rylan and Lennox exchanged a grim look. She knew what they were thinking, but she couldn't bear to hear them say it out loud. Her hands were suddenly moved off Kade's abdomen as Rylan took her place at the man's side. Pike joined them, his expression hard as he knelt beside his injured friend.

"We need to get him out of here," Pike said tersely.

"We shouldn't move him." But even as Jamie voiced the protest, she knew they had no other choice. What else were they supposed to do? Let Kade bleed to death on the cold pavement?

She rose unsteadily to her feet, her gaze falling on Sara. "We need to find Gideon," she told Lennox. "Sara needs her father. And—" Jamie's breath caught in her throat as she remembered the unthinkable. "Bethany. Oh my God. Someone needs to tell Bethany about Arch."

"I'll do it," Lennox said gruffly.

Pain squeezed her chest, so tight she could barely speak. She thought about the couple, the adoration in their eyes whenever they had looked at each other. "No. I'll do it."

"Are you sure?"

She gulped through the agony in her throat. "Yes."

He swept his hand over her cheek and she sagged into his touch, momentarily blocking out the chaos around them. The shouts. The footsteps. The sharp voices of Rylan and Pike as they enlisted Beckett and Travis to help them lift Kade.

She focused instead on Lennox's familiar face. His strong grip on her waist as he pulled her close. His comforting lips on the side of her neck.

She allowed herself this moment. She drew strength from him. Then she stepped out of the embrace and whispered, "Go help Rylan take care of Kade. I'll find you after I talk to Bethany."

Nodding, he kissed her temple, then went to join the others.

Jamie took a breath and walked in the opposite direction. She didn't want to do this. She *didn't*. But she had no choice.

Somebody needed to tell Bethany that the man she loved was dead.

The town infirmary was located in the basement of the building next to the restaurant. It had fluorescent lighting that made Lennox's eyes hurt, and the ever-present smell of mold and antiseptic that burned his nostrils each time he inhaled. More important, it had cabinets full of medical supplies that had been amassed on raids, and two fairly competent medics who'd once fought in the People's Army.

And yet with all the tools at their disposal, Kade remained in critical condition.

"We're not equipped to deal with this," John, one of the medics, admitted to the small group that had gathered in the corridor.

Before anyone could answer, the group got a little bigger as Reese and Sloan burst through the metal doors at the end of the hall.

"How's Randy?" Reese demanded.

"The bullet grazed his arm," John reported. "We cleaned him up, slapped a bandage on it, and sent him home. Ethan's mother will look after him tonight. But he'll be fine."

"And Kade?" she said flatly.

"He's lost a lot of blood," said the other medic, a stocky man named Frank. "The bullet's still in his gut, and there's no way of getting it out without causing more damage."

Lennox peered through the open doorway of the room beside them, where Kade was lying on a long metal table. His eyes were closed, his chest covered in blood, but at least that chest was still rising and falling. He was still breathing.

"He's gonna need surgery," John told his leader. "Or at the very least, a blood transfusion."

"Then give him a blood transfusion," Reese snapped.

"We can't," Frank said grimly.

"Why the hell not?"

"Because our universal donor is dead." Pain flickered in the medic's eyes. "Arch is—was—the only one whose blood type we knew for sure. He was type O. We don't know Kade's, and we can't risk giving him incompatible blood."

The reminder that Arch was dead split Lennox's chest in two. Arch was *dead*. Jesus. His concern for Kade had overshadowed that bleak truth, but now it was all his brain was capable of registering. Arch. Dead. And Jamie was the one who had to tell Bethany.

Bethany, who was seven months pregnant.

Lennox suddenly felt sick.

"Hudson is a universal donor." Pike spoke up in a

gravelly voice, causing everyone to look over in surprise.

"Shit, you're right." Rylan focused on Reese. "She gave us a whole lesson on blood typing a while back. And she was trained in the city hospital." He paused. "She might be able to help him."

"She's five hours away," Lennox pointed out. "We can reach them on the sat phone, but even if they left right this second, it'll still take a while for her to get here." The eddy of queasiness in his gut churned harder. "We don't know if he has that long."

Reese glanced at the doorway, at Kade, then turned to Pike. "Take the chopper."

He looked startled. "You sure?"

Lennox was equally surprised. It was no secret that Reese had a military-grade chopper stashed on a helipad they'd built out on the farm, but she rarely allowed her people to use it. The cost of fuel was too damn high; even a short flight could cripple the town of its fuel supplies.

"I promised Connor that his men would be safe here," she muttered. "And I owe it to Kade to give him the best possible treatment." She cleared her throat, then scowled at Pike. "Why are you still here? Go to the farm and get on that chopper. Bring Connor's woman here."

Pike took a step forward, but Reese stopped him. "Just her, Pike. Any extra weight will eat up more fuel. Connor will have to stay at the camp."

Lennox wasn't holding his breath about that happening, but Pike nodded and stalked off.

Reese wasn't done giving orders. "You're on cleanup," she told Sloan. "We need to take care of the bodies before rigor mortis sets in. The scene needs to look right."

Rylan frowned. "What scene?"

She gave an impatient shake of her head. "Don't worry about it. Sloan will take care of it."

"I'm going with him," Rylan said before shifting his gaze to Lennox. "You'll stay with Kade?"

"I won't leave his side," he promised.

With a look of gratitude, Rylan clapped his hand over Lennox's arm, then glanced at Sloan. "Let's go."

The two men disappeared down the hall, and then both medics ducked into Kade's room, leaving Lennox alone with Reese.

"What kind of retaliation can we expect?" he asked quietly. "Dominik and Ferris will know something's up when Charlie and his crew don't report back to headquarters."

"They'll report back."

Her mysterious response made him frown. "What the hell does that mean?"

"For fuck's sake, why do I need to explain myself to everyone? I know what I'm doing." Reese jammed her finger in the center of his chest. "Save your questions for later, Lennox. Right now your job is to keep Kade alive. Connor will have my head if his man doesn't survive." She spun on her heel and marched toward the door, her red hair swinging like a pendulum with each brisk step.

Lennox took a breath and went to check on Kade. John had just replaced the bandage, but already it was more pink than white. Kade was still bleeding, not as much as before, but still fucking bleeding, damn it.

Christ. Tonight had been a bloodbath.

Lennox rubbed his eyes, then raked his hands through his hair as he collapsed on the chair next to Kade. Arch was dead. Kade was hurt. And yet Lennox couldn't help thanking whatever higher power had spared everyone else. Jamie. Sara. Randy, whom Lennox had tackled to the ground when the guns went off. The boy had still gotten shot, but luckily it was just a flesh wound.

A wheezy noise captured his attention. It was Kade's breathing. Shit. If Kade's respiratory system was starting to shut down, that definitely wasn't a good sign.

Lennox had never felt more powerless in his life as he sat at the man's side. He couldn't do a damn thing to help Kade.

He wasn't sure anybody could.

Bethany didn't cry.

She didn't scream.

She didn't pound her fists against the wall and shout at the heavens for taking Arch from her.

All she did was sink down on the couch, press both hands to her belly, and close her eyes.

Jamie had been sitting with the woman for more than an hour, and she'd reached a point where she truly had no idea what to do.

Arch is dead.

Those were the only words she'd been able to choke out before Bethany fell into her trance. The longer Bethany stayed silent, the more worried Jamie got, but what was she supposed to do? What was the proper etiquette you were supposed to follow after you had just told a close friend that her man was dead? Should she hug her? Rub her back? Make her something to eat?

Jamie had already voiced each one of those suggestions. Bethany hadn't responded. Hell, she didn't even seem to register Jamie's presence.

"Bethy," she whispered. "Please. Talk to me. I need to know you're here with me."

The woman's eyes didn't open, but for the first time since Jamie had entered the bedroom Bethany had shared with Arch, her friend finally spoke.

"Go help Kade." It was a dismissal. Brief. Hoarse.

The agony stabbing Jamie's heart only intensified. "No. You shouldn't be alone right now."

"I'm not alone." Bethany was rubbing her stomach almost hypnotically. "I'm with my baby."

Tears stung Jamie's eyes, then spilled over and streamed down her cheeks. But Bethany wasn't looking at her. Bethany wasn't even in the room. She was somewhere else, somewhere that Jamie couldn't access.

"I don't want to leave you."

"You have to. They might need you in the infirmary." Bethany finally slitted her eyes open, and the overpowering grief Jamie saw in them ripped her insides to shreds.

"*You* need me."

"I'll be all right." Bethany's eyelids closed again.

No, she wouldn't be all right. How could she be? She'd lost the man she loved, the father of her baby. One of the best men Jamie had ever known. Her heart ached at the thought of never seeing Arch again. Never hearing his gruff voice. Never feeling those big bear paws he called hands gripping her waist when he hugged her.

But it was obvious there was nothing she could do for Bethany right now. The woman had completely shut down.

"I'll come back to check on you in a bit," she said softly.

That didn't garner a response from Bethany.

Jamie's knees wobbled as she stood up. She hesitated, then leaned down and kissed the woman's forehead. Bethany's skin was ice-cold beneath Jamie's lips. Her eyes remained closed.

God, Jamie truly had no idea how Bethany was ever going to come back from this.

It was pitch-black out when Jamie exited the storefront where Bethany and Arch lived. With the torches extinguished and the moon nowhere in sight, it was too dark to see even two feet in front of her, so she clicked on her flashlight and carefully made her way to the building that housed the infirmary. It was alarmingly quiet inside, but as she neared the end of the hall, she heard a murmur of voices. When she turned the corner, she found Lennox sitting on the floor, leaning his head against the cinder block wall.

"How is he?" Jamie asked urgently.

Her heart jumped when he didn't answer.

She poked her head into the doorway two feet from where he sat, and was overcome with relief when she spotted one of the medics changing Kade's bandage. He was alive, then. They wouldn't bother changing the dressings of a dead man.

Lennox didn't stand up, so she slid down beside him. After a beat, he wrapped his arm around her.

"Where is everyone?" Jamie tucked her head against his shoulder.

"Pike went to get Hudson," Lennox mumbled. "Reese gave him the chopper. It'll take him less than an hour to fly to camp." He checked the watch strapped to his wrist. "They should be back soon. It's been nearly two hours since he left."

"And the others?"

"Sloan and Rylan are taking care of the bodies. Randy and Sara are at home." Lennox's arm tightened around her. "How's Bethany?"

Jamie exhaled slowly. "Not good."

He didn't ask for more details. In fact, he didn't say another word. He went silent and stared straight ahead, and each minute that ticked by heightened Jamie's concern. He was shutting down on her the way Bethany had done. Maybe he was in shock?

But no, she knew Lennox. He possessed the kind of steely strength other men only dreamed of. He didn't go into shock. He didn't withdraw after something dangerous had gone down. Just a few months ago their home had been ambushed. They'd watched one of their friends die—Nell, one of the most beautiful, vibrant women Jamie had ever known. Lennox hadn't shut down then, so she couldn't understand why he was shutting down now.

His head suddenly snapped toward her, and the clarity swimming in his gray eyes startled her.

"It's not safe here," he said roughly.

Her brow furrowed. "Len—"

"It's not safe here," he repeated, and then he turned his head and went back to staring at the wall.

23

Lennox jolted to attention when he heard the slamming of doors above them, followed by hurried footsteps that vibrated in the ceiling. Thank fuck. Hopefully that meant Pike was back.

He and Jamie had been sitting in silence for the past ten minutes. Kade was still alive, but not doing well judging by the increasingly agitated murmurs floating out of his room. John and Frank couldn't do more than try to control the bleeding and keep him conscious.

Loud thumps sounded from the stairwell. The metal doors burst open and Xander appeared. "Where is he?" the bearded outlaw demanded.

Lennox and Jamie quickly hopped to their feet. There was a blur of blond hair at the door. Hudson flew through it, racing after Xander. Lennox waited for Connor to appear, but the doorway remained empty.

"Where's Con?" he asked with a frown.

Hudson answered while giving Jamie a quick hug.

"Back at camp. Someone needed to stay with Piper and Layla."

Lennox had been certain Connor wouldn't let Hudson out of his sight, but apparently the man trusted Xander with her care.

The four of them entered Kade's room, and Xander's face paled the moment he saw his friend. He wasted no time touching the man's ashen cheeks. "Kade. You with us?"

A pair of dark eyes slit open. "Xan?" the patient said weakly.

"I'm right here, man. So's Hudson." Xander looked sharply at the medics. "Pike said you need blood?"

John nodded, then glanced at Hudson. "You sure you're a universal donor?"

"A hundred percent." She was already rolling up the sleeves of her oversize flannel shirt, which must have belonged to Connor, because it hung all the way to her jean-clad knees. "You have the right equipment to do this?"

"Yeah. Take a seat."

The medics pushed Lennox and the others out of the way as Hudson settled in the chair next to Kade. They were relegated to the wall, and Lennox's throat tightened when he saw Hudson reach for Kade's hand. She squeezed it, her gray eyes focusing on the wounded man's face.

"You're going to be okay," she murmured.

Frank was bustling over Kade, shifting the man's arm so he could insert a small needle into the artery at Kade's wrist. A long tube was connected to the needle, and John quickly snapped a second needle to the other end and flicked the inside of Hudson's elbow with his free hand. Once he found the vein, the needle slid in, and within seconds, Hudson's blood began flowing through the tube, trickling slowly toward Kade's wrist.

"How do you know how much to give him?" Jamie asked tentatively.

"We don't," Hudson answered in a soft voice, her gaze still glued to Kade. "We just have to wait and see if there's any improvement."

"Xan . . ." Kade's pained plea was barely above a whisper. "You still here?"

Xander sank to his knees so that his face was close to Kade's. "Still here, man. I'm not going anywhere."

Kade let out a breath that sounded distressingly wheezy. "You still have the letter I gave you?"

Lennox saw Xander's broad shoulders tense, but the man's tone was gentle as he said, "Yeah."

"You'll . . . give it to him if anything happens to me?"

"Nothing's going to happen to you," Xander said firmly. "You're going to be fine."

Lennox didn't share the other man's conviction. Kade looked like he was knocking on death's door. There was no color in his face. Maybe because it had all gathered at his side, which was red and swollen. And his breathing was weak and raspy.

"This isn't going as fast as I'd like," Frank said, frowning as he studied the sluggish flow of blood traveling through the tube.

"It'll pick up," Hudson assured him, but she sounded worried too.

Time passed. Lennox wasn't sure how much, because his mind was elsewhere. No longer in the room with Kade, but back in the town square. He heard the crack of gunfire. He saw the bullets. He felt the fear. The sheer, absolute terror that had consumed him when he was crouching behind cover, not knowing where Jamie was, not knowing if she was dead or alive.

They needed to get out of Foxworth. There would be retaliation coming their way. There *had* to be. The GC didn't take kindly to dead Enforcers in the free land, no matter how Reese ended up staging the scene.

"Enough."

The harsh command jerked Lennox from his internal panic. Pike was looming in the doorway, his impossibly dark eyes narrowed at the center of the room.

"She's given him too much," he told the medics. "You need to stop."

"I'm okay," Hudson tried to protest, and Lennox was suddenly horrified when he noticed her face.

She was whiter than snow. Her eyes were glazed. And either he was imagining it, or she was swaying in her chair, about to keel over even though she was seated.

"It's been two hours," Pike snapped, charging toward her. "Time to stop."

Two hours? Jesus. Lennox had no idea it'd been that long.

"He's right, doll." Xander spoke up in a tired voice. "Con will kill us if we bring his woman back to him in a coffin."

Hudson continued to object, but the men—and the medics—weren't hearing it. The needle was efficiently removed from her arm. Pike helped her to her feet. She swayed so wildly that Pike cursed and lifted her up into his arms, but her arms were too weak to wrap around him. They dangled at her sides as he carried her out the door.

"I'll take her upstairs, make sure she gets some rest," he barked over his shoulder.

Once they were gone, Xander took the chair Hudson had been sitting on, his gaze sweeping over Kade's face. "It looks like he's got some color in his cheeks, no?"

No, it didn't. If anything, Kade's skin was gray now. But Lennox didn't have the heart to say it, so he nodded and said, "He's looking better."

He felt Jamie's hand slipping into his own. Her fingers were freezing. "Now what?" she whispered, her worried eyes focused on Kade.

Lennox swallowed. "We wait."

Jamie woke up with a start, confused to find that they were out in the hall again. She was curled up on the floor beside Lennox with her head in his lap, but she didn't remember getting there, or falling asleep. She blinked a couple of times. Spotted Pike and Xander, who'd dragged chairs out into the corridor and were sitting in absolute silence, staring at Kade's door. She shifted her gaze and found Rylan leaning against the wall a few feet away.

She wasn't sure what time it was, but she remembered being awake when Rylan and Sloan had returned from their mysterious errand about an hour ago. She'd been too exhausted to focus on the details, but from the low murmur of their conversation, she had gleaned that they'd driven a hundred miles east, where they'd created a visual narrative with the dead bodies from the town square, setting it up to look as if the unit had been attacked by bandits. Then they'd used the radio in the truck to contact Enforcer headquarters and make a desperate plea for backup. But it would be too late. When reinforcements arrived, they would discover that their fellow soldiers had already lost the battle.

Or at least that was the story Reese was hoping they'd buy.

Jamie prayed like hell it worked. That the Enforcers who found the truck didn't somehow piece it together that their men had died at Foxworth and not on the road.

But at the moment, she was far more worried about Kade, who had been drifting in and out of consciousness since the blood transfusion.

Jamie sat up and rubbed her eyes just as Hudson emerged from Kade's room to give them another report. Thankfully the blonde was looking steady on her feet again. Jamie had been truly concerned about her earlier. Hudson had given Kade way too much blood, and it was a miracle she hadn't died herself.

"Xan," Hudson said softly.

The man shot up from his chair. "Time for another transfusion?" When Hudson slowly shook her head, Xander's eyes widened in horror. "Is he . . . ?"

"No," the blonde said quickly. "He's alive." There was an agonizingly long pause. "But I'm not sure how long he'll stay that way."

Jamie's heart dropped to the pit of her stomach. *No.* She stumbled to her feet. Lennox did the same, his warm hand resting on her hip to steady her.

"Then give him another transfusion." Xander's desperation thickened the air in the corridor.

"It won't help."

"You don't know that! We can at least *try*, god-damn it!"

Hudson repeated herself. Low and weary. "It won't help."

The small group followed her into Kade's room, where she gingerly removed the dressing over his bullet wound. Jamie tried not to gasp when she glimpsed Kade's abdomen. It was distended. And turning purple. The signs of internal bleeding were impossible to miss, and a strangled sob lodged in her throat when she recognized the implications of that.

Hudson confirmed Jamie's suspicions. "He's bleed-ing internally. I don't know if even surgery would help at this point, but that's not an option. We're not equipped to operate."

"How long?" Xander whispered, and they all knew what he meant.

"I don't know," Hudson said helplessly. "Minutes? Hours?"

"Is he in pain?" Rylan asked from the door. His expression was as stricken as everyone else's.

"I gave him some painkillers, but . . ." Hudson bit her lip. "He's suffering."

Xander let out a tortured groan. "Give him more, then," he burst out. "Don't you have anything stron-ger?"

"We've got some morphine, but not a lot. Which means either we inject him with small doses, which won't help much with the pain. Or we give him one massive dose and . . ." She trailed off.

This time Jamie did gasp. One massive dose? That would . . . fuck, it would kill him.

Her gaze landed on Kade. His face was grayer than the cinder block walls. His breaths were so shallow his chest was scarcely moving anymore.

No, the morphine wouldn't kill him.

It would put him out of his misery.

At Kade's side, Xander had evidently reached the same conclusion. His entire face collapsed as another anguished sound escaped his lips. Everyone went silent. It felt like hours. Days. And then Xander's head turned sharply toward Hudson.

"Give me the morphine."

"Xan—" she protested.

"Just give it to me and leave," he bit out. "All of you. Just leave."

Jamie's hands began to shake, so hard that Lennox took both of them in his palms and squeezed tightly. "Jamie," he murmured. "Let's go."

God. She didn't want to leave. But Xander was already pushing away from the table, forcibly shoving everyone but Hudson to the door.

In the hallway, the tears spilled over, soaking her cheeks and prompting her to bury her face against Lennox's chest. "I can't believe this is happening," she whispered.

His shaky hand stroked her hair. "I know."

There was a loud click. Jamie raised her head to find that Xander had kicked Hudson out too. The blonde looked so ravaged that Jamie moved from Lennox's arms to Hudson's, holding the other woman tight. "You did everything you could, Hudson."

"But it wasn't enough," Hudson mumbled.

Jamie heard a low voice from behind the door. Xander, as he spoke quietly to Kade. She was dreading the moment when he stopped talking, because that would mean that he'd . . .

Another sob flew out, and she released Hudson so abruptly the woman staggered backward. Jamie whirled around to Lennox. "I can't be here," she choked out. "I *can't*—"

He had his arm around her before she could get another word out. "It's okay, love. It's okay. We don't have to be here."

She didn't remember leaving the infirmary or heading back to their room. She didn't remember Lennox pulling a blanket over her and sliding in beside her. She didn't remember what they said to each other, or exactly when it was that the first light of dawn streamed in through the window.

All she knew was that when she opened her eyes that morning, Kade was dead.

24

Foxworth was in mourning. *Lennox* was in mourning. Even as he went through his usual morning routine— got dressed, washed up, grabbed a cup of coffee from the restaurant—it didn't escape him that his world had once again been rocked off its axis. He'd lost two close friends last night.

Arch. Kade.

Jesus, *Kade*. The grief he felt at the loss of Arch was crushing, but the loss of Kade . . . the knowledge that Xander had been forced to inject the lethal dose of morphine that took their friend's life . . . it would haunt Lennox for the rest of his life.

He forced himself to stay productive. He helped Beckett and Travis clean up the debris littering the town square. He checked in on Jamie, who was spending the day hovering over Bethany. And now he was heading to the restaurant, because he'd been told Randy was there, and he wanted to make sure the kid's arm was holding up well.

But Randy wasn't alone when Lennox strode into

the restaurant. The boy was sitting in a corner booth with Sara.

Shit. After everything that had happened last night, Lennox knew Sara's father would be even more determined now to keep his daughter away from Randy.

Just as Lennox took a tense step toward the booth, a large hand clamped onto his shoulder. He turned, surprised to find Gideon there. The man had been holed up in the booth behind Lennox, judging by the lone steaming mug on the tabletop.

"It's all right," Gideon murmured, following Lennox's gaze. "I told him he could sit with her."

He couldn't mask his surprise. "You did?"

"He saved her life last night. That Enforcer bastard tried to"—Gideon's voice cracked—"rape her. If Randy hadn't shown up . . ." Relief and agony warred in the man's gaze.

Lennox nodded in understanding. "What was she even doing out last night? We had a curfew in effect."

"She was looking for that goddamn necklace."

"What are you talking about?" he asked with a frown.

"Your woman gave her a necklace. Those pearls? I guess the clasp was loose and the damn thing fell off somewhere in the rec center." Gideon angrily shook his head. "She snuck out to get it, said she didn't want the Enforcers finding the necklace and stealing it from her."

Lennox stifled a sigh.

"Trust me, I'm not happy with that bit of foolishness." Gideon's tone softened. "But I don't have the heart to punish her for it. She was already punished enough last night." He sighed. "I'm damn grateful Randy showed up when he did."

Lennox glanced toward the booth again, where Randy and Sara were talking quietly. Neither one was smiling, but they looked far more relaxed than they'd been last night.

His stomach clenched when he remembered their pale faces. Sara's tears. Randy's bloodstained sleeve. Gideon had almost lost his daughter yesterday.

Lennox had almost lost Jamie.

"You leaving?"

The abrupt question snapped his head up. "What?"

"You and your people," Gideon clarified. "Are you heading back to your camp now that training is over?"

"Yeah. In a few hours, actually." Agony clogged his throat. "Ry and Xan are preparing Kade's body. They want to bury him at our camp."

Gideon's expression grew pained. "I'm sorry for your loss, Lennox."

"You lost someone too last night," he said roughly. "Arch."

They both fell silent as they thought about their fallen friends. Lennox knew there was a funeral being planned for Arch tomorrow, but as much as it pained him not to attend, he was getting the hell out of Foxworth as soon as Rylan and the others were ready to go.

It was so fucking ironic. He'd always felt safest here in Foxworth, but how foolish was that? For all his preaching about safety being an illusion, he'd taken Foxworth for granted. He'd allowed himself to believe that nothing bad could touch this town, that the gates and Reese's deals with the city were enough to protect the people living here.

He'd been wrong. There were no safe places in the free land. Danger was everywhere, and now it looked as though Foxworth might be the most dangerous place of all.

Jamie could have died yesterday. Other people *had* died.

Which meant it was time to go.

But first, there was one more person he needed to check in with.

He found Reese in the courtyard. She was murmuring instructions to Travis, who had taken over Arch's duties of manning the gate. Trav had a rifle slung over his shoulder and was listening intently to every word Reese said.

Lennox waited until they were done, then cornered Reese on the sidewalk. "Did you hear from your other reps?" he asked in lieu of greeting.

She gave a brisk nod. "I got in touch with Nestor about an hour ago."

"And?"

"They found Charlie's unit." Her lips quirked. "Nestor asked me whether I was aware that there were bandits this close to Foxworth."

Lennox breathed in relief. "He wasn't suspicious?"

"Not in the slightest. Turns out the last time Charlie reported in, he told headquarters they were on their way back to base. They must have had their run-in with the bandits right after that, and he didn't bother checking in again to let anyone know his team was coming to Foxworth."

"What about your alliances? Still intact?"

"For now. Nestor still isn't happy about what happened on his last visit, but he assured me that Charlie's replacement would abide by the rules of our deal." She slanted her head. "What about you?"

He narrowed his eyes. "What about me?"

"You ready to give me an answer yet?"

"No."

She ran a frustrated hand through her copper hair. "Len. Come on. After last night, it's even more important for all of us to stand together. The Enforcers are out of control." Fury lit her eyes. "That bastard Cruz shot Arch in cold blood. These people need to be stopped."

"I'll be in touch," was all he said.

Her annoyed curse told him she didn't like that answer, but he didn't give a shit if she was displeased. He wasn't committing to anything until he'd considered every angle. Even so, he knew Reese was right. Surviving in the free land was becoming increasingly hazardous. The Enforcers *were* out of control. But Lennox had bigger concerns. Priorities that ran deeper than helping Reese form a united stand against the council.

He wasn't throwing himself in the line of fire unless he was absolutely sure he could keep Jamie *out* of the line of fire.

"I'll find you before we leave." He touched Reese's arm and then headed off to see Jamie.

She was exiting Bethany's door when he reached the one-story building, and Lennox wasted no time pulling her into his arms. "Hey." He buried his face in her hair.

"Hey," she murmured back.

He breathed in her familiar scent and once again uttered a silent prayer that she was all right. Christ, he'd almost lost her last night.

The memory only fueled his need to get going. To speed away from Foxworth's gates and take her back to Connor's camp. To their hidden fortress in the mountains. Maybe there it would be safe. Maybe he could *make* it safe.

"We should start packing." He released her abruptly. "We have a long drive ahead of us."

Jamie hesitated.

"What?" he said instantly.

"I wanted to talk to you about that. I was coming to find you, actually."

Her timid expression raised his hackles. Jamie was *never* timid. Unless she was about to tell him something she knew he wouldn't like.

"Jamie . . ." His tone held a warning. And his pulse had kicked up a notch.

She puffed out a hurried breath. "I want to stay here."

Lennox blinked.

Then blinked again.

"Bethany needs me," she said when he didn't respond. "She's in such a bad place right now. And she's seven months pregnant. In two months she's going to be taking care of a baby. *Alone.*"

He blinked.

Then blinked again.

"She needs our help," Jamie pleaded. "Arch is gone. The others are going to be too busy protecting the gates and keeping everyone safe. She's our friend, Len. She needs us."

He blinked.

Then blinked again.

"Damn it, Lennox! Would you stop blinking like an owl and start *talking*?"

The annoyed demand snapped him out of his trance. "Absolutely not," he ground out.

Her blue eyes flickered with annoyance. "Lennox."

"Absolutely not," he echoed, and his thunderous tone made her flinch. "We're not staying here."

"Yes, we are." She planted her hands on her hips. "Or at least, *I* am. You can go back to Connor if you want, but I'm not going anywhere. Bethany—"

"Someone else can take care of Bethany," he interrupted. "It's not your responsibility, Jamie."

"She's our friend." Jamie stared at him with astonished eyes. *"Arch* was our friend. He would want us to take care of his woman."

"I don't give a shit what he would've wanted! You're *my* woman, and I take care of *you*, you understand me? And we're fucking leaving. Today."

Defiance hardened her face. "No. I'm staying to take care of my friend. At least until the baby is born—"

"Until the baby is born?" he burst out in disbelief. "That's two months!"

Didn't she realize how long that was? How much shit could happen to her in that time? Lennox didn't give a damn if Nestor had bought the bandit story Reese had orchestrated on the road. As long as Reese maintained her alliance with the Enforcers, Foxworth would always be on their radar. Connor's camp wasn't. End of fucking story.

"You're not staying here," he hissed out. "I mean

it, Jamie. You're coming with me and we're getting the hell out of here."

She met his eyes. "No." Calm and resolute.

And just like that, something inside him snapped. As if a piece of rope that had become more and more frayed over time, the thin threads ripping apart into jagged, severed pieces.

"If you stay . . ." He struggled for breath. "If you stay, then it's over between us."

Jamie's shocked gaze flew to his. "You don't mean that."

"Yes. I do." Lennox was surprised his voice could be so steady when he'd lost every shred of control. "I can't do this anymore."

"Do what?" she said pleadingly.

"Watch you put your life at risk. I can't keep you safe if you don't *let* me." He shuddered out a breath. "I can't let myself love you knowing you don't give a shit about your own life. That you're willing to risk it so you can raid a goddamn house, or stay in a place that's crawling with Enforcers just to hold someone's hand."

"*Let* yourself love me?" Her eyes blazed at him. "You need to give yourself permission to love me? Bullshit. You *do* love me. You always have, and you're being ridiculous right now. It *is* safe here—"

"It's not!" he roared.

"It's as safe as it's gonna get," she shot back. "And yes, right now I'm not thinking about my own self-preservation. I'm thinking about Bethany, who's going to have a baby soon, who just lost her man. What's the point of making connections with people if you're not going to be there for them when they need you the most?"

His heart rattled his rib cage, each erratic beat thudding between his ears. He drew a deep breath. Another one. And another. It didn't calm him down. It just made him dizzy.

"Come with me," he whispered. "Right now, Jamie. Please."

"No."

She might as well have slapped him. His heart fractured, sharp pieces slicing down to his gut.

"Now what? Does that mean it's over?" she said sardonically.

Lennox exhaled. Then he nodded.

Her eyes went wide again. "What happened to *I go where you go*?" Anguish rang in her voice. "Doesn't the opposite of that apply? *I stay where you stay?*"

"Not here," he choked out. "We can't stay here."

"Well, that's what I'm doing, Lennox. I'm staying with Bethany. And Reese will do everything in her power to protect this town."

He was so frustrated he wanted to grab her by the shoulders and shake her. "This *town*? It's not a town, Jamie. It's a goddamn illusion. We're still in outlaw territory. We're still living in a fucking wasteland, and we're still being hunted by those bastards in the city. This perfect little dream of yours? A baby? A home? There's no such thing as *home*. Bethany and Arch tried building one, and look where it got them. Arch is fucking dead. And Bethany's kid? Next time the Enforcers come here to crash and drink and screw, they're gonna hear that goddamn baby crying, rip it right out of Bethany's arms, and haul it to the city."

Jamie jerked as if he'd hit her. "Reese won't let that happen."

"Reese is powerless." He growled at her. "*She has no power.* And you're a fool if you believe otherwise."

He stumbled backward, the anger and panic and frustration finally winning the battle inside him.

"I'm leaving in an hour," he muttered. "Find me if you come to your senses. But I'm leaving, goddamn it. With or without you."

Rylan looked at the papers strewn on the desk, then at the woman whose deep brown eyes were fixed on his face. Sloan, of course, was the silent shadow in the corner of the room. He hadn't spoken a word since Reese outlined her plan to raid one of the most heavily guarded munitions depots in West Colony.

"This is suicide," Rylan said flatly.

She shrugged. "It's suicide if we do nothing. We need more weapons. And once we get them, we'll have a fighting chance."

The careless response irked him. When Reese summoned him to her quarters, he'd had an inkling of what she wanted to discuss, but having her plan spelled out to him in blunt, no-nonsense terms only highlighted the sheer amount of risk involved in orchestrating it.

But he couldn't deny she was right. Foxworth's alliances with the Enforcers were beginning to deteriorate. Outlaws were dying. Kade—Rylan forcibly pushed away the thought of his friend. Not now. He couldn't grieve for Kade right now.

They were heading out soon. Him, Hudson, Pike, Xan . . . Fuck, Xan. He'd barely spoken a word since— nope, not thinking about that either. He could mourn on the ride back. He could mourn when they put Kade in the ground.

"How many of the others are on board?" he asked Reese.

"Five hundred or so."

He rubbed the stubble on his jaw. "That's not enough."

"There are only two hundred Enforcers in West City," she pointed out.

"And thousands of citizens—"

"Who can't defend themselves. At least the bulk of them. If we have enough firepower to take out the Enforcers, the citizens will be left unprotected."

He shot a quick glance at Sloan, but the man didn't offer an opinion. His dark eyes remained shuttered.

"You're talking about starting a war," Rylan muttered.

"No, I'm talking about stealing some weapons."

"To start a war."

His continued reluctance brought a smile to Reese's lips. "One step at a time, honey." She pointed to the desk. "First we take care of this. Then we worry about the next step." Her head tilted. "You'll run this by Connor?"

"Do I have a choice?"

She shrugged. "You can say no."

To this woman? Impossible.

Rylan stepped toward her, smiling when he noticed the flare of heat in her expression. He grazed her bottom lip with his fingertips. Now was not the time, he knew that, but if he didn't forcefully turn his attention away from all the death and focus on something positive, the grief might engulf him.

"I'm going to get you naked one of these days," he informed her.

Reese's eyes darted toward Sloan, then back to Rylan. "Maybe."

"Oh, there's no maybe about it, gorgeous." He let that linger in the air for a moment, before his expression grew somber. "I'll talk to Connor on your behalf, but I'm not making any promises."

"Didn't expect you to."

With a nod, he eased away from her but halted when he reached the doorway. "Reese."

"Yeah?"

"I *will* fuck you." He dragged his tongue over his lips. "It's going to be soon." He locked his gaze to hers. "And you're going to love every second of it."

As he slid out the door, he heard Sloan's low chuckle echoing behind him.

25

"You let him go?"

Bethany's shout thundered in the bedroom. It was the first show of emotion she'd displayed since last night, and Jamie was so startled that she dropped the coffee cup she'd been about to give the woman. It crashed to the floor and broke into two pieces, dark liquid staining the weathered wood.

"Shit. I'm sorry. Let me find something to clean this mess—"

"Forget about the mess!" Bethany's dark eyes flashed. "What do you mean, Lennox is gone? Why didn't you go with him?"

Jamie was stunned by the question. She hadn't expected Bethany to be this upset by the news. If anyone should be upset, it was Jamie.

She was the one who'd watched the taillights of the Jeep disappearing beyond the gate an hour ago.

She was the one who'd tried one last time to convince Lennox to stay.

She was the one he hadn't even kissed good-bye.

God, she couldn't believe he'd actually left. She'd

thought he was bluffing. That he wouldn't possibly leave her behind and head back to Connor's camp with the others. *I go where you go.* It was their motto, damn it. The longest they'd ever been apart was a few days, and now he was leaving her in Foxworth for two months? Maybe longer?

But he had to have been bluffing about the ultimatum, right? It wasn't *really* over between them. It couldn't be.

"Jamie," Bethany snapped. "Answer me. Why didn't you go with him?"

"Because . . ." She gulped. "Because you need me. You . . ." Another gulp. "You lost Arch, sweetie. You're having a *baby*. Someone needs to be here to take care of you."

The woman's jaw twitched. "I can take care of myself."

Jamie bit the inside of her cheek. "I know you think that, but—"

"I don't think it—I *know* it." Bethany's ponytail moved in an angry swish as she barreled forward. With her huge belly and awkward steps, she posed the least threatening picture Jamie had ever seen. "I was with Arch for fifteen years, Jamie. You really think he didn't make sure I could take care of myself in all that time? He taught me how to be strong, damn it. I *am* strong. And I'm going to be strong for our baby, you hear me?"

Jamie opened her mouth, only to get cut off again.

"Last night was rough. It was the worst night of my life." Bethany curved her palms over her stomach. "But I'll get through this. I don't need you to stay here and hold my hand. I'm not going to sit in this room and wither away, all right? Arch would strangle me if I did that. And he'd strangle *you* if he knew you'd stood by and let your man drive out of here."

She clenched her teeth. "Lennox could have stayed. He *chose* to leave."

"Then you should've gone with him."

"He didn't exactly make the idea appealing when he was yelling and giving ultimatums and telling me I don't value my own life," Jamie grumbled.

Bethany shook her head in dismay. "Do you realize how rare it is to find a worthy man to love in this world? Lennox has his faults, of course he does. Arch did too. He could be a real asshole sometimes— remind me to tell you about the time he lost his shit at me because I forgot to drop a purifying tablet in the water supply at our last camp. But that's what men do. They yell and grumble and pound their fists against their chests and do whatever they can to protect their women. And we protect *them*. Trust me, they know that. They *know* they need us, even if they don't always say it."

Jamie faltered. "He said it was over between us."

Bethany snorted. "Sweetie, it's not over until *we* say it's over."

Laughter bubbled in Jamie's throat but didn't breach the surface. She was too distraught to laugh. And too confused by the sudden change in her friend. The pale emotionless robot from last night had transformed into a living, breathing woman in front of her eyes.

"I'm going to be okay." The humor faded as Bethany voiced the soft assurance. "I promise you, I will. But if you stay here in town, I'll be furious with you.

You belong with your man. Life is too short. You need to hold on to Lennox and never let him go."

Jamie's heart clenched as she remembered Arch's heavy body hitting the ground. The bullet hole in his forehead. The blood. Her mind suddenly replaced Arch's face with Lennox's, and a wave of agony nearly knocked her over.

Bethany was right. She should've thrown herself into the backseat of that Jeep and held on to Lennox for dear life.

She should never have let him go.

"You left her behind?"

Hudson's enraged voice once again blasted over the rumble of the Jeep's engine. It was the tenth time in the last hour that she'd twisted around in the front seat and hurled the accusation at Lennox, and he was getting tired of hearing it.

What other choice did he have? Stay in Foxworth and wait for the next Enforcer attack? Watch Jamie die in the cross fire?

He couldn't put himself through this torture anymore. The constant fear that he might lose her. The sheer frustration every time she made a choice that placed her life in danger.

"Why wouldn't you stay in Foxworth?" Hudson was still railing into him. "She didn't say she was staying there forever, just until Bethany's baby is born. You should've just stayed behind!"

"I agree." Rylan's curt voice came from the driver's seat. "I have no doubt Reese will keep her safe, but Jamie can be stubborn sometimes. You're the only person who's able to talk sense into her when she gets

all pissy. Or . . . well, maybe Beckett can too." A pause.
"I guess Beck can take care of her until she's ready to
come home—"

A growl tore from Lennox's throat, causing Rylan
to stop talking.

"Pull over," Lennox snapped.

Rylan's perplexed gaze found Lennox's in the
rearview mirror, but rather than argue, he swiftly
steered the Jeep toward the shoulder of the road. A
sharp honk of the horn alerted Pike, who was driving a borrowed pickup truck with Kade's body, and
Xander, who was riding up ahead on a motorcycle.
Lennox had left his Harley in Foxworth so Jamie
would have means of transportation when—*if?*—
she chose to return to camp, but now he regretted
not taking his bike, because it was way fucking
faster than Xan's beat-up Ducati.

He was already out of the Jeep before Xander had
even come to a complete stop. "What's going on?"
the other man asked warily.

"I need the bike. You can ride in the Jeep."

Like Rylan, Xander didn't question the orders.
He simply knocked the kickstand down and slid off
the Ducati.

A second later, Lennox was straddling the motorcycle.

"Where are you going?" Xander demanded.

"Where do you think?" Then he squeezed the
clutch and sped off, because Jesus Christ, he'd already
wasted enough time.

The last thing Rylan had said . . . it had gotten to
him. *Until she's ready to come home.*

Home. He'd told Jamie that building a home was

nothing more than a dream. He'd told her it didn't exist. But he'd been wrong, damn it.

So fucking wrong.

And the fear? It was still there, lodged in his throat like a wad of spoiled food. For more than twenty years his goal—his *only* goal—had been to keep Jamie safe. And he'd left her alone in Foxworth? He was such an idiot. He'd left because he was too scared to lose her, but he'd lost her regardless.

Goddamn idiot.

The urgency to return to Jamie had him speeding faster than he'd normally risk, but he was only thirty minutes into the drive when he heard another engine. His muscles stiffened, fingers tightening around the brakes. Shit. Traveling in the daylight posed the risk of running into Enforcers, but he and the others had been willing to take the chance because they were all eager to get back to camp.

He slowed the Ducati, debating whether to ride out of sight or speed past the oncoming vehicle. As another bike crested over the top of the sloped road, he relaxed. Not Enforcers, then. But that could still be a bandit tearing toward him—

Lennox came to a grinding stop when he glimpsed golden hair streaming out of a black helmet.

Son of a bitch.

The Harley slowed when its driver caught sight of Lennox. Within seconds, she was off the bike and shrugging the helmet off as she raced toward him.

"What are you doing here?" Lennox asked, his gaze eating up the sight of her.

Jamie's lips quirked. "I go where you go."

The joy that soared inside him was so powerful it

made him light-headed. With a desperate noise, he yanked her into his arms and hugged her tight enough to make her gasp. Her fists pounded on his shoulders as she tried to ease away from his crushing embrace.

"I can't breathe, Len."

"I was wrong," he blurted in response.

Her big blue eyes peered up at him, and the familiar sight unleashed a rush of warmth in his chest. "No kidding. But just out of curiosity, what do you think you were wrong about?"

"Home," he said hoarsely.

Jamie frowned. "What?"

"I was wrong when I told you it didn't exist. It does." His throat closed up. "But it's not a house, or a camp, or a fucking town. It's right *here*." He reached out and placed his hand over her chest. He felt her steady heartbeat against his palm, the rise and fall of her breasts with every breath she took. "You're my home, Jamie. It doesn't matter where we go or what happens. As long as you're with me, I'm home."

A wondrous smile stretched across her rosebud mouth. "So you finally figured that out, huh?"

He choked out a laugh. "Took me a while, but . . . yeah."

She tilted her head to the side, her long hair falling over one shoulder. "Hey, remember when you called me stupid?"

Remorse fluttered through him. "I shouldn't have—"

Jamie interrupted him. "Well, you're the stupid one, Len. You're a big dumb man who makes big dumb decisions sometimes." She lifted one eyebrow. "But that's okay. Want to know why?"

He pressed his lips together to stop another laugh. "Why?"

She offered a cocky grin. "Because I'm here to make sure your stupidity doesn't get out of line."

His laughter spilled over. "And I thank my lucky stars for that every day, my love."

Her breath hitched.

"What?" he demanded.

"You called me your love."

He frowned. "I always call you that."

"No. You call me *love*. You call everyone that. But you just said '*my* love.'" Jamie beamed at him. "Because you love me."

An indulgent smile tugged on his lips. "Because I love you," he concurred.

"Good, because I love you too." She stood up on her tiptoes and kissed him square on the mouth. "Let's get back on the road. We're sitting ducks out here."

"Where are we going?" he asked gruffly. "Foxworth?"

Jamie shook her head. "Connor's." Her voice went soft. "Bethany is doing okay, but I want to go back to Foxworth when the baby is born."

"*We'll* go back to Foxworth when the baby is born."

She hesitated.

"What is it?"

Her expression became even more agitated, which brought a frown to his lips.

"What's wrong?" he demanded.

"I . . ." She bit her lip. "I still want a baby, Len. Not right now, but someday. I haven't changed my mind about that."

A lump rose in his throat. "I know."

Jamie leaned in and rested her forehead against his chin, her breath fluttering over his throat. "I get how dangerous it is. Trust me, I get it. And maybe you were right—maybe it is naive of me to think that I could raise a child in this world." She pressed her cheek to his chest. "But I can't let the danger stop me from living my life the way I want to live it. We take a risk every single day just by living outside the city walls. Having a baby is another risk I'm willing to take."

"I know."

She lifted her head, a wry smile playing on her lips. "And you can deny it all you want, but I know you want a family too."

He gulped. She was wrong. He didn't. He—

"You loved the way we grew up," she said softly. "You loved all the children running around our camp, and the school lessons, and the games our parents would make up for us. And you loved being a father figure to Randy this month. Don't tell me you didn't."

Lennox swallowed again. She was wrong. He didn't. He—

He *did*.

Fucking hell.

Jamie's quiet laughter tickled his collarbone through his shirt. "Yeah, sweetie, I know you as well as you know me." She touched his cheek in a soothing motion. "You want the same things I do. So stop being afraid. We can have everything we want, as long as we stick together. As long as we protect each other. Love each other." She brushed her lips over his. "Can you do that for me?"

Emotion flooded his heart. "Anything," he whispered. "I can do anything for you."

Her smile was brighter than the sun shining down on them. "Good. Now let's go." Before he could blink, she was hurrying toward the Harley. "Race you back?" she called over her shoulder.

Her reckless laughter warmed his heart. Christ. This woman. Just . . . this woman. She was everything to him. She was his heart, his soul, absolutely *everything*.

And even in this dangerous land, that made him the luckiest man in the world.

It was hard to look at anything in Foxworth without thinking of Jake. He was ingrained in every inch of this town. He was the one who'd found it, the one who'd convinced Reese that a permanent base didn't mean instant death. It had been his idea to raid the nearby factories for sheet metal, his idea to erect the gates around the main stretch of town. His idea to form alliances with the shadier Enforcers, offering them sex and booze in exchange for protection and invisibility.

Foxworth was Jake's creation. He had been its king, and Reese his queen. A queen who'd murdered him for the crown.

No, not for the crown. For *them*—Reese looked around at the thirty or so people filling the room.

A little more than eighty people resided in Foxworth, but not all of them were original members of the group. Some were nomads who'd wandered up to the gates long after Jake's death. Others were old acquaintances who'd found their way back to the area. But the ones who'd known Jake—the ones who'd suffered at his hands—they were the ones she'd saved from the man she'd loved.

Jake had needed to be stopped.

She'd stopped him.

"So who's it going to be?"

Reese tensed as Rylan came up beside her. He held a tumbler of amber liquid in one big hand, tapping his thumb against the glass.

"Who's going to be what?" she muttered. As always, his presence had thrown her guard up a hundred feet.

"The man who'll be getting the gift of your pussy tonight." His blue eyes flickered with irritation. "I'd be happy if you chose me, but that's probably hoping for too much, huh?"

"You're right about that."

"Anyone ever tell you you're a real ballbuster?"

She fought a smile, but it broke free when she noticed the very obvious bulge in his pants. The man seemed to sport a permanent hard-on, as if he expected he might have to whip out his dick at a moment's notice and always wanted to be prepared.

"Seriously, gorgeous, would it kill you to say yes?" Rylan leaned in so close that his lips brushed her ear. "You know I'd make it good for you."

She had no doubt. But Rylan was too damn dangerous to spread her legs for. Forget the fact that he physically resembled her ex-lover, with his golden hair and vivid blue eyes. That was an issue, sure, but not an insurmountable one. He and Jake might look vaguely the same, but Reese knew from experience that no man fucked the same.

No, it was the *other* resemblance between Rylan

and Jake that scared her—the reckless streak. Rylan didn't seem to give a shit whether he lived or died. He breezed through life as if it were a game. One he evidently didn't care about winning. Otherwise he wouldn't throw himself headfirst into dangerous situations without a single care for his well-being. And although he took orders from Connor Mackenzie, Reese knew without a doubt that he'd disobey his leader in a heartbeat if it struck his fancy.

Granted, he didn't seem to crave power the way Jake had, but the motives behind Rylan's actions didn't matter. Like Jake, he was too impulsive. Dangerously so.

A man who didn't think before he acted was a man who couldn't be controlled.

And for a woman who carefully planned every move she made, *that* was the issue. She refused to let another loose cannon into her bed, especially when she was well aware that men like Jake and Rylan were her weakness.

"You know who else would make it good for me?" she said sweetly. "Beckett."

Rylan followed her gaze to the tattooed man across the room. Beckett was laughing at something his friend Travis had just said. "Beck's a decent lay," Rylan agreed. "But he's not what you need tonight. Too playful."

She raised an eyebrow. "And what do I need tonight?"

"With all the adrenaline from the raid still burning in your blood? You need a good, hard dicking, gorgeous." He shrugged, nodding to their left. "Nash could probably give it to you."

Reese glanced at the man in question. Nash's rugged features and lean frame were definitely appealing, but she wasn't really feeling him tonight.

"It's too bad Lennox isn't here. He'd give it to you as rough as you wanted." Rylan grinned. "But he's a one-woman man these days, so maybe it's a good thing he's at Con's camp. This way, your poor ego doesn't have to take a hit every time he rejects you."

She narrowed her eyes. But she couldn't argue with that. Lennox had made it clear that he was with Jamie now and was not interested in screwing anyone else. And Jamie had made it clear what would happen if Reese graced Lennox's bed ever again—that little bitch had beaten the shit out of Reese the last time they'd crossed paths.

Not that Reese held a grudge. She'd be possessive of Lennox too, if he were her man. He fucked like a dream.

"I don't mind rejection," she answered with a shrug. "It's character building."

Rylan chuckled and handed her his glass. "Drink."

"You trying to liquor me up, honey?"

He blinked innocently. "Nah, you just looked thirsty."

A laugh slipped out, but she still accepted the glass and took a long swig. Bourbon, she noted, as the alcohol slid down her throat. She wondered if Rylan had picked it because he knew she had a hard-on for bourbon, or if it was just a coincidence.

After another sip, she handed the glass back. "Getting me drunk won't impair my judgment, you know. I'm even more stubborn when I'm wasted."

He laughed too, and the deep husky sound tickled a place she didn't want associated with this man.

Reese turned away from his twinkling blue eyes and searched the room for Sloan, who was never far from her side—usually lurking in the shadows somewhere, his watchful gaze fixed on her.

When she couldn't see him anywhere, a pang of unease tugged at her insides. He must have ducked out right after he'd walked her over to the rec hall, which was odd, because Sloan rarely left her alone.

Then again, it *was* late. He'd probably gone to bed. The room felt unbalanced somehow without Sloan.

"Too stubborn to dance with me?" Rylan countered, drawing her from her thoughts.

Rather than give her the chance to reply, he took her hand and yanked her against him. Reese grabbed onto his broad shoulders by instinct, and she was still battling annoyance when he shoved one thigh between her legs so their bodies were plastered together.

Her traitorous hormones instantly kicked in, her pussy tingling, thanks to the hard thigh pressed against it. The last time she and Rylan were in this position, she'd been seconds away from taking him to bed, a foolish decision that had been interrupted by the arrival of the Enforcers. The events that followed had been a total shit storm. People had died. Good people, like Arch, whose death had left his pregnant woman all alone in this world. Like Kade, whose death had been the push Connor had needed to join Reese's cause.

"Get out of your head," Rylan murmured.

She clenched her fingers over his shoulders, but, for some stupid reason, didn't shove him away. "I'm not . . ." She trailed off.

"Not thinking about your next move?" he mocked. "Planning the next attack? Mentally counting all the bodies you might leave in your wake?"

His soft laughter grated. And fuck him for knowing what was eating at her. Before his extended stay at Foxworth two months ago, when he'd come to train her people in the art of guns and combat, she never would've used the word *perceptive* to describe this man. But he'd proven her wrong during that visit. Rylan was far more observant than she'd ever given him credit for.

His rough fingertips traced a path up her neck to her mouth. He rubbed her lower lip slowly, seductively. "You need to fuck," he whispered.

Tension gathered inside her, tightening her muscles, pulsing in her core. He was absolutely right. Sex was a surefire way to release all the volatile energy surging through her veins.

"Use me tonight, Reese." He buried his face in her neck as he continued to rub up against her like a dog in heat. He wasn't moving in time to the fast-paced beat pulsing out of the rec hall speakers but to his own slow, sensual rhythm, each grind of his hips weakening her resolve. "Use me however you want. Fuck me however you want. Just . . . say yes."

A shiver racked her body as his warm mouth latched onto the side of her throat. He kissed her hot flesh, then sucked hard enough to make her moan.

That got her a quiet chuckle. "You know you want

to." His tongue licked a path along her jaw and upward, until their lips were a mere inch apart. "We'll burn so hot together, baby."

She didn't answer. She couldn't, because her throat was clamped shut. God, of course they'd be hot together. Her entire body was already close to going up in flames. Just the feel of his erection against her thigh made her weak-kneed and achy.

But . . . she didn't trust herself when she was around this man.

The truth was, there was a reason she was drawn to loose cannons.

Because she *was* one.

She was only careful because she *forced* herself to be, but those wild tendencies that had gravitated toward Jake lived inside her too. She was driven by base urges just like Jake had been, and she struggled every second of every day to hold on to restraint and be the kind of leader her people deserved. The kind of leader Jake had failed to be.

Rylan tested that restraint, and she didn't like it.

Where was Sloan, damn it? Panic rolled through her as she peered past Rylan's broad shoulder and once again searched the room. Sloan grounded her. He was the only one who— Her panic faded when she spotted him near the door. A breath of relief slid past her lips.

"I'm down with Sloan joining us. The more, the merrier," Rylan murmured after he'd twisted his head to track her gaze.

Sloan stared back at them, his gaze steady and reassuring. *I'm here*, his eyes telegraphed from across the room. Reese watched as he settled his broad shoulders against the wall, crossing his arms and resting one ankle on the other.

She turned to Rylan, who took her renewed attention as an invitation. He shifted her around so she couldn't see Sloan anymore and nuzzled her neck again, whispering, "What's it going to be, gorgeous?"

No.

Yes.

Her body was a fuse waiting for a spark. Primed for sex. Aching for it.

She felt the unshakable gaze of Sloan at her back. Yeah, she was deep into her head and if she didn't pull out of this maelstrom of guilt and worry, she wasn't going to be good for anything.

Now, more than ever, she needed to be sharp and ready. She looked up into Rylan's heated gaze. He never took anything too seriously, was rumored to be one of the best fucks in the Colonies. Sex with him would be the best distraction she could ask for.

Except . . . she still didn't trust herself. She didn't trust that she could give in to Rylan and come out of it unscathed.

Abruptly, she pulled out of his arms. "Follow me."

She turned on her heel, not waiting to see if he followed. The hard boots hitting the floor answered for him. Sloan straightened as she arrowed in his direction, and by the time she pulled to a stop in front of him, he'd reached his full, towering height.

"You said I needed a man tonight," Reese muttered. "Is he the one I need?"

Sloan's hazel eyes locked with hers. "I can't think

of a better person in this room to pull you out of your head."

Rylan's breath was hot on her neck and Reese had to fight to keep from shivering in sexual delight. She shook her head instead. "He's reckless."

Sloan nodded.

"It's not wise."

"If we did everything that was wise, we would've been dead a long time ago." Sloan lifted his hand as if to cup her cheek, but the touch never landed. It never did. He always held himself back.

She knew, because she wasn't dumb or blind, that he lusted after her. And even though he'd never made a move to scratch that itch, it was always there between them, like the caress that never happened. Reese had become accustomed to it, as much as she expected the sun to rise and the rain to fall. Sloan was the one constant in her life.

Rylan coughed. "I'm right here, you know."

They both ignored him. Reese kept her eyes on Sloan. If he was with her . . . then maybe she could hold on to some shred of control. Maybe the fiery lust, the recklessness Rylan stirred in her, wouldn't spill over into other more vulnerable areas.

"Only if you're there," she whispered to Sloan. "I don't trust myself." In other words, she needed him to be the lifeline he'd always been to pull her out of the quicksand when it threatened to swallow her.

Sloan searched her face, looking for what, she wasn't sure. He could read her like a book. He was the only one. Slowly, as if he'd turned the proposition over in his head a few dozen times, he nodded.

"If that's what it takes to ease your mind, then I'm there. Nothing will happen that you don't need."

"Interesting choice of words there, brother," Rylan noted. "What about giving Reese what she wants?"

Sloan's gaze hardened when it shifted from her to Rylan. "She gets it all."